SOUND OF A FURIOUS SKY

AN FBI AGENT DOM WALKER NOVEL

HN WAKE

SIGN UP for the HN Wake newsletter to get a **FREE** book from the Mac Ambrose series.

Go to www.hnwake.com

or

in your ebook click here or on the image.

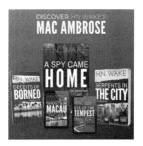

For my friends near and dear who may happen to live far and wide. You are valued.

Twenty years ago

Five cardboard boxes from *Mario's Bakery* sat at the base of a grimy wall in the barren apartment. Domini Walker watched her brother race into the first bedroom and hop between feet, blond hair fluttering and long arms flailing. Compared to the proper beds they had at home, the mattress on the floor resembled a campsite. He tap-danced inside the empty closet and closed the door like an excited Boy Scout.

Aunt Lucille's voice was clipped. "Beecher seems to like it."

"He's ten."

"Shall we sit, Dom?"

They sat on the prickly upholstery at opposite ends of the sun-seared brown sofa. Dom didn't know much about Aunt Lucille, other than her husband always stank of beer and her two deranged boys threw rocks at cats, but she imagined the woman's belongings would not fit into five boxes.

Beecher raced past them and into the second bedroom.

Aunt Lucille stared out the bare window. "This is just temporary. This way you can both remain in the same school. Keep some continuity. We will change the address on the school files when you start back up in the fall. No need to make a fuss."

"She's not coming back, is she?"

In the other room, Beecher stilled.

Aunt Lucille blinked. "Some time in Florida will do your mother good. We are all lucky that Esther may have found someone. What with everything that's happened this year ... with your father. Oh, my lord."

"She's not coming back, is she?"

Beecher's small face appeared around the door frame.

Aunt Lucille stood quickly and smoothed a white shirt over a flat chest. "No. Your mother is not coming back."

A coldness crept over Dom's skin.

Beecher tiptoed into the room and placed his hands on the bristly sofa arm.

Aunt Lucille wrested a folded envelope from her purse and dropped it on a cushion. "The utilities are paid. There's a supermarket down the block. I'll get you spending money every week."

"I'm fifteen."

The sofa cushion shifted as Beecher settled beside her.

"Esther wasn't exactly a shining example of motherhood, Dom. You've been taking care of yourself and Beecher for years. It won't be any different." Aunt Lucille spun and marched to the door before clapping it shut in her wake.

As Beecher's arm reached for her, Dom noticed the tiny blond hairs quivering as if his skin were ice cold. Six months ago, when Chief Hester from Precinct 9 had called the apartment above the bakery with a raspy "I've got some terrible news ... " Dom had fixated on the letter magnets on the refrigerator. It was only in that moment she had realized the bright primary colors had faded.

In the barren living room, she whispered, "It will be completely different."

TUESDAY MORNING

When the passenger pigeon began to decline in this country during the latter decades of the nineteenth century, the market gunners turned their attention to the larger shore birds, such as the golden plovers and the Eskimo Curlews or "prairie pigeons," as they were called by settlers in the prairie states. The curlews apparently knew no fear of man and had the touching habit of circling over their wounded companions, so that entire flocks were sometimes annihilated by hunters.

—Thomas Foster, "Circling to Doom"

1

IT WAS a long-standing New York FBI tradition to assign the picnic cases to agents returning from a leave of absence. Early Tuesday morning, Assistant Director in Charge Yves Fontaine received a call about the twenty-five-year-old daughter of a wealthy family that had gone missing. Having been around the Agency for twenty-one years, rising through Criminal Division to head of the Bureau's busiest field office, Fontaine knew what to do. He threw the assignment to Special Agent Domini Walker.

At noon, Dom flashed identification at the uniformed doorman outside 15 Central Park West, one of the city's most extravagant addresses. White gloves yanked open the heavy brass door and ushered her into a softly lit lobby. In the rarefied silence, the spongy soles of her work shoes squished loudly against the opulent marble. From behind an enormous reception desk, a thin bespectacled man watched her progression. She tugged down on the lightweight navy jacket with the bright yellow FBI across the back. *Fidelity. Bravery. Integrity.*

After reaching the desk, she flashed her badge. "I'm here for the Van Burens." *Please do not give me a hard time, friend. It's*

*my first case back after three months, I haven't found my sea legs,
and I've drawn the short straw on a Richie Rich runaway case.*

"Of course, Agent." White teeth gleamed from a broad
smile as his right hand indicated an elevator lobby to the side.
"I'll let them know you are on the way. Eleventh floor."

Look at that. Blue-collar stiffs sticking together. She gave him
a smile.

The elevator door slid open on the eleventh floor to a maid
in a pressed white dress and an expanse of polished taupe-
colored wood. A huge living room awash in beige swept to a
wall of windows and a dazzling bird's-eye view of the rolling
green fields of Central Park. If she had been alone, Dom would
have whistled a tribute to the extravagance.

The maid led Dom past a twenty-seat dining table with a
huge unruly bouquet of cream flowers to an arrangement of pale
leather sofas littered with tan pillows. The room's only color
was a massive oil painting of vibrant red blooms.

"I'll get the Van Burens," the maid said softly.

The Van Burens did not keep her waiting. Claude Van
Buren's long strides ate up the distance. Thick gray hair swept
away from a high forehead, a round face, and a thick rugby player's neck. "Thank you for coming." His grip was vise-like.

"Special Agent Domini Walker, sir. I'll be in charge if an
investigation should prove necessary."

"Exactly." Deep grooves fanned gray scowling eyes. "If.
There will be no need for any of this. When Hettie returns
home from whatever adventure she's cooked up, this will all be
sorted."

Optimism and bravado were good. "Let's hope that's
true, sir."

"How long have you been with the FBI?" He examined her.

At thirty-five, Dom looked younger. It was decidedly not an
advantage. "Ten years, sir."

"Really? You don't look old enough."

Like a draft against a gauzy curtain, the upbeat voice of Dom's late father, Stewart Walker, rippled her unconsciousness. *Don't be intimidated, my Dom. We're all born the same way— naked and terrified. You are enough.* She nodded. "Yes, I've heard that before."

From around Claude Van Buren's shadow, his wife appeared. Dressed in a pale silk shirt over ivory slacks, Yvette Van Buren had exquisite features and silky shoulder-length blonde hair. She was beautiful enough to be either vapid or brilliant. Her handshake was soft but sure, and her voice was tender. "Please, let's sit."

"I'm sorry we have to meet under these circumstances," Dom said.

Claude took up a large space at the end of the sofa. "Special Agent Walker. Let me start by saying there may not be circumstances to begin with. This will all turn out to be a big misunderstanding. It's a shame to have involved law enforcement at all."

Yvette sat four feet away with her back pressed against the sofa's leather and her hands clasped together. There was a stillness about her and a hint of melancholy in her pale eyes. The distance from her husband was telling.

Dom softly cleared her throat. "Why don't you tell me what's going on?"

"We've decided to err on the side of caution." Yvette's voice was mild, and the accent was cultured. "I would rather us be overly protective than negligent. You see, Hettie did not arrive at work yesterday, and no one has heard from her."

This poised beautiful woman didn't sound stupid. "You think something untoward has happened?"

Claude squinted.

Yvette nodded. "Yes, I believe something has happened to her."

"And you, Mr. Van Buren?"

"I think Hettie is a young woman who has forgotten to tell her mother that she is off on holiday somewhere."

Yvette pressed lips in a practiced reflex.

That was interesting. "When was the last time you saw Hettie?"

"Last week, Wednesday." Claude sighed. "She came by my office."

"Two days ago. Sunday." Yvette clasped her hands tighter. "We went shopping. We walked the bags up to her apartment together. I left around four pm."

"Is she irresponsible? Could she have run away? Any reason to not tell you she's gone on a trip?"

Claude stiffened. "No. Not at all."

"No," Yvette added softly. "She is quite responsible, and there is nothing she keeps from us."

Kids keep lots of secrets. But let's move on. "Is she thoughtful?"

"Yes," Claude replied. "She's a good kid. Listens. Follows the rules. Never really any problem."

"Yes," Yvette agreed. "She's a lovely young woman."

"Could you tell me more?"

"We had a very easy baby." Claude nodded. "We doted on her as an only child. She was perfectly normal in elementary school. Neither head of the class nor a troublemaker. She always followed the teachers' instructions. She played dolls as girls do." He swayed as he spoke, unconsciously expanding his territory on the sofa. "She had lessons. Yvette saw to that. Horses, tennis, golf, swimming. Yvette raised a very fine daughter. No real significant problems growing up, I'd say."

Everyone has tells—unconscious micro-movements of nonverbal communication. Tells can't establish if a person is lying, but they can indicate anxiety. Dom watched for early baseline tells but there was very little anxiety from either of them on this topic. No ticks. No calming touches.

"Growing up, Hettie never lacked for anything," Claude continued. "She did and had all the things a girl deserves. We visited family for the holidays, hosted New Year's every year. Never any trouble. Hettie is a good girl. She got good grades because we got her tutors. She made it to Bryn Mawr, and we were happy with that. Studied botany and the sciences. I tried to talk her into something more professional, but she was quite determined at that point—" He shook his head as if it was inconsequential and rubbed one hand lightly on a thigh.

That thigh rub, was that a tell? "You didn't like her choice of profession?"

"I would have preferred she go into something more ... substantial." Both hands rubbed thighs.

"You don't think the sciences are substantial?"

His lips pursed. "Scientific research is tedious. Especially as a career." He cracked his knuckles.

Hettie's career was definitely an issue. "Would you have preferred if she had done something else?"

Yvette intervened. "Hettie has a job she loves and a good lifestyle in New York. She is happy."

"Mrs. Van Buren, are you supportive of her job?"

"It's a fine job. A fine career. It's not as exciting as it could be, I agree with my husband on that score, but it works with Hettie's quiet lifestyle."

"Can you explain her lifestyle for me?"

"Hettie isn't a social butterfly. She does not do the social scene—the gallery openings, the Met, the parties, the Hamptons in the summer. She has her close friends and stays fairly quiet."

"She avoids the party scene?"

Yvette nodded. "Oh yes. That's not her way."

"Boyfriend?" Dom asked them both.

Claude stretched his back and smoothed his tie. Yvette squeezed her hand. Both stared at Dom silently.

Well, well, well. What have we here? "There *is* a boyfriend?"

"Yes," Claude snapped. "She is seeing someone. He is someone neither her mother nor I approve of."

"Can you explain that?"

"He's a student over at NYC."

Dom turned to Yvette. "You don't approve?"

Yvette released a tired sigh. "My side, the Lowrances, have been a family of privilege ever since my great-grandfather discovered oil. We must protect our family."

Dom waited.

"His family does not have money."

Oh, my. They really didn't like the gold-digging boyfriend. "What's his name?"

"Micah something." Claude huffed.

"You've not met him?"

Yvette touched her neck. "No."

Claude cleared his throat. "No."

Like really, really didn't like him. "Did you fight with Hettie about seeing this Micah?"

"It happened, yes." Yvette's hand petted her neck. "I'm simply not happy Hettie is wrapped up with a man who may not have her best interests at heart."

"Often? Did you fight often?"

Yvette returned her hands to a clasp and the knuckles whitened. "Hettie and I have fought, yes. But Hettie is a woman now. She can certainly see whomever she wants to see. I have no control over that."

"Did you try to dissuade your daughter from dating this boy?"

Yvette remained mute.

"Did you try to dissuade her?"

Yvette's lips clenched. "In my way."

"And what way is that?"

"Hettie is aware I do not approve of that boy. I've asked her not to speak of him to me."

"Could Micah be the reason Hettie has not been in touch?"

Silence.

Well, well. Lots of family dynamics at play here. But let's move on. "Mr. Van Buren, what do you and Hettie tend to chat about?"

"Everyday issues. Some politics."

"Did you and Hettie share the same politics?"

"Mostly."

Dom cocked her head. "What do you do, Mr. Van Buren?"

"I'm in private equity. I'm the Managing Partner of a private equity firm."

"Was Hettie ever interested in pursuing your line of work?"

He scowled. "No. Never. I wish she had been."

Dom turned to Yvette. "What types of things do you and Hettie discuss?"

"We talk about her work. At the American Museum of Natural History. I'm on the board there. It's a very prestigious board. We oversee all things about the museum. It's very demanding, but I consider it a service to my country—"

"Hettie works there." Claude shook his head. "Hettie is an Ornithologist. Birds. That sort of thing. Yvette arranged that."

"How so?"

"The way a proper family arranges a position for their child." He shrugged.

In sum, Hettie was an obedient girl with a quiet career as a bird scientist, an overbearing father, and a polished and subdued mother. Hettie was dating someone who caused a great deal of anxiety for a super wealthy family who thought he was a gold digger. *Yup, a Richie Rich runaway case.* Hettie and this disliked boyfriend were probably holed up on some beach drinking lime margaritas with their cell phones turned off.

But the key at the early stage of an investigation was to be open to all possibilities, to not race down one rabbit hole in case it dead-ended. "Is there anything else I should know about? Is there anyone you imagine would have an issue with Hettie? Someone from work, or college?"

Claude squinted. "No, no. Nothing like that."

"What about any incidents in the last, say, few weeks that—for any reason—stand out?"

"No, nothing that stands out, or we would have told you," he said.

"Any unusual conversations?"

"No."

"Did she mention getting in touch with anyone from her past?"

"No."

"Did she mention any fights she had?"

"No."

"Any unusual meetings?"

"No." He barked.

Dom turned to Yvette. "Your husband thinks your daughter has gone off on a holiday. That she has gone away with this Micah and did not want you to know that?"

Yvette squinted. "My husband and I *do* disagree at times."

Lots of family dynamics. "Your husband's theory that she's off somewhere on a secret vacation, that doesn't sit well with you? You feel something is amiss with Hettie?"

Yvette's eyes moistened. "Yes. I feel it."

"You've tried calling her?"

"Oh yes, I've been calling her since Monday morning, but her voicemail picks up. I went around there last night, but when I went in, her apartment was dark. She wasn't home."

"You have a key?"

Claude said, "We pay the rent."

"Mr. Van Buren, have *you* tried to call your daughter?"

"Yes. When I found out last night that Yvette had been looking for her, I did try to call her. She never picked up."

"Anything else I should know?"

They both shook their heads.

"Well then, trust me when I say that Hettie is the number one priority for the Bureau."

He wagged his finger in the air. "When you find her, tell her the FBI has spent good resources chasing a goose."

"I will update you regularly—"

"I'm sure she'll call in today," he grumbled.

"You let me know immediately if you hear from her. Can I get her number?"

He relayed the number from memory.

Dom stood, and the Van Burens rose from the sofa. "Is there someone at the museum I can speak to? I'll want to check in with her colleagues."

Yvette smoothed her hair. "The Executive Director, Mr. Blaulicht. I know him well."

"I'd like your permission to enter Hettie's apartment."

"Of course." Claude yelled at a far door. "Marla, can you bring Hettie's apartment key?"

The maid in the white dress scurried across the living room and handed Dom a key.

Time to go find the runaway rich kid. But keep the possibilities open. "One more thing. If you hear from anyone, anyone you're unfamiliar with, please call me first—"

"What do you mean?" Yvette blinked rapidly.

It was a common physical expression of confusion, a forced delay that allowed the brain to digest new information. "Just in the off chance—"

"A ransom note." Claude placed his hand on Yvette's arm. "You mean if we get some kind of ransom note or call?"

Dom nodded.

Yvette petted her neck. Claude cleared his throat and was finally silent.

As they walked to the door, Dom said, "Let's assume that Hettie is just fine. Let's not jump to any conclusions. You should know I have a 90 percent clearance rate. I am the lead specialist on missing persons for the FBI in New York. I'm the right agent to find Hettie."

Spoken out loud, the last line actually sounded convincing. But still, Special Agent Domini Walker tugged down on her navy jacket.

2

IN THE HEART of Greenwich Village, Hettie Van Buren's building sat on the corner of Fifth Avenue and Waverly Place overlooking Washington Square Park. Dom pulled the red antique Lancia Fulvia Coupé into the circular drive and turned off the ignition. In the silenced interior, the thick smell of oil and gasoline buffeted loose an overly saturated memory of her father. Stewart Walker had smiled from behind the same wheel with a huge grin while speeding them along in a car rally. *To win the race, my Dom, you have to push past the fear.* Despite everything that had happened fifteen years ago, despite everything that he had done, she welcomed the flashbacks. They were all she had left of him.

A scowling doorman with wiry Albert Einstein hair approached from the lobby door wagging his finger. Hettie had traded in her parents' Central Park luxury for a similarly elite building in a swank downtown neighborhood.

Dom stood from the race car and flashed her badge. "I'm going up to Hettie Van Buren's apartment."

He paused. "Ah. Okay. 10E."

"Were you on duty on Sunday?" she asked as they walked up the drive.

"Yes, sure. Why?"

"Do you remember seeing Hettie?"

"Yes. Is everything okay?"

"We're not sure. What do you remember?"

"Well, her mother, Mrs. Van Buren, came by in the afternoon, then she and Hettie went out. They came back with shopping bags and went upstairs. A little while later, Mrs. Van Buren left. Alone. I remember the mother leaving because she insists on parking that boat of a Cadillac in the drive. Insists on it. So, I am aware when she comes and goes. It's kinda front and center."

"Normally people don't park in the drive?"

"Oh, they park there." He rolled his eyes. "They just don't leave their car there for hours. There's a fifteen-minute loading and unloading rule."

She smiled. "That doesn't apply to Mrs. Van Buren?"

He winked at her. "Correct."

"You have security cameras?"

"Nope. Afraid not."

"You on duty all day Sunday?"

He opened the door for her. "Yup. I left around eight pm."

She stepped into the lobby. "And Monday all day?"

"Yup. That's me."

"Did you see Hettie on Monday?"

He frowned. "I don't think so. No."

"Who was on night duty on Sunday?"

"Carl."

"Can you have him call me at this number?" She handed him her card.

The lobby was a study in gold. Shiny golden wallpaper, gleaming gold lights, and tall, oriental vases decorated with gilt lace. Greenwich Village wasn't Central Park, but it was still cultured. The paneled elevator smelled of cedar and the bronze carpeted hallway of the tenth floor was hushed. Gold sconces lit the way to the corner apartment. The door was secure—no scratches, no marks, no sign of forced entry.

After unlocking the door, she pushed into a bright and airy apartment with wall-to-wall windows overlooking the park. "Hettie Van Buren? This is the FBI. I'm coming in."

There was only silence. Through the window, a flock of pigeons drifted over the monument like a school of fish on a current.

Softly she shut the door. "Hettie, are you here?"

Dom wanted this case to be a simple misunderstanding. Hettie was on a long romantic weekend in a private villa on a beach with palm trees with the disputed boyfriend. Or maybe they were partying with friends in a Vegas penthouse. The wealthy had lots of insulated ways to entertain themselves. In the best-case scenario, Dom would find the missing young woman and everyone could go back to their sheltered lives. Lord knew, Dom needed an easy first case back from leave. Fontaine had taken a risk giving this to her and she didn't want to let him down. What if her skill set had atrophied over the preceding three months? *Fake it till you make it, my Dom,* her father whispered in her ear. Stewart Walker had been corny.

She focused on the details in the room as she pulled plastic gloves from her jacket and snapped them on. The space smelled of a pungent flower. On the far end of a large white-and-gray marble counter that divided the open-plan kitchen from the living area, a vase was filled with tall lilies. Bright green stems held taupe blossoms. *Who buys tan flowers?* The water in the vase had evaporated to nearly empty. *How long does it take water to evaporate?*

The room was a wash of white except for a huge blue and

yellow print on the far wall. Pale wood floors had a glossy polish. Centered around a plush white carpet, a white sectional sofa faced the far wall. Magazines were stacked neatly on a coffee table. Plumped cushions on the white couch sat under a neatly folded fur blanket. Books stood like a picket fence, alternating tall and short, on the shelves of a white bookshelf. *Who arranges books like that? A designer, maybe.* Interspersed on the shelves were twenty framed photos.

All in all, the apartment reminded Dom of the parents' style —monochromatic, modern, and spotless. It was too stylized for a woman as young as twenty-five and the bright painting felt forced, almost like faked happiness.

In the kitchen, the counter had been cleaned recently. Organic kitchen disinfectants stood sentry, like soldiers in a row, along the back of the sink. A fully stocked cupboard displayed soda cans, spices, oils and vinegars, and a box of trash bags. Inside the refrigerator, sausages were wrapped in cling wrap, the drawers were full of crisp vegetables, and a large bottle of fresh juice sat in the door shelf. Opening the dishwasher, she was hit with the smell of mildew. Three dirty plates and eight glasses were spiked along the upper and lower drawers. This wasn't the refrigerator or the dishwasher of someone planning an out-of-town vacation.

Dom stepped to the bookshelf and examined the photos. Three smiling friends appeared over the years. Up close, Hettie's blue eyes were piercing, and her thin blond hair framed a round face with chunky cheekbones. The daughter was nowhere near as exceptional looking as her mother—not ugly, more plain—and the comparisons would not have been kind.

As she snapped photos of the crowded book shelf, her cell phone rang. It was Carl, the night doorman.

Dom moved down a silent hallway. "Did you work Sunday and Monday nights?"

"Yes, both nights."

A white guest room was dominated by splashes of yellow. Yellow pillows were arranged on jaunty angles on a white bed, and a huge photograph of snow-covered mountain peaks rose over an aquamarine lake. "Do you remember Hettie Van Buren coming or going?"

"No. That's definitely a no. She didn't come or go while I was on duty. In fact, her mother came by last night and asked the same thing."

That confirmed what Yvette had said earlier.

Carl asked, "Is Hettie okay?"

"I'm not sure yet. We're just making sure."

"She's a lovely young lady. I hope she's okay."

"Thanks." They clicked off.

A polished wood floor led further down the hallway toward a master bedroom. Five photos, enlarged and framed, hung on the wall near the open door. In each, Hettie stood with a strikingly good-looking young Latino man with tousled dark hair, sparkling eyes, and a large white smile. His shoulders were broad and athletic. In one of the shots, the two lovebirds were dressed in sweaty khakis in the middle of a green jungle, their eyes laughing at the camera. Hettie had found happiness with a man her parents disliked. Instead of putting that love on display in the living room, she hung it down this private hall. *Was she ashamed or avoiding conflict?*

Hettie's bedroom was singularly white and stark. White walls, white carpet, and a white plump bed. A huge photo of the same peaked mountains and lake at sunset dominated the far wall. Everything was neat and tidy.

Except it wasn't.

By the bathroom door, a framed photo on the wall was canted at a jarring angle, its glass smashed as if a shoulder had careened into it. A colorful china bowl lay on the carpet along-side scattered coins and jewelry. Someone had been on their way into the bathroom when they stumbled. Or had been pushed.

Dom's heart rate spiked. Nobody had seen Hettie in two days, the flowers were dying, the dishwasher was dirty, there was fresh food in the refrigerator, and now there were signs of a struggle.

Dom's chest tightened. It was the familiar twinge at the start of the hunt. Stewart Walker grinned. *You ready for this, my Dom?*

She turned and strode to the hallway. In one of the photos of Micah and Hettie, the smiling boyfriend's arms were around Hettie's shoulders, pulling her close by her neck. The gesture could be interpreted as dominating. *What do we know about you, Mr. I'm-Super-Hot-And-Have-A-Seductive-Smile Boyfriend?*

It was time to answer both those questions.

3

MILA PASCALE LIKED ROUTINE. Upon waking, she mentally forecasted the day's events: the protein shake thoroughly blended, the backpack correctly packed—the cell phone, laptop, cords, and pens in the proper pockets with zippers flushed—the ride to the museum uneventful, the tasks from the museum librarian completed, the lunch eaten, and the home route determined. Only when the day had been properly projected, did she get out of bed. Order reduced surprises, and most importantly, it meant she never left anything behind.

That morning's routine had been perfectly predictable. She had pumped hard up Seventh Avenue and passed Times Square with the city noises thumping her chest, the cars brushing near her thigh, and the taxis blaring warnings. At Columbus Circle the traffic thinned, and she pedaled into the curve to hit the sidewalk entrance of Central Park at top speed.

The last five minutes of the morning commute through the park were the most exhilarating. Today the green hills smelled of cut grass. A dog owner's whistle pierced the sky. The sun beamed down on rolling fields. It was only until the 77th Street Stone Arch that her regular groove was interrupted. Something metallic glinted from spiked grass. Hands clamped on brakes and skidding tires threw clumps of dirt into the air. She circled back, leaned down, and picked up a shiny new penny. *All day long you'll have good luck.* She slipped it in her pocket.

Just after lunch, Mila's orderly day was interrupted for a second time. Through the jarringly loud throngs circling the rearing dinosaur skeleton in the immense Roosevelt Rotunda of the American Museum of Natural History, Mila noticed the dark navy of an FBI jacket. The memory of a young boy's blue eyes and rabbit grin sucked the air from her chest. Her feet fused to the floor. *Had the FBI found Jimmy?* Mila's hand slipped into the front pocket of her jeans to clasp the solitary penny.

The navy jacket was worn by a tall, slender woman speaking to the museum's Executive Director Harold Blaulicht, aka The Bootlicker. A testy type on a good day, Bootlicker jiggled his fingers in the air like a distressed pastry chef. When a high-pitched squeal from a group of elementary schoolers rattled off stone walls, Bootlicker's lips twitched and his eyes bulged. The FBI agent, cool as a cucumber, touched his shoulder and asked him a direct question. As if by magic, Bootlicker calmed.

A chunky cigarette-smelling guy from Mammalogy passed by Mila. "Some girl down in ornithology is missing. Blaulicht's freaking out."

The air conditioning chilled Mila's face. The odds of the FBI being in the museum about anything other than Jimmy were mathematically enormous but not impossible.

"Hey," she shouted after Cigarette-Smelling Guy. "Who down in ornithology?"

"Some girl named Hettie."

Mila knew Hettie Van Buren. They had chatted once in the coffee line and walked together through the museum. Hettie was nice, smart, shy, and everybody knew her mom was on the board. Mila had never had any reason to do research for her because the museum scientists did far more advanced work than anything a summer intern would assist. But Hettie had been very friendly to her.

Miss Timid Hettie was missing? The odds were inconceivable. But not impossible.

Mila watched as Bootlicker summoned a stout museum guide and spoke quickly at him. Agent Cool Cucumber shook goodbye to Bootlicker and accompanied the guide into the Hall of African Mammals. Mila followed as they made their way through the crowds toward the broad staircase in the back of the building. Under the navy jacket with the bright yellow letters, the agent had on slim dark jeans and a white cotton button-down shirt. Her face was pretty without makeup and her dark hair was pulled back in a long ponytail that swung between her shoulder blades. At five eight-ish, her long legs took the stairs in an easy athletic gait, arms rocking freely. Such a self-assured woman was probably at home in any situation and in control in the most social anxiety inducing and unpredictable environments. Agent Cool Cucumber with the observant eyes was probably a kidnapping specialist who read gory forensics reports over breakfast. They would have assigned a kidnapping specialist to a missing person case, especially when it was Hettie Van Buren that was missing. Nobody messed with Miss Timid Hettie.

Mila wanted to run up, introduce herself, and ask questions. How had the agent gotten into the FBI? Was it a tough screening process? What types of people did they look for?

Instead, feeling like a sneak, she followed the woman at a distance into the darkened Hall of African Mammals where mothers holding infants gazed at exhibits and high-octane children laughed and screeched. They passed under the eight charging elephants and banked down a small corridor into the long Hall of African Peoples. Lighted dioramas displayed ancient masks, tribal clothes, and pounded metal trinkets. They progressed to the Hall of Birds where king penguins, Andean condors, and a Secretary Bird stared blankly from behind glass. A teenage mother texted on a phone while her baby whimpered from a stroller. Just past the Hall of Birds, the stout guide pulled open the door leading to the east wing's staff section and Agent Cool Cucumber disappeared.

Mila stood in the shadows staring at the closed *PRIVATE - STAFF ONLY* door. She should have pushed aside the stout guide and introduced herself. She could have offered to walk the agent to ornithology. She could have used that walk to ask all kinds of questions. What happened to cold cases of young smiling boys named Jimmy that had been snatched off the street in broad daylight? Would such a cold case ever be reassigned to a self-assured agent who just happened to be working the Hettie Van Buren case? What if the missing Miss Timid Hettie case provided a once-in-a-lifetime opportunity for a family member of the missing boy to get a cold case reopened?

Mila's routine day had just capsized.

4

ONE OF HETTIE'S COLLEAGUES, a young man named Jonathan, waited on the quiet side of the *PRIVATE - STAFF ONLY* door. He had a sharp nose over a thin goatee and was lethargic as he led her down a quiet hall to a wooden door with a frosted glass pane with stenciled *Ornithology Department*. They pushed into a brightly lit cavernous space with rows of black lab tables, clusters of cubicles, and towering shelves strewn with glass vials, white skeletons, chrome machines, and scientific books. Bird posters and colorful maps dominated the far wall.

"Is Hettie okay?" Jonathan frowned.

"Yes, as far as we know. I'm just checking in since we haven't heard from her in a bit." Misrepresenting was in every FBI job description.

"Oh, God. I hope so." He led her past a group of scientists in white lab coats huddled together, their hands fluttering over vials.

"Do you know her well?"

"Oh, my God," he squeaked. "That sounds so ominous."

"I'm just ticking off the boxes. I'm sure she went on a holiday and turned her cell phone off." Except for that overturned dish in the bedroom and that broken glass in the frame. "When did you last see her?"

"Friday. I haven't seen her since the weekend."

The smell of chemicals hung in the room and stung the inside of her nostrils. "Do you know her well?"

"Uh, well? No, not really. But we all work together, you know. Hettie is lovely."

It was the same mild description Hettie's doorman had used —positive yet unimaginative, as if the person was uninteresting. "How would you describe her?"

He wobbled his head back and forth. "She's nice. She's quiet. I would even say shy. She comes and works, and sometimes stays late. Just all around a nice gal."

That sounded a lot like uninteresting. "So not necessarily a strong personality?"

"Strong? No, I wouldn't say strong. Just nice."

They arrived at a tidy desk under a wall littered with dozens of stuffed exotic birds suspended in action. An outstretched white eagle swooped to the floor. A fat gray goose craned its neck. Not a single dirty New York City pigeon was stuck on the wall. Dom turned to Jonathan. "Does she have friends here at work?"

"Uh, more coworkers." He shrugged. "Like normal."

"She seem happy?"

"Oh, yeah, fine. I know she has a boyfriend. I can hear her chatting on the phone with him sometimes. She smiles when she's talking to him."

"Have you met her boyfriend?"

"No. Hettie and I aren't that close."

"Are there other colleagues that are closer to her?"

He frowned. "Nah, she's pretty solitary. But many of us are, to be fair. You know, scientists and all." He gave her a self-depreciating smile.

"No work-related happy hours?"

"I mean … maybe … once a year?" His brow furrowed.

"So Hettie doesn't go to work parties?"

"Not really, no. She's not real into going out."

"She ever talk about her parents?"

He reared back. "No, not to me." There was a pregnant pause. "But we all know about them."

She leaned forward. "How's that?"

"Her mom is on the board here. Yvette Van Buren. They are big donors. They come to all the parties." His voice dropped to a low whisper. "Nobody would ever cross Hettie, not with that lineage. Blaulicht loves her."

"Anything else you can think of?"

"She's just a really nice person. Super into birds. But so are most of us here. I sure hope she's okay."

"I'm sure it will be fine. Thanks for your help, Jonathan."

Dom slid out the desk's rolling chair and settled in. From overhead, beady glass eyes examined her with the critical gaze of guardians protecting a shy young woman with a domineering father, a passive mother, and an aversion to New York's wealthy socialite scene. *Give me a break here, would ya? I've only had this case for three hours.* She took a deep breath to block out the noise of the lab and slowly examined the area.

The desk was tidy. A few documents were piled in the upper right corner next to a small organizer that held pens, scissors, and tape measures in neat compartments. A travel coffee mug appeared to have been cleaned recently. Inside, the drawer was littered with office items—notepads, crumpled tissues, scattered pens, thumbtacks, a green music player with earphones—but no notes, no passwords scribbled on pieces of paper. Jiggling the mouse, Dom woke the computer. A lot of people didn't turn off their computer after a work day. Hettie had not either. The home screen displayed the Outlook desktop with the email and calendar systems open. No need for a login password. It was a common mistake.

She scanned the emails in Hettie's inbox. Messages about birds, research, and notes from other ornithologists. There didn't appear to be any emails from personal contacts. It looked like Hettie kept her private and professional lives separate. A quiet, studious woman who avoided the limelight. Dom pulled up the Outlook calendar to the current day's view and the plans for the evening. *Madeline. B day. Blue Hill. 8 pm.* A friend's birthday.

On her cell phone, Dom looked up the number for Blue Hill over by Washington Square Park, called it, and confirmed there was still a reservation for Hettie Van Buren. A pit formed in her stomach. The mess at the apartment with the strewn china bowl and smashed picture frame, and now a missed birthday date. Two strikes. Not good. *Where are you, Hettie?*

Dom scrolled the calendar back day by day. Hettie kept a full schedule with meetings, one-on-one dinners, and salon and gym appointments.

Micah play Broadway. 8 pm

Foundation proposal due.

Dentist. 3 pm

Boot camp work out. 5:30 pm

Shopping w/ Whitney. 6 pm

WRF mtg on migration patterns, LA. 2 pm

Hair. 5 pm

Dinner M&D Tea Room. 7 pm

Scrolling back through the calendar, Dom's finger paused on the period three weeks ago. Five days that were left blank. For five days there were no meetings, no dinners. Did Hettie take a vacation? Scrolling further through the remainder of the year, it appeared that those five days were the only blank ones in an otherwise fully scheduled life. Did her parents not know anything about those five days? Dom asked specifically if Hettie had any plans. Maybe they forgot?

She found Jonathan at his desk. "Would you know if Hettie took a vacation a few weeks back?"

His brow wrinkled. "I can't remember."

"Okay, thanks."

Returning to the desk, Dom scrolled the calendar into the future. For the next month, the schedule was very busy. Hettie did not plan on being away. Strike three. And three strikes were no longer a coincidence.

Dom needed to find the boyfriend. Quickly. In the best-case scenario, he would direct Dom to Hettie's location. In the worst-case scenario, he was involved in her increasingly suspicious disappearance. In Hettie's address book, she ran a search for Micah and was rewarded with *Micah Zapata, 212 Bronxdale Ave, Bronx* and a telephone number. She dialed the number. It went straight to voicemail. A call only went straight to voicemail when the mailbox was full or the phone was dead.

From overhead, the flying battalion of exotic birds glared at her with sharp, demanding eyes. *Okay, guys, I get, I get it. Something's wrong with your Hettie. I'm on it.*

5

MICAH ZAPATA, Hettie's boyfriend, lived in an upper apartment of a Bronx fourplex on a small, well-kept street with the remarkably unoriginal name of Bronxdale Avenue. Dom parked the Lancia by the curb and checked her phone. Her brother had texted. *How's the case going?*

Three months ago, when the Bureau put Dom on administrative leave, Beecher Walker moved back home. He had been going through a big life transition. A year earlier, and after much angst, Beecher decided that being an economist for a big investment bank was no longer professionally fulfilling. He quit his job. At which point, his young wife decided that Beecher was no longer personally fulfilling. The divorce settlement was still being vigorously contested. Dom's forced leave of absence was the perfect excuse for him to regroup from home. Beecher and Dom fell back into their familial ways. This morning he cooked a stack of blueberry pancakes to celebrate her official return to work. While his enthusiasm was endearing, it unnerved her. She didn't like the idea of her younger brother trying to boost her confidence.

She texted, *Still too early to say.*

But you feel solid?

Sometimes Beecher was too smart for his own good. She typed *Still too early to say.*

She slipped the phone in her jeans pocket, retrieved a pancake holster from the glove compartment, clipped it on her belt just over the kidney near the small of her back, and unfolded from the sports car. From the trunk's safe, she pulled a Glock 17m, secured it in the holster, and shut the trunk. Jogging up the external stairs, she cornered onto the small landing of Micah's apartment.

The front door was ajar one inch.

In her mind, alarm bells shrilled. Doors ajar were never a good thing. She unsheathed the Glock, held it right-handed pointed skyward, brushed her index finger against the passive safety lever on the trigger, and banged on the thin door. "FBI. We're coming in!" Better for an intruder to think she wasn't alone.

Silence.

Double gripping the Glock, she lunged back before leaning over and smashing her foot into the door. Better for an intruder to know she meant business. The flimsy door slammed against the interior wall with a rattling boom. She cornered into the apartment, swept the gun left to right, and settled in a fighting stance—torso square to the room, feet shoulder width apart, right foot behind left. A ratty orange sofa and a haggard coffee table sat on an ugly brown carpet. A flat-screen television stood upright on a forlorn console. Sweatshirts and baseball hats hung by the door. A small galley kitchen extended off the living room. There was nothing but an empty silence.

"FBI, coming in!"

She sighted the gun down the hallway to a closed bedroom door. It was a dangerous funnel to where a perp could be waiting. Adrenaline kicked up a notch. Her heartbeat spiked as she darted down the dim hall. Pausing in front of the closed door, she sucked in three sharp breaths. Leaning back like a kick boxer, she delivered a roundhouse kick into the door and dropped into a fighting stance with the Glock sweeping the room. A rancid, putrid stench bit her nostrils. *Fuck.*

Her stomach flipped, and she gagged. "FBI!" But she knew there would be no response. With that smell, she knew what she would find.

A silent and still Micah Zapata was stretched awkwardly across the floor and the far wall, legs splayed, head canted. A red bloom stretched across the center of his white shirt. The purple of rigor mortis had colored both arms. His eyes were open and staring blankly. *Fuck.*

She crab-stepped to the closet door, yanked it open, and swept the gun across the empty space. She rushed into the bathroom, Glock ready. It was also empty. The apartment was clear.

While striding down the hallway, she holstered the gun, snatched her phone, and punched in the numbers for HQ. After stopping by the front door, she breathed in the fresh air as the phone rang out on the other side.

A woman answered the line. "Javits Dispatch."

Dom pressed her shoulder against the phone and fumbled in her jacket pocket for plastic gloves. "This is Special Agent Domini Walker. I've got a homicide. Location, 212 Bronxdale Avenue, Apt 4. I need NYPD and ERT. On the double." ERT stood for the Evidence Response Team.

Her heart hammered in her chest as her fingers fumbled for the gloves.

Dispatch confirmed the address and Dom clicked off the call.

After snapping the gloves on her trembling fingers, she dialed Fontaine's office.

His secretary patched her through immediately.

"Sir, it's Walker. I've got a homicide. Hettie Van Buren's boyfriend. Male, twenty-something, Latino. Gunshot wound to the chest. Possibly twenty-four hours."

"Jesus." Fontaine's voice was deep and gravely. "ERT?"

"They're on their way." Her breathing was shallow, and her legs felt leaden.

"NYPD?"

She pushed her spine against the hardness of the wall, willing her fingers to still. "Dispatched."

All the proper initial steps had been taken. There was silence on the line.

Dom had worked with Fontaine on her last operation, St. Christopher's. Her actions in that case had attracted FBI's internal affairs, the Office of Professional Responsibility, had triggered an internal investigation, and had grounded her for the last three months. Fontaine was working to get the internal investigation dropped, and she appreciated his efforts. But all assistant directors in charge of New York had been political beasts, and Fontaine was no exception. Rumors of his political connections swirled among the rank and file. She didn't trust him. But to be fair, Domini Walker didn't trust most people.

His deep voice broke the silence. "You want this? I can take you off it."

This morning, the Van Buren case had appeared to be a simple rich-girl-gone-partying scenario—perfect for someone coming off leave. Within three hours, it became a homicide with a likely kidnapping. She closed her eyes. A flash of Stewart Walker's smile blinked across the insides of her lids. In the memory, he was in the Brooklyn swimming pool surrounded by water with his wet hands stretched to his five-year-old daughter on the cement deck while nodding encouragement. *Keep your eyes open when you jump, my Dom. You gotta live it.*

In her ear, Fontaine repeated, "I can take you off this case."

She popped her eyes open to the brightness in the apartment like a Polaroid snapping a meaningful instant. Her heartbeat settled into a manageable pounding and her fingers stilled. "No. I've got it."

"I can take you off this."

"No, I want it." She pulled a Blistex from her jacket pocket and rubbed the menthol into each nostril.

"Are you sure?"

The pulse in her neck was stable. "Yes."

"You sure?"

It was time to come back in. "Yes, I'm sure."

"Okay. What have you found so far?"

"The parents are touchy. The father is a big personality. They don't like the boyfriend. They haven't seen Hettie since Sunday. Signs of a struggle at Hettie's apartment. Overturned dish. Smashed frame. Water in a vase drying. Fresh food in the fridge. Musty dishwasher. Two days. My sense is a kidnapping."

"Witnesses at her apartment?"

"No. Not at Hettie's apartment. She went in with her mother on Sunday, the mother left alone, Hettie never came out." The menthol cleared her airways.

"Okay."

"Hettie works at the Museum of Natural History. They don't know anything. Haven't seen her since last week. Boyfriend lives in this location. Bronx. Upper floor. Lower income. Cursory exam looks clean. No drug paraphernalia, no guns. Door was ajar. Victim in the bedroom, slid against the wall."

"Anything else?"

"Not yet."

"Okay."

Silence. "Dom, do this by the book. There will be eyes on you."

The Van Burens were very prominent in the city. "Of course."

"You need a field partner on this one?"

It was not always an FBI custom to assign partners. In some instances, the investigating agent worked alone. "I'm better on my own." That was an understatement. She wasn't good with partners.

In the silence, she could sense his deliberations. On the one hand, he wouldn't want to break her winning streak as a lone wolf. But an influential, politically connected family was now involved in a murder and kidnap investigation, and it would be high profile. Two agents on the case would be more people to share the blame if it went south.

She bent at her waist and pushed the phone tighter against her ear. "Sir, I'll close this. I'm better on my own."

"Okay. Agreed. For now."

"Can I choose my support?" On the St. Christopher operation, Dom had worked with a young staff operations specialist named Lea Peck. Lea was fresh out of a Southern college, all enthusiasm, brains, and sass, and she had provided thorough case support by deftly managing streams of raw data. "I want the SOS I worked with on the last operation."

"Done. I'll call the Van Burens now and let them know about the boyfriend."

Kidnapping cases worked against a stopwatch and were high on tension. The strong-willed Claude would undoubtedly insert both himself and his powerful friends. When a ransom note was inevitably sent, conversations would get heated, tempers would rise, and blame would be meted out. The goal, in the face of this extra noise, was to stay focused on finding Hettie.

She stood up. "Sir, my priority is Hettie. Nothing or nobody else."

"You just do your job, Agent. I'll deal with the family."

"You'll deal with the politics, sir?"

He hung up.

Staff Operations Specialist Lea Peck picked up her phone on the second ring. "Dom. How-the-hell-in-Alabama are you? Please tell me you're back."

Amidst the drifting stench of death, Lea's thick Southern accent was a calming salve. "I am. And I've asked for you."

"Hell, yes, you did! Girls are back together! Talk to me."

"You at the office?"

"You bet. What have we got?"

Dom imagined Lea at a desk in the huge brightly lit analyst floor of the downtown Jacob J. Javits Federal Building. She was a twenty-three-year-old African American woman whose parents' credentials, a Baptist minister and a third-grade English teacher, were remarkably upstanding. At five ten with broad shoulders and a muscled body, she was a four-time all-American in track and field and an NCAA champion for Louisiana State University's Lady Tigers in the 60- and 200-meter events and the 4x400-meter relay. Lea strongly believed in justice, civil rights, God, and the inimitable power of a full-bodied curse word.

Over the torturous twelve months of operation St. Christopher, Dom and Lea spent endless days and nights under fluorescent lighting huddled across desks as they gamed out moves. What would happen if they rolled up on this perp's girlfriend or chased down that kingpin's enemy? Only once on that case had Lea missed a trick, and she called Dom immediately.

Lea's call had come at three am. "I missed something. It's big. It's bad."

"Tell me," Dom said.

"Our guy in Chicago purchased plastic ties at Home Depot, a plastic bed cover at Walmart, and a video recorder at Best Buy.

I didn't catch it on his credit card records. I just saw it. I'm sorry, Dom. I fucked up."

Two days earlier, Dom stood outside the suspect's Chicago house and talked to him through a screen door. She did not ask to go inside because they had no cause.

Lea's oversight cost the life of a small child. Dom said softly. "Listen, stay focused. Don't beat yourself up."

"How can I not?"

"Because we're gonna get him. And the others." She sniffed. "Remember, you did not do this. They did this. They're the bad guys. We're the good guys. Good guys are gonna win this. Do you hear me? Do you hear me?"

"Yes."

"You got this. We got this. We don't have time to beat ourselves up. We move on. We'll get 'em."

"You promise?"

"Yes. I promise. We will get them."

Lea's voice gained strength. "We'll get 'em like cock-sucking rats in a trap?"

"Like rats in a trap," Dom responded.

Now, standing in Micah Zapata's forlorn apartment, Dom was glad Lea was back. "The team is back together."

"Tits and ass. We are back together."

"You ready for this?"

"As I'll ever be. Big deal family on this one, am I right? Gonna be lots of moving parts. Where you at?"

"I'm at the boyfriend's apartment. Homicide. He's been shot."

Lea whistled. "Hell's bells."

"I'm calling Hettie Van Buren a kidnapping. And now the boyfriend. Three strikes—"

"Clock's on."

For the FBI, a kidnapping was considered a murder waiting

to happen. The sooner an investigator found a motive and a suspect, the better a victim's chances of survival. Dom and Lea both knew the odds were against them.

Dom paced across the living room. "I need a tap on Claude and Yvette Van Buren's cell phones and any landlines at their apartment. Stat."

"You expecting a ransom call?"

She spun and returned across the room. "I'm expecting something."

"On it like a righteous angel."

"I'll need subpoenas and toll records going back a month for Hettie, the Van Burens, and one Micah Zapata." She relayed his address.

"Moses has spoken. Consider it done."

She started across the floor again. "ERT is on the way. I'll have them send it all to the labs marked for you."

"Manna from heaven."

She circled into the galley kitchen. "Then I'll need ERT to do a sweep of Hettie's apartment. I didn't find her phone. If she's on the move and she has her phone, we need to track that immediately. Also, I need to know where her phone last pinged on a tower."

"Roger."

"When they're finished with Hettie's apartment, have them grab her work stuff at the Museum of Natural History. Her computer and anything from her desk. I'm gonna do a sweep here at the boyfriend's. I'll keep you posted."

"Fire it up, Dom. We got this."

Hanging up the call, Dom glanced down the silent gloom to the bedroom. *Micah, what did you and Hettie get yourselves into?*

She needed an answer soon. Murderers had a way of killing kidnapped victims.

6

DOM MOVED down the hallway's worn carpet with one deliberate foot in front of the other. Maybe it was that Stewart Walker died when she and Beecher were so young and fragile. Maybe it was that Esther disappeared without a goodbye. For whatever reason, being in a room with an empty human shell brought on profound feelings of vulnerability and sadness. The examination of a homicide victim was the toughest part of her job. She hated it.

She stepped into the bedroom and scrutinized Micah's body. Staring down the barrel of an intruder's gun in his bedroom, Micah would have backed up against the wall and pleaded for his life. He probably hadn't even tried to fight back. The shot would have thrown him against the wall where he slid into a seated position. Although his shoulders slipped sideways, the skeleton retained some stiffness with the torso still upright. Two wooden legs extended across the carpet with toes pointed to the ceiling, and a blood bloom seeped out across his white shirt and fanned down over the belt line. The crotch of his pants appeared yellowed, and his hands lay empty on either side of the hips.

A cold fog slithered up through Dom's gut. Dank and malignant, the rising fog drained heat as it passed into her chest. Her legs froze, and her arms felt numb.

Dom raised her gaze to Micah's face. His open eyes were sunken, and his pupils had whitened. Loose gray skin along his cheeks and the neck bore a wet sheen from ruptured blisters.

Tears stung her eyelids as a warm drop escaped. Like a high-definition movie, imaginary snippets of Micah in happier days swarmed into the void. Micah running along a beach, holding Hettie's hand; Micah driving a car, cocky and self-assured with an elbow out the window and sun streaming on tan skin; Micah surrounded by friends, watching a soccer game, laughing with beautiful teeth, chest heaving in delight; Micah grinning over a wine at a fancy restaurant with Hettie. In her mind, Micah Zapata had been a vibrant, cheerful young man madly in love with a shy young woman. His future had been bright.

The fog in her chest suddenly contracted, drawing her ribs in on themselves in a painful cinch. She coughed into the silence and rattled her head. *That's enough of that, Dom.*

Taking a step ahead, she knelt at the feet and examined the wound. The bullet had hit dead center, equidistant from either side. It was an unusually clean shot. It may have been luck, but it was more likely the shooter was a professional. It was a malevolent and cowardly kill.

Dom sat back on her haunches. *Micah, what have you and Hettie gotten yourselves into?*

Which of the two victims—Hettie or Micah—were more likely to be affiliated in some way with professional killers? Surely not Hettie Van Buren, a high-society trust-fund debutante with a silver spoon. No, it was far more plausible that these crimes originated from someone connected to Micah Zapata. Call it intuition or a hunch, but it was a bet Dom felt fairly confident about.

She leaned over the stiff legs, slid her right hand around the left hip, and felt an empty jean pocket. Trying the left side, she felt a cell phone and edged it out. The battery was dead. She slipped it into her coat pocket and stood.

Turning a slow 360 degrees, she took in the sparsely furnished room. The bed was a simple box set on an iron frame with a dingy cream sheet and a brown cotton blanket. Hettie's apartment on Washington Square Park was a completely different world. It was no surprise there was only one pillow. On the single bedside table were two silver-framed photos. In one, Hettie sat on Micah's lap at an outdoor restaurant over-looking a large green canyon under a bright summer sun. Upstate New York, maybe? Hettie's arm was around his shoul-ders, and she wore a devious grin as if, moments earlier, she kissed him deeply. The second photo was a black-and-white close-up of Hettie. Taken from the vantage point of a lover in a bed, she gave the photographer a sultry stare. Above a sheet around her chest, her shoulders were bare.

Dom swallowed to push some warmth into the cold dank fog in her chest.

There was nothing under the bed. In the closet, T-shirts were stacked on the shelf, shoes were kicked haphazardly, and long sleeve button-down shirts drooped on cheap hangers. The dresser drawers held a smattering of loose gray socks, balled underwear, and crammed white T-shirts. A single prescription bottle of antibiotics was the only thing of interest in the medi-cine cabinet. Micah appeared to have been a normal young man —no hoarding, no porn, no guns.

Dom made her way down the hallway into the living room and did a quick search. Three dirty coffee mugs were leaving rings on the wooden coffee table. A crumpled T-shirt hung over the arm of the couch. In the refrigerator, two soda cans sat along-side condiments from take-out places and a solitary jar of ketchup. In the freezer, four homemade packages with Spanish words in black ink—*pollo, pescado*—were gathering frost. A box of trash bags sat forsaken under the sink.

The apartment felt perfectly normal. There were no hidden drugs, no cache of cash, not even a cabinet full of liquor. In fact, it all appeared too normal. *What young man in his twenties didn't have junk?* No video game consoles, no car magazines, no CDs. The apartment felt flat. Maybe Micah, a college kid on scholarship who was trying to climb out of a low-income background, had only ever intended this home to be temporary.

Two shelves swayed under heavy books with the titles *The Ecology of Capitalism, Sustainability*, and *Forget Fossil Fuels*. The Van Burens mentioned Micah was a student at NYU, and the text books spoke of an environmental major. She stepped to the shelves. Jammed in the middle of the text books was a tall yellow book that appeared to be a high school yearbook.

She pulled the yellow book, sat on the sofa, and opened the front cover. A collage of boldly colored photos captured the mischievous gleaming eyes and optimistic sparkling smiles of carefree teenagers. The cold fog returned to her chest and crept down her arms. Dom's high school memories had not been carefree. Those lonely, somber days had been spent hiding an ominous secret.

A long dormant memory from fifteen years earlier barreled into her consciousness. In the bright empty apartment, Dom and Beecher sat silently watching the dust motes twirl on a current from Aunt Lucille's sudden departure.

Beecher whispered, "Dom, what does it mean?"

She wanted to say *We're abandoned*, but the words caught in her throat. Instead, there was silence, frozen arms, and the prickly upholstery against her legs.

The hapless spin of the motes slowed.

"Dom, what does it mean?"

The high pitch of Beecher's voice unstuck her, and she smoothed the hair on his arm with a soft stroke. "It means it's just you and me now."

"What do we do?"

"I guess we go grocery shopping." Her voice sounded brave despite her cold fear.

Later, they carried six bags of groceries ten blocks and up three flights of stairs. They had eaten cheap spaghetti on soggy paper plates, and that night they had moved the two bare mattresses into one room.

Flipping through the pages of the yellow yearbook, Dom found Micah Zapata among the rows of formal portraits. The younger version, a few pounds thinner, had been just as good-looking. He must have been a lady-killer in high school. His smile was broad, his eyes were bright, and his dark hair was tousled. Hettie would have easily fallen for those looks. *Who the heck were you, Micah Zapata? Did you have a dark side?*

Among the candid shots in the back of the yearbook, he smiled devilishly with his arms slung over the shoulders of two friends. On his right, a fresh-faced white boy wore a Yankees baseball hat, a black T-shirt, and a large gold necklace. To the left of Micah, a Hispanic face looked tough under a clean-shaven head. The edge of a tattoo crept along the bicep of the clean-shaven friend. Tattoos were common among gang members. *Who do we have here?*

Setting the book on the couch, Dom snapped a close-up of the trio and fired off a message to Lea. *Any way to identify that tat on the guy to the left?*

Outside on the cement stairs, shoes clomped up to the open apartment door.

Jolting upright, Dom reached across her chest for the Glock, stepped over the coffee table, crossed the room in three strides, jammed her back up against the wall, and double-gripped the gun to the ceiling. Better to be overly cautious. Better not to present your center body mass target in a direct line of sight to an unknown person entering a crime scene. Especially when that body mass was not protected by body armor, there was a dead body in the bedroom, and the stomping up the stairs was of two unidentified individuals.

7

OUTSIDE MICAH ZAPATA'S apartment a male voice shouted, "NYPD!"

Dom lowered the Glock and took a deep breath. Shoving off from the wall, she said loudly, "FBI. We're clear." She rolled her shoulders and cracked her neck. Better to not give off a tense vibe.

Two detectives stepped through the door, one black and large, the other Hispanic and smaller. The black one noticed as she holstered her Glock. "Sorry, did we give you a scare?"

She shrugged. "Just being prepared."

He introduced himself as Detective Johns and his Hispanic partner as Detective Rodriguez. Both from Homicide. They scanned the scene with smart, inquisitive eyes and sniffed the putrid smell.

"You come up through Narcotics?" she asked.

They both nodded with the unruffled confidence of long tenures. Johns was huge, maybe six four, and had the calm energy of a man accustomed to getting his way. She imagined him at home on a La-Z-Boy watching Saturday afternoon football with a happy wife making nachos, a cold beer in his hand,

and at least five screaming kids bouncing off walls. Rodriguez was the polar opposite at five eight with the slim build of a boxer and critical eyes that flicked left and right across the living room. He probably lived in a very tidy apartment in a clean building with a large Doberman and a boyfriend.

She nodded down the hall. "Victim in the bedroom. Single gunshot to the chest. The apartment looks pretty clean."

Lots of older guys in the NYPD hadn't bought in yet to the idea of women law enforcement, but neither eyed her sideways or displayed the common micro expressions of disapproval—squinting or the one-sided pull of pressed lips. These two acted nonplussed. It was a small win. "Okay, see what you think. I'll wait outside."

Twenty minutes later, they stepped out on the landing.

She asked, "Whatta ya think?"

"Mm-hmm. Not a whole lot. Clean kill, like you said. Chest. Thirty-five caliber. Maybe two days ago?" Johns spoke with a calm confidence, unperturbed by the body inside.

Rodriguez stood as the silent partner, taking the measure of her.

Johns scanned the room and hummed like a father that soothed multiple children. "Mm-hmm. We usually see crime scenes that are all messed up. Overturned beds, trashed closets. You know the drill. Hoods come in, take the shot, look around for reward. No associated burglary. This had none of that. Also, the home is clean, tidy. Mostly we see poverty, grime, paraphernalia. You know what I'm talking about."

She nodded. "Too clean. Guy seems real normal."

They both nodded.

"Mm-hmm. Shooter came in, did the job, left. Intent was the kill shot."

"Agreed. Anything that tweaked a motive for you?"

Johns shook his head.

She counted off with her fingers. "Personal dispute. A wronged girlfriend. A heavy collecting a gambling debt. Drug related."

Johns nodded. "I feel you. Could be any of those, but—"

"But the shot looks professional."

"Agreed. Doesn't smell like a novice."

She cracked her knuckles. "Here's the hinky. The vic is related to a kidnapping."

"How's that?" Johns asked.

"Rich white girl. Washington Square Park."

Both men frowned.

"I think the perp took the girlfriend. Somehow connected. The timing is way too coincidental."

"No shit. A kid from the Bronx tapping a Village girl? He gets hit and the girl's a 134?" 134 was police code for a kidnapping.

She nodded.

Johns whistled. "I don't envy you. That case ain't for the fainthearted."

She pulled out her phone and showed them the photo of the friend's tattoo. "You recognize this?"

Rodriguez scratched his cheek. "Can't tell." He had an unusually high-pitched voice, which is probably why he didn't talk much. He pointed at the photo. "Could be a clown. That's something. A crying clown tat stands for 'laugh now, cry later,' as in they're winning now out on the streets but they know it will catch up with them. But you can't really tell from that photo. Could be something else."

All three stood silently considering the possibilities of a West Village rich girl tied up in something gang related.

Dom slid her phone in her pocket. "It might be gang?"

Both men nodded.

Rodriguez spoke again. "It jives with the Honduran thing."

Dom and Johns gave him questioning looks.

Rodriguez nodded back into the apartment. "The T-shirt in the living room. It's a soccer jersey. For the Honduran soccer team."

Johns hummed.

She nodded at Rodriguez. "Nice catch. What's the situation with the Honduran gang in this neighborhood?"

Johns said. "Mostly local crews. Crack, heroin. The big gangs don't mess around too much over here. Not poor enough. The market isn't big enough. About ten blocks away you've got some projects owned by the Cholos, but that's really small-scale stuff. This hood over here ... it ain't their scene. We were surprised, to be honest, by the address."

Rodriguez nodded toward the living room. "But the apartment is really clean, so if your vic is gang, it's gotta be on a higher order. Like maybe he was the accountant or in logistics."

The detectives shifted impatiently on their feet.

Time to wrap this up. "Tell you what, I'll take the lab work since it's related to my other case, but do you mind taking the street on this? To rule out witnesses?" It was polite of her to ask. Technically, since a homicide was NYPD territory, it would default to their jurisdiction.

They both shrugged. Homicide detectives in New York were used to taking orders even if they had a huge case backlog.

Johns said, "Mm-hmm. Sure."

"I appreciate it. I've got our techs on the way."

They swapped cards and the two detectives shuffled down the stairs.

Dom rang Lea. "I need some research on drugs coming out of Honduras."

"I can do you one better. I'll get you a Border Control guy on the line. Give me five."

Ten minutes later Dom's phone rang.

"Special Agent Walker, this is Albert Castillo with the US Customs and Border Patrol in Miami. What can I do for you?" He had a pleasant voice.

Dom stepped into the living room and glanced at the soccer jersey hanging on a hook. "If you've got a few minutes, I need a quick lesson on Honduras."

"Sure. It's mostly drugs when we're talking Honduras. It's a major transit point for transnational drugs. We see Columbian cartels using it as a handover point to the Mexican cartels. It's not the number one handover location, more like number four or five. It's mostly cocaine. 140-300 tons a year, by our estimates. There are some very local groups in Honduras that are tied up with the political elites and businessmen. By all accounts, their police are one of the most corrupt in Latin America. We hear they may be cracking down. On the other hand, the military has upped its effort there, including coastal patrols. They are also using radar to track drug flights. But hey, it's still all very dirty. Crooked with a capital C." He paused. "Does that help?"

She looked around the apartment. "So with all that comes violence?"

"You betcha. Honduras is one of the poorest in Latin America. It's plagued by violence and crime. I've heard of whole neighborhoods being butchered. Lots and lots of civilians getting killed. A real tragedy."

"We get people moving here?"

"Oh, yeah. To avoid the violence. But remember these families are also moving to Mexico, Belize, other safe zones, too. Not just the US."

She stepped to the door and checked outside. Better to not get surprised again. "One last question, do you hear a lot about kidnapping?"

"Not specifically, but those cartels and gangs are savages. I wouldn't put anything past them."

"Okay, thanks, Agent Castillo. I appreciate the quick response."

"Sure, any time." He clicked off.

Footfalls sounded from outside. She stepped out onto the cement landing to see two ERTs climbing the stairs. She had worked with Christopher Locke before. "Hey, Christopher. How you doing?"

"Hi, Dom. All good." He nodded over his shoulder to his partner as they passed into the living room. "This here is Becky Turnball."

The two women acknowledged each other with silent chin lifts, two women sticking together in the male-dominated Bureau. "The body is in the bedroom."

"We'll look for telltales." Locke meant hair, nails, fibers, and blood or anything left behind by the perp.

"I've got Lea Peck on this."

"Got it." He shook his head with a wide grin. "She's a whippersnapper. Full of spit fire, that one."

Turnball closed her eyes for a beat and gave a tiny shake of the head. Locke wouldn't have used those phrases to describe a male colleague, and both women knew it. Dom liked her immediately.

Dom held up Micah's cell phone. "I'll need Lea on this asap, too."

Turnball snapped on plastic gloves and zipped the phone inside an evidence bag. "I'll get it to her pronto."

"This is related to a kidnapping. Rich girl over in Greenwich Village. Some disturbance in her bedroom."

"Sure," Locke nodded. "We'll head there next."

"And when you can fit it in, Lea will need you up at the

Museum of Natural History to grab the rich girl's work computer."

They both nodded.

"Okay," Dom said, "I'll leave you to it."

Time to start fitting the pieces together on Micah Zapata. The clock was running.

TUESDAY AFTERNOON

Now the flocks of swift-flying curlews that used to wing their way each fall from the Arctic tundra to Labrador and then out over 2,500 miles of the Atlantic to South America and back in the spring up through Texas and Mississippi Valley are gone.

—Thomas Foster, "Circling to Doom"

8

RURAL HONDURAS

The sway of the bus rumbling along the highway made her sleepy. Despite the hot, gritty wind that rushed through the open windows, she didn't close her eyes. She needed to stay vigilant.

Maria Cardona had woken before sunrise and had listened to the morning noises—the whistle in Ines' snores, the scratch of the rooster outside the door, the screech of a macaw in the distance. She needed to feed the chickens and make sure the water tank was full. If the chilis and tomatoes looked ripe in the garden, she would bring some to Aunt Alma's as a gift. A four-year-old was a handful, especially for five days. The special *semita* sweet bread, purchased from the market yesterday, would be their breakfast. She needed to remember to also take the extra milk to Aunt Alma's or it would go bad.

From the hanger on the peg, she took down her best dress, washed earlier in the week, and slipped it over her head. Outside, the sun was rising over the mountains and the breeze was dry. There wouldn't be rain while she was gone. Not in the dry season. It felt like it was always the dry season now. She had to be careful with the water in the outhouse. After, with the thin broom, she swept the hardened dirt by the door of the one-room house and tossed feed to the clucking chickens.

Inside, she folded away their clothes from yesterday and made her bed. Only when the morning chores were finished did she wake Ines with a tight hug, clutching the small body to her chest and searing to memory the feel of her daughter against her heart. Anything could go wrong on this trip. Anything could always go wrong. She had learned that.

After dropping Ines at Aunt Alma's, she had walked the two hours to the market. The packed bag was small, but heavy, so when she arrived she sat on a bench and waited for the local bus. While there was a faster, more expensive bus, and they had said they would pay for transport and meals, she hedged. What if they didn't pay? No, she would take the local bus with the open windows.

The grit on the wind scratched her eyes. Only five more hours to go.

Her cousin was sending the nephew to the bus terminal on the outskirts of Tegucigalpa. It was arranged that he would wait by the Super El Rey across the street. It was safer for the twelve-year-old city boy to wait at the supermarket for a few hours than to have straight-from-the-village Maria lost at the terminal.

The bus roared past a roadside stall. Over forlorn piles of corn, a young woman watched with a blank face, unimpressed with yet another passage of poor people hurtling to the big city.

Maria had never been on a cross-country bus. There had never been a need. But everyone knew what they looked like from the outside: crammed with dazed travelers, bags lashed on the roof, open windows yawning. Rumors warned that the men's fingers could become slithering snakes, so Maria stood behind the driver for an hour until a seat next to a woman opened up.

Maria Cardona may be from the village, but she was not naive.

9

AT A SECOND BRONX apartment not far from Micah Zapata's, Dom knocked on the door. Telling a parent their child had been killed was a heartbreaking part of her job. It never got easier, and it never got normal.

Opening the door, the older Mr. Zapata knew instantly that something was wrong. Fear shot through his gentle dark eyes. "What is it?" He had a pleasant round face, a shock of black hair, and a crisp blue-collared shirt. His accent was thick.

Dom flashed her badge. "Sir, I'm FBI. May I come in?"

Mr. Zapata opened the door wide and ushered her into the small apartment with fluttery hands. From a galley kitchen, Mrs. Zapata appeared, a tiny woman behind heavy glasses with salt-and-pepper hair pulled back in a tight bun. She wiped her hands on a red-and-white checkered apron.

Dom took a deep breath. "I'm afraid I've got some terrible news."

Their eyes widened to saucers.

Say it twice, so the brain can prepare. "I have some terrible news."

Both parents blinked.

"I'm afraid your son, Micah, has been the victim of a shooting. Micah is gone. Micah is dead."

Dom closed her eyes. *Wait for it, wait for it.* A banshee howl filled the room. Dom opened her eyes just as the older woman fell to her knees. The mother's scream choked her up, and tears stung for the second time that day. Mr. Zapata moved quickly to grab his wife and get her to the couch. It was a good sign. At least as a united couple, they had each other. It would make things easier. There were few things that made this easier. Dom whispered, "I am so, so sorry,"

"Oh, Dios mío, mi hijo, mi hijo," wailed Mrs. Zapata. "Oh, my God, my boy, my boy."

Dom sat in a near chair. "We believe he passed Sunday or yesterday, but I'll let you know when I have more details."

Mr. Zapata, blinking in shock and fear, put his arms around his wife who rocked between wails. "What happened?"

"I'm not sure yet. It looks like someone forced their way into his apartment."

"What? What do you mean? In his apartment?"

"Yes. Someone forced their way in. Shot Micah."

"Oh, Dios mío, Oh, Dios mío, mi hijo!" wailed Mrs. Zapata.

Tears streamed down Mr. Zapata's cheeks. "In his apartment?"

When a brain has received a shock, it skips like a scratched record. Sometimes it took a number of attempts to explain. "Yes, he was in his apartment."

"You mean my boy was alone?" Mr. Zapata's tears dripped faster.

Dom swallowed against a thick throat. "Sir, I believe Micah died quickly. I believe he did not suffer."

"Who did this?"

"I don't know yet."

Mrs. Zapata wailed into balled fists. "Oh, Dios mío."

"Who do you think did this?" He swallowed.

"I don't know yet. I am in charge of the investigation. I am going to find the person that did this to Micah and I am going to put him in jail. That's my promise to you."

Mrs. Zapata's howls descended into a guttural sob as her brain shut down in shock.

Mr. Zapata wheezed, "How could this happen?"

Dom touched Mr. Zapata's knee. "Is there anyone that disliked your son?"

"No. Nothing like that. Micah is a good boy." Mr. Zapata shook his head, and his face contorted in confusion through the stream of tears. "We came from Honduras. It is bad there. Much violence. We came here for Roberto and Micah. When they were small. We came here to get away."

The wife's sobs wracked at the irony.

"Micah is a good boy. We came here and he is a good boy. Did good in high school. Even though he bad."

There it was. "When you say Micah was bad, what do you mean?"

"The drugs. The smoking."

She had guessed it. It was the same tragic story across swathes of poor America, urban or rural. "Micah had gotten into drugs in high school?"

He nodded. "But he never let grades go bad. He got good grades. He smart."

Many parents had rosier perceptions of their children than reality confirmed.

"He accepted to NYU. They pay for him. Scholarship. Because we from Honduras they give him special scholarship. He get better. Clean up. Went to NYU. Once he was in college—"

Mrs. Zapata's shoulders heaved.

"Once he got into college"—Mr. Zapata struggled to speak through the shock—"he was a new boy."

"Can you explain this change to me?"

He waved his right hand frantically. "He leave those bad friends. He move into his apartment, he take scholarship money, he study. All the time. He leave those bad friends behind. We so proud of him. He a good kid. Good man."

"What was he studying?"

"The environment. Climate. He plans on stopping the climate change."

It sounded like Micah had turned his life around, had chosen an academic path to an admirable career. Did he have any residual secrets? "Are you sure that he did not stay in touch with his old friends?"

He waved his hand again. "Yes. Very sure. Micah tell us he want a good life. He see the other students at NYU, he want their life."

A more complex picture of Micah Zapata was forming. He was a young man from the wrong side of the tracks who had gotten an opportunity for a new life and had moved past his modest beginnings. "So, none of Micah's friends from high school—none of them—are still around?"

Mrs. Zapata sobbed.

"No." Mr. Zapata sat straight and squared his shoulders.

Dom pulled up the photo from the year book, Micah with his arms around two friends. She gently handed the phone to Mr. Zapata. He sobbed when he saw his son. Mrs. Zapata leaned over his arm, caught the image of her son, and wailed, throwing her hands over her face.

Dom asked quietly, "Mr. Zapata, are these the bad friends from high school?"

Mr. Zapata nodded.

"The ones that used drugs?"

He nodded again.

"Do you know their names?"

"Only their nicknames." He pointed to the one with a cheerful face wearing the baseball cap, "That Maynor. Yes, Maynor." His finger moved slowly to the one with the harsh look and the clown tattoo. "That one bad. He named Toro."

"As in bull?"

He nodded. "He no good."

She slid the phone back into her jacket pocket. "You think maybe one of his old friends is jealous of Micah's success? His going to NYU? His new life?"

"I don't know. He never talk about anything like that."

"Any fights with anyone that you know of?"

"No. No. He go to school. He do his homework. He study. No fights."

"So no one you can think of that would have a reason to hurt Micah?"

"No. Micah is our pride and joy."

"You have another son? Older?"

Mr. Zapata nodded through his tears.

"And is he a good boy too?"

They both shook their heads. Mrs. Zapata's wails softened. She hid her face in her hands. They both felt nervous about the other son. "Tell me about him."

"Roberto is a mechanic. At Jiffy Lube. He live in Harlem. He don't make so much money. He no have a wife. He have one kid. We never see the baby."

Mrs. Zapata cried into her hands.

"Would Roberto know about this Toro?"

"Yes, maybe," Mr. Zapata said.

"Okay. And what about Micah's girlfriend Hettie? What can you tell me about her? About their relationship. Did they fight?"

Both the parents went quiet. Mr. Zapata said, "No, no. They are both good people. They no fight too much."

"How long were Hettie and Micah together as boyfriend and girlfriend?"

"A year?" Mr. Zapata wrapped his arms around his chest and rocked gently.

"They were in love?"

"Yes. He say to me that he wanted to someday marry her."

Mrs. Zapata's crying started again.

"Okay, is there anyone that didn't like Micah being with Hettie?"

He rocked harder. "No, no. We all very happy. They very happy," he whispered. "Only her parents don't like Micah."

"Have you met the Van Burens?"

"No. No. Hettie's parents no approve that we are from Honduras. Her parents no approve."

Mrs. Zapata began rocking.

Dom reached out to touch Mr. Zapata's arm. "I'll go see Roberto now. Is there anything I should know about him?"

They both stared at the floor.

Huh. Interesting. "Does Roberto have a history? With the police?"

Mr. Zapata nodded.

"Has he been to jail, Mr. Zapata?"

Mr. Zapata nodded.

"For what?"

"Assault. Drugs." He hung his head.

"Okay, then let's do it this way. Don't call him. Let me go talk to him without warning."

Mr. Zapata understood the request. The FBI did not want Roberto to flee. He nodded.

"Thank you, Mr. Zapata." She took his hand. "I will be in touch soon. You will be able to see Micah soon, to prepare him."

Mr. Zapata's red-rimmed eyes bored into her as the rivers of tears carved into his cheeks. "You find them. Those that killed my son. You find them. I bring my family here to be safe. Now this. You promise you find them?"

"I will find them."

Mr. Zapata dropped his face against his wife's shoulder, and the two sobbed together.

Out on the street, she leaned against her car and dialed Lea Peck. She didn't wait for Lea to speak. "I need the rap sheet on one Roberto Zapata at the same address as the vic's parents. He works at a Jiffy Lube in Harlem. I'm heading over there."

"Roger that."

Next, Dom called Fontaine.

After the wails in the Zapata apartment, his voice was cream butter. "What have you got?"

"Not much. But the vic—the boyfriend—had a history. Not sure how heavy. He did some drugs in high school, but it sounds like college turned him around. The parents are confident he was on the straight and narrow, and his apartment was squeaky clean. But maybe old friends have come back to haunt him."

"Okay, that sounds like a rabbit hole."

"Also, there's a tough guy brother who's done some time."

"Huh. Follow both leads. I've apprised the Van Burens of the situation. They're going to keep working with us. For the moment."

"Understood."

"But, Dom, we need to find Hettie fast. The clock is on. I don't need to tell you that."

10

THE JIFFY LUBE ON HARLEM'S BROADHURST
AVENUE did not appear commercially viable. The two garage
bays were empty, and the only car on the small cement lot was a
rusted 1990s VW Rabbit. A long twisting crack in the office
window was taped with silver duct tape. Debris took flight on a
breeze wafting through one of two alleys on either side of the
small building. It was a struggling business in a neighborhood
ransacked by poverty and brutality.

Dom parked a few hundred yards past the garage as a long
Lincoln rolled past, four windows open, two heads nodding, and
a deep bass thumping. She stretched out of the sports car and
with a practiced gesture, tapped the holstered Glock. As she
approached the ramshackle Jiffy Lube, her skin tightened. Guys
with rap sheets were tricky. They were used to bucking authority, defending territory, and if threatened, making unpredictable
decisions. Few had qualms resorting to violence.

Dom slid the pair of sunglasses to the top of her head. It was
better to look casual and calm than a lone hard-nosed Feddie in
a precarious situation. *Nothing to see here. Just coming to ask a
few easy questions.*

Something darted behind the bandaged garage window. She slowed. Through the dirty glass, two dark eyes narrowed into a hard stare. She stepped onto the cement of the Jiffy Lube's lot and stopped, hands empty by her thighs. *Just a single unintimidating female Feddie here to have a nice calm chat.* She nodded to the window.

The eyes disappeared. A minute later, a man in gray, dirty coveralls flew through the doorway and raced to the far alley.

Seriously? She leaned and lunged into a sprint. Racing past the VW, she cornered right into the alley at full speed, pulling her Glock and training it ahead. Up ahead, the man in the gray coveralls moved fast, arms scissoring. The chain-link fence flew past. Her thighs pumped. "FBI. Freeze, freeze!"

Under the coveralls, the body was tight and lean, and the sprint was fast. He covered ground quickly, opening the distance between them with every stride.

She leaned into the sprint and pushed harder on her feet as her chest heaved.

Reaching the alley's opening, he glanced over his shoulder and his left hand fanned out.

"FBI, freeze!"

At full sprint, his hand seized the corner pole. His momentum yanked his arm straight, pitched his body up, and swung him left in a wide arc around the corner. He was out of sight.

She pumped her burning legs harder. After reaching the end of the alley, she grasped the pole and pitched herself around the corner—fast and blind.

Three feet ahead, Roberto faced her. His chest heaved and his right arm was stretched overhead with a steel pole poised to smash her head.

Landing on her feet, she trained the gun on his chest, threw her left palm up, and coughed through gasps, "This is about Micah."

Roberto froze.

The fight or flight theory is incomplete. In the face of something frightening, one doesn't immediately flee or fight. A person freezes. The instant paralysis is a subconscious holdover from when early humans, walking the plains, sighted a predator.

Roberto stood frozen with wide eyes.

She flared her left fingers wide with a conciliatory palm by her shoulder. "This is about Micah. This isn't about you, Roberto. I don't want you."

Micah was as still as a wary gazelle.

"It's about Micah."

He glared, the outstretched arm stiffened, and the neck tattoos stretched across straining muscles.

"It's about your brother. I'm not here for you."

He blinked.

Say it again to let it sink in. "I'm not here for you. Your parents sent me."

His left foot stepped back in a tiny but recognizable step. It was a good sign. In the face of fear, the second subconscious survival reaction was flight.

She lowered her left palm slowly. "Lower. The. Pole. Let's talk." She didn't want him to run.

His breathing normalized, and the pole began to tremble.

"Roberto, something has happened to Micah. Now please lower the pole, and we'll talk."

His face softened a fraction, and the pole descended. From behind and down the block, someone yelled, "Pig, go home!"

The pole shot back up, his nostrils flared, his eyes darted to the distance, and Roberto took a step toward her.

Uh-oh. When neither freezing nor fleeing relieves the fear, the next animal instinct was to fight. When a body prepares to fight, it makes a movement toward the opponent.

She yelled to grab his attention. "Roberto! We're good! Lower the pole again. Ignore the bystanders. They got nothing to do with this. I'm here about your brother. Look at me, we're good."

He glanced at her.

She lowered her outstretched hand. "I need you to lower your weapon, then I'll lower mine, and we'll talk."

Cold onyx eyes glared.

"Your parents sent me. This is about Micah. Ignore the bystander. This is not about you."

He canted on his heels and lowered the pole.

She took a deep breath. "Okay. Roberto, I need you to put the pole on the ground. You with me? Then I can lower my gun."

With wary eyes, Roberto knelt and placed the pole on the ground.

She lowered her gun. Her heart raced, sweat dripped down her neck, and her shirt was soaked. She kicked the pole, sending it clanging heavily on the cement. "We're going to go back into the Jiffy Lube, and we're going to have a nice conversation. Got it?"

Roberto cocked his chin begrudgingly.

She jerked back down the alley. "Okay, let's do it."

Eyes hard and chin jutted, he walked past with a warning sneer.

Roberto Zapata may have clues, conscious or otherwise, that would help fill in the jigsaw puzzle about Micah and Hettie. But guys with rap sheets were tricky. This could go either way. He could clam up, or he could decide to be helpful. She needed to exert just enough authority to impress but threaten. She holstered the Glock and followed at a distance.

11

LEA PECK LEFT her desk on the eighth floor of Jacob J. Javits Federal Building in downtown Manhattan, rode the elevator to the first floor, and stepped outside into the afternoon air. Taking a deep breath of city air, she rolled her neck to dislodge the kinks, stepped out from the overhang, and walked slowly to the corner. High kick knee bends pressed thighs to chest and stretched the gluts. At the corner, she grabbed her left knee and rolled her leg out to stretch the adductors. She repeated the stretch on the right.

She felt the eyes of the guards near the lobby. They knew her. This was a regular routine every two hours. The ad stretch got 'em every time. *It's a free country, cuddle cakes, so you take a good long stare at my swag while I exercise my rights to exercise. Lock a cheetah up in a cage for too long and they lose their fight.*

She'd been digging into Hettie Van Buren's social media. The search was tedious and unrevealing. The girl posted the same damn things every damn day: some repost from an earnest environmental activist group—Worldwildlife Fund, World Resources Institute—about some damn depressing state-of-the-world shit, followed by a funny repost of a random joke. Please.

Only rich folks had time for that. During the last year, Hettie sporadically posted a photo smiling with the formerly delicious Micah at a fancy restaurant somewhere. Nowhere in the posts, the back chats, or the likes did Hettie so much as peep with any personality. All happy, all the damn time. Please.

Lea didn't do social media. That was for civilians. She knew how much data was collected, scrubbed, used, and sold. Ain't no damn corporation was gonna get rich off her activity data. No, sir.

She crossed the street and took off at a high-speed sprint. Clunky black earrings that read *Queen* bounced against her jawbone all the way to the end to the end of the block. She pressed a finger to her neck. The sprint had barely registered a heartbeat. Time to go back to work.

On the second floor, Lea Peck strode under the bright glare of fluorescent lighting and past rows of white lab tables surrounded by robed technicians. Machines whirred, and the space smelled of formaldehyde and singed hair. Because of its size, the New York field office contained its own forensic lab. For most jurisdictions, evidence was transported to the FBI Lab in Quantico, one of the world's largest crime labs with warehouse-sized rooms and hundreds of scientific experts. But the New York field office had an exponentially large number of high-priority, fast-moving cases that needed immediate initial diagnostics. The kidnapping of Hettie Van Buren was one of those cases.

At the far end, Lea found Becky Turnball staring down various pieces of evidence dispersed across a long counter. Cardboard boxes were stacked up near her feet. "Hey, Becky."

"Lea Peck. How ya doing, kid?"

Lea wagged her head. "I am not complaining. We've got a high roller case thumping, my car is still running, and for lunch I had a sushi burrito from The Works. I'm all in today."

Becky laughed. "Big case is right. Didn't this come from Fontaine direct?"

"Indeed."

"Red carpet treatment."

"Indeed. Listen, if I go missing, I want this lottery treatment rolled out for my sorry Louisiana Baptist ass."

"I hear that."

Lea leaned over the counter, surveyed the wares and focused on a slice of carpet covered in dark blood. "Where's his body?"

"On the way to Quantico. But we won't need it. It was one clean shot through the chest."

Rows of photos were lined neatly into a grid that displayed the body of Micah Zapata as he was found, sitting awkwardly on the floor, his back against a white wall, his head tilted, blood spray behind him like a splatter art from a local fair. There was no visible clown ink to match his friend's tattoo.

"Any tats?" Lea asked.

"Nope."

Lea crooked her head past the photos to the toiletries. Advil, toothbrush, toothpaste, comb, deodorant. Normal guy stuff. "Anything in the bathroom?"

Becky swabbed a coffee mug. "Nah, the bathroom's clean. No hidden stuff, no drugs, no nothing." Her voice turned conspiratorial. "Check the last section at the end of the counter." She hooked her head to the far right.

Lea sidestepped to look at three photos—each a shot of a mangy shrub from different angles—next to a sealed evidence bag scribbled with a black Sharpie *"Zapata. External."* Inside was a Sturm Rugger 9mm. *What the fuck? Was that a gun in the bushes?*

Lea glanced at Becky. "You match this?"

Becky looked up slowly. "Yup." She wagged eyebrows.

"They left the gun?"

"Threw it in the bushes."

What kind of Keystone fucking crook drops a gun? "Prints?"

"Yup." Becky turned back to the mug with a smile. "Already sent them to Quantico."

"Holy shit." If they are able to match the prints, they could swoop in on the killer kidnappers and grab Hettie Van Buren in lightning speed. It was potentially a huge break.

Becky smiled to herself. "I was gonna call you when they come back. My guess, a few hours."

"Holy shit," Lea said before whistling her way out of the lab.

Back at her desk, an email from the cell phone forensic expert popped into her inbox. He would have pulled everything from Micah's phone: calls dialed and received, text messages, address book contacts, photos, and videos. She opened the photos and videos first. There were 1,342 photos. Lots of Micah with Hettie. Lots of Micah with his mom. Only a few appeared to be photos of friends, but that was normal—guys typically don't photograph friends. There were a lot of stylized shots of meals. Micah appeared to have been a bit of a foodie. Or a bit of a poor kid who dropped into a pot of butter with a rich lady who took him to high-end restaurants.

She closed the photos and opened his cellphone history. Micah had regularly texted with four people: his mother, Hettie, a friend listed as Raul, and a second friend named Mark. These conversations had been active as recent as Sunday with short updates. They all appeared normal. *where to meet?, omw, 5 minutes, kisses.* He and Hettie texted a lot of *I love you. Xoxo.* Lea sucked her cheek. It was a lot easier to love a minted lady than a poor girl.

A month ago, one conversation stood out. Micah and a guy named Toro had a twenty minute call. After, they had exchanged eighteen text messages.

Toro had started the text conversation with, *Bro, we need to talk.*

Not now, Micah had replied.

I'm telling you.

I can't now. Got lots on.

Bro, big $$$ on table.

Yo, I can't.

You know anybody can?

No.

How bout yo brother?

R aint' got no $

How bout yo lady?

Step off. Serious.

Just sayin. Need asap. Tick tock.

FO. He meant fuck off.

Will cut you in 40%.

FO. Leave me out.

Bro, we know about your lady.

FO.

Lea reread the conversation. She scanned Micah's call history for Toro's number. Prior to this exchange, Micah had not spoken to Toro in over twenty months.

Uh, hmm. Now we're getting somewhere. Correction. Now we've arrived somewhere. A smile tickled Lea's lips.

12

INSIDE THE JIFFY LUBE OFFICE, an ancient cash register fought for space with dirty papers on a decrepit desk. A credit card machine collected dust near the cracked window. Chained to a handmade shelf, a small twenty-inch television blared a Spanish game show. A haze of oil and gas hung in the air.

Roberto Zapata stood near the desk, feet wide and arms crossed. Tattoos climbed both arms and disappeared into short dirty sleeves only to emerge and crawl up his neck. He growled, "What's up with Micah?"

"There's been a missing person reported." Dom stood in the door frame. "It's your brother's girlfriend. Hettie Van Buren is missing."

Roberto blinked.

"I went to check Micah's apartment. I'm sorry to tell you this, but I found his body. Micah's dead."

Roberto's eyes widened, and his jaw tensed. He blinked repeatedly.

Roberto was displaying all physiological characteristics of shock as the brain digested alarming information. It meant he had nothing to do with his brother's death.

He cleared his throat with a quick cough. "How?"

It was the most common first question of innocent people. She said, "He was shot."

"Where?"

"In his chest."

"When?" He held his body extremely still.

Tough guys learned to contain their body movements as self-defense in dangerous environments. "I found him about four hours ago. I'll know more later tonight, maybe tomorrow."

"No. When was he popped?"

"Best guess is twenty-four hours ago."

He shook his head and blew out both cheeks.

The news was a bombshell, tough guy or not. She shuffled back to give him space.

"You talk to my parents?"

"Yeah. I was over there just now. That's how I knew to come talk to you. Do you have any ideas about who would want to hurt Micah?"

"I got nothin' to do with this," he said quickly.

Involvement with Feds was not a normal occurrence for guys like Roberto. She nodded.

He craned his neck. "I'm telling you, I got nothing to do with this."

"Yeah, I get that. That's not why I'm here. I'm here to find out if you know anyone who might have a grudge with Micah?"

"No."

"Any ideas where I should start to look?"

He sniffed. "No."

"Your parents mentioned Micah had some friends from high school, maybe some tough guys?"

He glanced up and to the left, playing the scenario out in his mind.

Eyes dart left when retrieving memories and to the right

when creating new scenarios. Roberto was taking this seriously. He was trying to help her.

"That was a long time ago," he said.

"Okay, what about more recently? Any gang affiliations in Micah's life now that you know about?"

"Not that I know about."

"Anybody maybe come round looking for money? Did he owe anyone?"

"Nah. Doubt it."

"He get in trouble lately? Gambling?"

He sucked his cheek. "Nah. He don't gamble."

"Drugs?"

He snapped long loose fingers against each other. "Nah, he been clean a long time now."

"How often did you see him?"

"Every few months?"

"When was the last time you saw him?"

"A few months ago." He glanced away.

"Where?"

He wouldn't look at her. "At our parents."

"What did you talk about?"

He closed his eyes. "Nothin." He held his eyes closed a second too long.

Eye blocking indicated avoidance. It was a baseline point of reference. Roberto didn't like the question. "Was it just you two and your parents?"

His eyes locked on her. "Yes."

That had been an easy question for him. She circled back to one that wasn't. "What did you talk about?"

He scratched his neck. "I can't remember."

This line of questioning was definitely making him anxious. "You can't remember anything you talked about?"

He cracked his neck. "Nah."

"Nothing?"

"Nah."

She didn't believe him. "Roberto, I need to know what you talked about. It may help find his killer."

He stared out the window. "Something about a project."

"What kind of project?"

"I dunno, something he and Hettie were doing."

"What was the project?"

"I don't remember."

"I don't believe you."

He turned on her with hard eyes and curled lips. "Yo, bitch, back up."

She stared him down.

"You need to step the fuck back." But he didn't move forward. "I said I don't remember." He finally glanced away.

"Roberto, I'm the law enforcement that's gonna find your brother's killer. You understand that, right? I'm not the one you've got an issue with. You want me on your side."

He moved to the window, his eyes downcast. "Like I said, it was just like any other family dinner. Parents hassling me, telling Micah how great he is." Pain crossed his features as he stared into the distance.

She fished out her cellphone and pulled up the photo of Micah with Toro. "Your dad called this guy Toro. Said he was bad news. You know him?"

Roberto glanced at the photo. "Yeah."

"You know how recently Micah saw him?"

He shrugged.

"It may be important."

"I dunno. That kid's a punk. He ain't no gangster."

"I'm not worried about his bona fides. I wanna know if Micah was still in touch with him recently."

He shrugged again.

"Do you know his full name?"

"Pena." His chin jutted as if Toro was insignificant. "Kelvin Pena. Punk."

"Where's he from?"

"Why ever'body gotta be from somewhere?"

She stepped away from him. "Roberto, we're on the same side. I'm just asking questions here."

"Yeah, he from Tegucigalpa."

He meant Tegucigalpa, Honduras. Honduras was emerging as a common theme. "Any idea where I can find him?"

"Nah."

"What about his parents?"

"Last I knew they over in Hunts Point." It was a Bronx neighborhood. "But he just a punk."

She pushed both hands into her jean pockets and softened her shoulders. *I'm just a nice Feddie asking easy questions.* "What was the project you discussed with Hettie and Micah?"

Roberto stared mutely across the Jiffy Lube lot. He was done with this interview. He spoke to the broken glass. "They kill my brother, they take Hettie?"

"That's what it looks like."

"They take the white girl but kill the cholo."

"That's what it looks like."

He turned and spat on the floor. "I'll put the word on the street. Maybe somebody knows somethin."

"I'm not averse to that." She handed him her card. "See what you find out."

He clicked his cheek. "Somebody's gonna pay."

"Yeah, one way or another. You're absolutely right."

The interior of the sports car muffled the noise from the outside. She knew a few things, but not a lot. The killer was probably experienced. They knew where both Micah Zapata and Hettie Van Buren lived, so this was planned. Micah had a past. Honduras could be an early lead. Kelvin Pena was worth pursuing. And a project of Micah and Hettie's caused Roberto discomfort. Dom would circle back to him once he had time to digest the news and get angry.

She pulled out her phone. There were two new items. First, Beecher had sent a text. *How's it going?*

The second was an email from Lea Peck at HQ. It was the NYPD criminal records on Roberto Zapata. Dom scanned his sheet.

October 2014: Zapata was charged with first-degree assault with intent to cause serious injury with a weapon and possession of a loaded firearm.

September 2014: Zapata pleaded guilty to operating as a major trafficker of controlled substance. He was arrested by US Customs and Border Patrol officers at John F. Kennedy Airport off an American Airline flight from Tegucigalpa, Honduras.

July 2013: Zapata was charged with third-degree felony possession with intent to sell while in prison.

July 2011: Zapata was arrested for alleged possession of marijuana.

November 2007: Zapata was charged with criminal possession of a controlled substance and intent to sell, a Class B felony. He pleaded guilty to a Class C felony.

August 2004: Zapata was charged with criminal possession and intent to sell. He pleaded guilty.

Roberto Zapata was a serious player who escalated his game over ten years. His most recent altercation was an assault with a weapon.

In the alley, Roberto very easily could have hit her across the head with a single fatal blow with that steel pole. Her heart hummed. Her father's voice whispered through the silence. *Everybody gets scared, my Dom.*

But her mind spun as she imagined an obituary. *Special Agent Domini Walker. Killed in the line of duty, protecting the American people. Fidelity, Bravery, and Integrity. She is survived by a single younger brother, Beecher Walker.*

In the rearview, the red taillights of a car receded down the street.

Who would take care of Beecher if Dom died?

The skin on her neck was clammy. *Beecher would not be okay without her.*

Her hands felt numb. *Beecher would not be okay on his own.*

She shook her hands. *Maybe Beecher would be okay?*

She cracked her knuckles. *Maybe Beecher would be fine because he was strong?*

Her fingers tingled as she squeezed the steering wheel. She blew against tight lips. *Yes, whatever happened to her, Beecher would be fine.*

She turned the key in the ignition and the race car growled. She felt older than she could handle.

13

THE GRIMY FLOOR tiles of the sixth floor of the Javits Building reminded Dom of Operation St. Christopher. Built over twelve months, St. Chris had culminated in thirty thumbtacks pinned to an enormous map of the country that covered a large portion of one wall in the fourth floor operations room. Each of the red thumbtacks represented a place she had surveilled—a burned-out house in Detroit, a decrepit tract home in Southern California, a rusted double-wide in Indiana—and each had been confirmed as a link in a larger network that bought and sold purity. Each red thumbtack indicated a bunker where a child was held and regularly raped. She had been staring at the map when Fontaine had summoned her to this hallway outside his office. It had been four months since he had given approval for the surgical strike that had lasted ten hours and crisscrossed the nation. St. Chris had been a righteous and exhilarating win.

But they had all moved on. She rubbed her stinging eyes. If you worked in the Bureau, you knew evil hung over the horizon like a desolate mist.

The ring of a desk phone broke Dom's reveries and she

peered through the door frame. Fontaine's executive assistant set the phone on the cradle and nodded to the inner door. "You can go in, Special Agent."

Dom cracked her neck and pushed through.

"Claude Van Buren called." Fontaine was a small, angular black man with a distinctive bald head and thick black-framed glasses that sat high on sharp cheek bones. He rarely smiled, and his eyes were bright and intense. A light French Haitian accent colored sharp barks.

She said, "Okay?"

"He wants a more senior agent. He also called the mayor."

Claude Van Buren was calling Fontaine directly—one rich man to a powerful one. That's how this town worked. She waited.

"I told him you were one of my best. He has acquiesced for now."

Dom was skeptical about Fontaine. The New York field office dealt with the most monied, lawyered, and crooked individuals in the country—white collar crime, financial crimes, mob rings, foreign influence. Many fingers were wriggling in this honey pot. By his very position as the New York ASIC, Fontaine would be highly political, but to date, Fontaine had treated her straight.

From behind the large wooden desk, he steepled his fingers and tapped his lips. "What have you got?"

"Hettie Van Buren has been missing since Sunday. She has a nice apartment, nice lifestyle—restaurants, friends, the regular rich gig—but she's no Paris Hilton. She works at the Museum of Natural History. She studies birds. By all accounts she's shy, well-behaved, polite." She shifted on her feet. "Hettie's parents have some nuances. The father is a banker. My sense is he's a bully—"

"Whoa there, Agent," Fontaine plunked his elbows on the

desk. "Or Claude Van Buren could just be very upset his daughter is missing."

Here we go. Politics coming in hot. Her jaw tensed. "Sir, that is a possibility. About the father. The mother is very polished, old school. My guess there is she's afraid of her husband. Emotionally remote—"

He held up a solitary finger. "Slow down, Special Agent. Watch yourself. The mother could simply be distraught."

Actually, family dynamics often provided a great deal of evidence in an investigation. But rather than push back on her ASIC, Dom continued. "Micah Zapata, the dead boyfriend, did some drugs in high school and had some bad friends, but, by all accounts, he has been free of that since attending NYU. I talked to his brother, guy named Roberto. Roberto is a bad hombre with a long record, but my sense is he wasn't involved in the murder of his brother." She didn't tell him that Roberto was also chasing down information among his gang contacts. A politically savvy ASIC may not want to know about nontraditional avenues of investigation. "One old friend has cropped up recently. This guy, Toro, was hitting Micah up for money. Even mentioned Hettie in some texts."

Fontaine thumped the steeple against his lips. "This friend from high school, that your most compelling lead?"

"I'm just not sure yet. It's too early for anything definitive."

"Okay. Keep me posted. And to be clear, the Van Burens are the one percent."

Politics were blazing hot on this one. She nodded.

"These people, they fly high. We need to be careful here."

How many warnings was he gonna give her? She straightened. What was he asking her to do? From deep within her ear, Stewart Walker whispered, *You do the right thing, my Dom. That's how you earn respect.* It was an ironic statement coming from the imaginary ghost of her father.

"You need to be careful here," Fontaine said.

She crossed her hands behind her back, a soldier reporting to a superior. "What exactly are you saying, sir? My job is to protect the American people. My job is to bring Hettie Van Buren home."

He squinted at her. "I know what your job is, Walker, but I need you to also be careful."

She was not going to make this easy for him. "Sir, I follow the evidence. I get the victim back. I lock up the bad guys. That's what I do. I'm not sure what you're suggesting I do differently."

He exhaled loudly. "Walker, you just need to be careful."

"I'm not understanding you, sir. Are you suggesting I don't turn over all the rocks that present themselves?"

He stared hard at her. "No, that's not what I'm suggesting, and yes, you do understand me. I'm telling you to not be a bull in a china shop around the family. Play nice with these people. They are very well connected in this town."

"Sir, playing nice is not my trademark." Everybody knew Dom's overly principled view of the world ruffled feathers.

He glared at her.

She bit her tongue. She was getting a feel for Hettie, she was narrowing in on leads, and she was regaining her confidence. She wanted this case and to be the one to find Hettie.

He sighed. "Okay, Walker. Follow the lead. The money, maybe drugs, whatever. If this begins to get close—in any way—to the family, you come tell me first. Before you do anything to disrupt the family, you come clear it with me. Is that English plain enough for you, Special Agent Walker?"

Sitting behind a big desk in HQ, that probably sounded like an appropriate compromise. Get advanced clearance of potentially difficult interactions with the family. But for a field agent, it might prove challenging to execute. But she nodded. She wanted the case.

As she turned to go, the hard edges of disapproval on his face slipped. She caught a faint sadness in his eyes and turned back. "Sir?"

He shook his head, reluctant to say something.

"Sir?"

He closed his eyes. "Darlin Montgomery is downstairs."

Her heart rate spiked. "What?"

"Office of Professional Responsibility brought her in, as part of the inquiry into St. Chris."

Her throat constricted. "Can I see her?"

"You can go try."

Behind one-way mirrors of the child psych room on the fifth floor, Dom watched as two Office of Professional Responsibility investigators closed their briefcases and nodded to the middle-aged social worker watching solemnly from a corner. In the center of the room a young black girl was making two Barbie dolls converse, dancing their bare arched feet on the white laminate of a child-sized table. Dom had found Darlin Montgomery in a dark, cold cellar outside Cleveland in a location marked by a red thumbtack.

The two officers stepped through the door.

Dom asked, "Can I see her?"

Their faces were sympathetic and the taller of the two said, "Yes. We're finished." He held the door for her.

Darlin set down the Barbies and watched Dom approach with stoic eyes.

"Hi, Darlin," Dom said as she squeezed into a small seat and gently placed both hands flat on the table in an unthreatening gesture. "So good to see you! How you doing?"

Darlin's face was a mask of seriousness. "I'm fine."

Darlin Montgomery had no home to go to and was in the foster system, which, at best, would be a long road to adoption. She was far from fine.

Dom swallowed. "You look really good. You back in school?"

Darlin nodded.

"You like it?"

Darlin shrugged. "I like my teacher. She's nice."

"What's her name?"

"Mrs. Grippi. She has long hair."

"That's nice. What else do you like about school?"

Darlin's face broke into a small devious smile. "They have lots of stuff for PE. We do lots of stuff in PE."

"Like what?"

"We have balls, and rolling seats, and stretchy bands." The smile grew.

Dom grinned. "That sounds fun."

"And we eat good food." Darlin smacked her lips. "Healthy."

Children were so resilient, persistent proof that life carried on. Dom chuckled. "Oh, yeah?"

"Yeah. We gotta eat a square meal. So they give us apples, and pasta with sauce, and string beans. I like the pasta. We don't get pizza every day."

Dom laughed, "Is that good? I mean, I kinda like pizza."

"Oh, I love pizza! But you gotta be healthy a lot."

"You're right. But are you allowed pizza at school?"

"Oh sure. Just not all the time."

"You like pepperoni?"

Darlin shook her head emphatically, "Hell no! I gotta have me Meat Lover's."

Dom laughed out loud. "You are so right. It's gotta, gotta be

Meat Lover's." Dom looked at the Barbies. "What were they talking about?"

Darlin's face dropped and Dom regretted changing the subject.

"Just stuff." Darlin shrugged. "Maybe college."

This was interesting. "Oh really?"

"Yeah, they have ta make a plan."

Dom waited.

"They have ta plan because they are strong and they are in charge of their destiny."

Someone had been working with Darlin. It was better to be strong and forceful than to be a victim. "Absolutely, Darlin. You are always super smart. You are strong, too." She gave her a gentle grin.

The child placed her hand on Dom's wrist. "You working, Dom?"

Dom's throat thickened. "Yes. I'm just starting back."

"You catchin' the bad guys?"

"I'm trying."

Darlin nodded sagely. "That's your job." The young girl pushed back her chair, stood, leaned over, and gave Dom a tight hug around the shoulders. "That's what you do."

14

DOM STARTED the hunt for Kelvin Pena, aka Toro, at the NYPD 52nd Precinct up in the Bronx. She parked on a side street, exchanged her Bureau jacket for a loose jean jacket, and slid the mirrored sunglasses on her head. By the main entrance, a uniform stood by the front door looking lazily up and down the street. It was a slow afternoon. Inside the quiet station, the ubiquitous near-retirement desk sergeant gave her a quick once-over and grumbled, "What can I do for you, lady?"

She flashed her badge. "Can I get a word with Detectives Johns and Rodriguez?"

His eyes widened, and he grunted as he picked up the phone.

Johns and Rodriguez emerged from the back.

Johns spoke first. "What have you got?"

"A lead. I've got the name and an address for the one with the tattoo in the photo. Named Kelvin Pena, aka Toro. My vic spoke to him a month ago. Toro wanted money. The vic said no."

"Mm-hmm. What are you thinking?"

"Maybe this Toro wanted that money real bad. He wasn't

happy Micah had turned him down. Scenario A: Maybe he went to see Micah Zapata and things got heated.

Johns shook his head. "That shot was too clean. This wasn't an emotional shooting."

"Scenario B: Maybe Micah turned him down and Toro left, cooled down, got a gun, and went back in later. This time they talked it out over a gun. But Micah still said no. Toro shot his friend."

Johns frowned.

"Scenario C: This Toro owes money, and the bad guys are watching him. The bad guys follow Toro to Micah's. Once Toro leaves, they decide to hit up Micah themselves. They go in on their own. Later. It ends up in a hit."

Both Johns and Rodriguez shrugged.

She shifted on her feet. "I'm not sure these make sense, but Toro is at the center of each one."

"How's the girl fit?" Johns asked.

"It fits any of these scenarios. Toro knows Hettie is rich. After Micah is dead, he or they go for Hettie instead. Holding her for ransom."

"Is there a ransom request?"

"Not yet."

Johns cast a glance to Rodriguez. "The scenarios are...thin... but plausible."

Rodriguez said softly, "Either way it went down, Toro sounds like a lead. What's the address?"

"Over on East 161 and Trinity Avenue."

Johns nodded. "Let's go find him."

The unmarked NYPD sedan smelled like stale cigarettes and melting plastic. The black seats were sticky against her jeans. Outside, six towering and characterless buildings circled a cement drive and a dusty park. In an empty basketball court, the backboards barely held on to mangled baskets. Cheap flowered curtains ruffled from a few open windows. Having been in other projects, Dom imagined raised voices through thin walls, hallways stinking of urine, and stairwells dark because of smashed lightbulbs. The poor didn't have a lot of options.

Across the street, patrons straggled in and out of a local bodega, *Fernandez Grocery*, whose window display was jammed with toiletries and Spanish-covered tin cans. A neon sign advertised twenty-four-hour lottery tickets. The poor didn't have a lot of options.

This part of the Bronx was a long way from Washington Square Park. Had Micah told Hettie that his friend Toro had reemerged? Had Micah asked Hettie for money?

From the driver seat, Johns' elbow sat on the window ledge catching sun. Calm dark eyes watched her in the rearview mirror. "You been a Fed a long time?"

"Just over ten years," she said it quickly. She didn't like talking about herself.

"Mostly kidnapping?"

"Mostly domestic."

"No counter-terrorism?" His eyes watched her.

"No, I stayed away from that."

Rodriguez jerked his chin in agreement.

"Yeah, mm-hmm. I feel you. Too heavy these days. What's the pension situation at the Bureau these days?"

"It's good if you stick it out twenty years."

"You gonna go desk jockey at some point?"

He wanted to know if she would move away from field work as she advanced. She hadn't thought about it too much. She had given herself another five years before making a decision about a less dangerous specialty. "Not sure yet."

"Family?" Johns grinned.

Law enforcement types always asked if she was married. What they really wanted to know was if she was sleeping with anyone. The personal lives of female field agents were a source of constant curiosity. "No, uh-uh." Dom kept her private life private.

"Mm-hmm. I'm married. Great lady. Keeps me on my toes. Count my blessings every morning she stays with me. Tough on the wife. And the four girls."

Dom had guessed five kids. She grinned to herself. "All girls?"

Johns nodded.

Rodriguez was keeping an eye on passing pedestrians.

"You got a picture of the vic's girlfriend?" Johns raised his eyebrows. "The missing girl?"

She slid out her phone, opened a photo of Hettie, and passed it to him.

He stared at the photo. "When she go missing?"

"We think Sunday."

"Same day as the boyfriend got shot?"

She nodded.

"Shame. She's got a gentle look about her."

"My thoughts exactly."

Rodriguez straightened against the seat and Johns followed his gaze. Across the street, a lean black man with a nappy head turned the corner and was walking toward them on abnormally long legs like a daddy-long-legs spider.

Johns said, "They call him Gust, as in *a gust of wind will knock him over*. Round here, that's not a compliment."

Through the open window, Rodriguez blasted a short whistle, and Gust glanced before turning on his heels and heading in the opposite direction. Johns turned the key on the ignition, and they trailed at a distance.

Tires crunched over crumbling cement as the car rolled down an alley and came to rest. A train clacked in the distance.

Gust, painfully skinny with a ropey neck, dirty hair, and dazed eyes, leaned into the passenger side window by Rodriguez. "Yo yo yo. What's happin' my bacon?" The reference to cops was unoriginal.

Johns leaned back against his seat. "Gust, we need you for a second. Hop in."

A lanky arm yanked opened the door and rangy legs and body odor filled the back seat. Examining Dom, Gust licked cracked lips. "Hello, fine filly."

Johns reached out and snapped his fingers inches in front of Gust's eyes. "We're looking for a guy named Toro. Kelvin Pena. Lives up in here."

Ignoring Johns, Gust sniffed the air around Dom. "Who have we here?"

Johns cleared his throat. "Just a friend."

Gust's teeth were rotten and his breath was rank. "You a lady cop?"

"She's a social worker. Looking for a lost patient."

"I love me some official-type pussy."

Dom didn't blink. She heard a lot worse. Had used a lot worse.

"Gust." Johns barked. "Shut your mouth before I come back there and shut it for you."

"Easy, bacon, easy. Just 'preciatin' the view."

"So you know this Toro or what?"

Rodriguez held up two twenties and waggled them over the seat.

Two dirty, spindly fingers pincered the cash and slid the money in a front jean pocket. Gust's hand stayed against his crotch and he jiggled his eyebrows at Dom. "Sure, man. You come to me cause I know everybody up in here."

"Talk to me," Johns said.

"Honduran. Two-bit. He used to think he gangsta, but he ain't. Wanted all thirteen but didn't cut it." He meant MS-13, a heavy-duty international gang in New York made up of mostly Latinos.

"So he's not gang?" Johns asked.

"Nah, he didn't cut it. They mostly ignored him."

"What's he do now?"

"Two-bit shit. I dunno."

"I need to find him."

"That's all I know."

"I need you to know more."

Gust let out a long breath, rancid and dead. "Yeah, yeah, don't get your bacon bits all in a rumble. Hold on." He pulled out a clam phone and dialed a number. He spoke in a low conspiratorial voice to the other end. "Yo, you know that Toro Pena dude, that two-bit dude?" They could hear the other voice through the phone before Gust snapped it closed. "He doin' somethin' out in Port Morris. Started up a few weeks ago."

Port Morris in Southern Bronx was a partially abandoned port with barren parking lots scattered with decrepit buildings and protected by rusted chain link fences. It would be a good place to hide a hostage—not many witnesses to see her arrival or to hear her screams. Adrenaline raced up Dom's spine.

Johns asked, "What's the something he's doing?"

"My guy didn't know."

"Where's he doing it?"

Gust licked his lips at Dom, momentarily distracted.

Johns raised his voice. "Gust, Port Morris ain't small."

"Yeah, you're right." Gust grinned at him. "I'd say it's big. Big as a twenty."

Rodriguez handed back another twenty. With his right hand, Gust revisited the pincer move, slid the bill into the pocket, and lingered over his crotch. His grimy left hand slithered to Dom's knee.

She snatched Gust's pinkie, wrenched it out, and jammed it back.

Gust's eyes bulged. "Ow, ow, ow!" he yelped.

Nobody touched her without permission. Nobody. She crushed down on the finger.

"Ow, ow, ow!"

Johns glanced into the rearview, raised his eyebrows.

"Ow, ow, ow!" Gust howled.

We. Do. Not. Have. Time. For. This. Hettie could be bound and gagged in some desolate cinder block building in Port Morris. She relieved the angle but held fast to the pinkie.

Gust whimpered, "My guy said he's heard Toro is in one of 'dem old buildings behind the FedEx."

She dropped the pinkie.

Gust cradled the hurt hand against a hollowed chest. "You broke my finger."

Nah I didn't. I could have, but I didn't. She gazed past him.

"Fucking cunt," Gust hissed.

Johns turned the ignition key and barked, "Out, Gust."

Gust threw open the door and rolled out of the car.

Johns slammed on the gas, the tires spun on the crushed cement as they peeled from the alley.

15

UNDER A SINISTER BLUE MOON, the buildings of Port Morris and their night shadows stood across the empty stretch like scattered tombstones in a forgotten cemetery. Enormous warehouses loomed among derelict buildings long ago ransacked by New York winters and homeless drifters. Two mammoth steel bridge cranes loomed over the East River waterfront, a funereal testament to a once thriving manufacturing hub.

In the back seat of the NYPD sedan, Dom pressed the phone to her ear.

Lea said, "It's the only building still standing within fifty feet of the new Fed Ex depot. It appears to have been part of a bankrupt shipping company. The lot butts up against the back perimeter of the Fed Ex warehouse. Let me know when you get to the alley. You'll want to take the left down the alley."

Johns slowed the car and squinted into the gloom.

"I see it," Dom said. "Johns, take the left down that alley."

Lea said, "In a hundred yards the alley ends at a gravel road. The gravel road leads to a back entrance to the east of the building. The main entrance is to the north. To the west is the Bronx Kill stream so nobody is exiting out the west side."

Headlights beamed over broken cement and piles of forgotten debris. At the end of the alley, a gravel road appeared.

Dom said, "I think we got it."

"You want backup?"

"No, there are three of us and we gotta go fast. Hettie may be in there."

"Copy that." Lea rang off.

Johns extinguished the head lights and rolled slowly onto the gravel road leading to the lot's east entrance. In the gloom, a beaten red Toyota Corolla and a white Audi were parked in front of a one-story cinder block box building. Tall weeds and a solitary scraggly bush had grown through the cracked cement of the lot. Two darkened windows, their glass long ago broken by vandals, watched guard. Johns rolled to a stop and killed the engine. "We recon for twenty, let it get darker, then we go in."

Please let Hettie be here. Cold glided through the empty space in Dom's chest. It had been two days since Hettie was taken. If she was inside, she would be bound and gagged. She would have defecated on herself. She would be exhausted past the point of crying. *Please don't let Hettie be here.*

Johns' voice was calm. "I'm thinking there is one outer room. Those are the busted windows and the reason for no light. My guess is there's a back room with no windows where they have light, which means a dark hallway." They would be breeching, hard and fast, through the dark and into bright light. It was a potentially blinding scenario. "Not good. But it's what we've got."

In the shadows of the car, Rodriguez nodded solemnly.

"I'm gonna roll up fast and quiet," Johns whispered. "No headlights. Leave the car doors open so they don't hear us. I'll take point. Rodriguez behind. Walker, you pull up rear. We keep as quiet as we can until we're all the way in."

"Affirmative," Dom said.

Rodriguez nodded.

"Guns drawn. Once in the light, I'll bank left. Rodriquez, you bank right." Johns would have a clear shot as he headed into the back room. Rodriguez would wait until Johns jumped left and out of his line of sight.

Her voice was strong and decisive. "I'll stay center." She would wait for Rodriguez to bank right to get a clear line of sight. "If he's got a gun, I don't care who takes the shot. My priority is getting Hettie."

There was movement at the front of the building. Dom's adrenaline surged. A single black male exited and walked to the Audi. The car's interior light flashed across a red track suit as he dropped into the driver's seat. The car's headlights flashed before it rolled back and turned to the north entrance. The beam shot across the light to their position.

Johns hissed, "Down."

They slid below window level. When the Audi's headlights flashed through the sedan, the adrenaline buffeted against Dom's neck.

Dark descended into the NYPD sedan, and they sat up.

Johns whispered, "Let's go now. There's only one car." He keyed the ignition, dropped the gear shift, and rolled the dark sedan onto the crumbling asphalt. They rolled slowly to the silent cinder block building. Ten feet from the building, Johns braked, killed the engine, cocked his gun, and whispered, "Keep it tight, stay frosty."

They rose from the car, guns high, and sprinted at the front door in a single line—Johns, Rodriguez, Dom.

The first room was empty. Ancient wind-blown trash on flattened cardboard boxes littered the floor. From down a single hallway, a light appeared. Hispanic rap music blared. Glass cracked under Dom's soft work shoes. *Please let Hettie be here so I can take her home.*

At the hallway, Johns checked over his shoulder. Dom glanced back across the dark lot. It was clear. She tapped Rodriguez's shoulder who tapped Johns. A high-pitched Spanish rapper wailed against a thumping staccato beat.

They raced toward the light.

"Freeze! NYPD. Freeze motherfucker!" Johns' huge shoulders cleared into the light, and he banked left.

Rodriguez banked right.

Johns barked, "Freeze, motherfucker! Hands in the air!"

Dom bolted into the light, trained the gun at the room's center, dropped into a low double- handed stance, and blinked to clear the spots from her eyes.

Sitting in front of a battered card table, a gaping Kelvin Pena waved both hands overhead.

Dom scanned left and right. Nothing. Pena was alone in the ten-by-ten-foot square room. Along four walls, tall metal shelving units were crammed with laundry detergent, infant formula, cigarette cartons, and liquor. The hideout was a cache of stolen staples.

Johns yelled, "Keep those hands up."

Pena waved both arms, his face in shock.

There was no Hettie. Just fucking groceries. Fucking black market groceries.

She let the Glock drop to her side.

16

OUTSIDE THE DOOR of the ornithology department, Mila heard only silence from the other side. It was 9:06 pm. Most, if not all, of the staff should have gone home. She should have gone home too. She should have gotten on her bike, peddled south, grabbed a slice of pizza—pepperoni and green peppers, slightly burned—at Prince Street pizza, and found a good book to chill with at home. It was exactly what she did most evenings. It was a clear pattern with very few surprises.

But earlier in the day, by the cafeteria's coffee counter, she heard a museum staffer describe a frantic conversation between Mr. Blaulicht and the Van Burens. Something happened to Hettie's boyfriend, and there were signs Hettie may have been kidnaped. Anxiety jolted Mila's gut. She had to do something. She couldn't sit back and let something horrible happen to yet another person within her existential orbit. And didn't she discover the gala video with the ominous protestor throwing blood on Mrs. Van Buren? What if that was related to these new crimes? It was almost as if destiny had looped her into proximity of the missing Hettie case.

Pushing into the quiet lab, chlorine and formaldehyde

swamped her nose. She liked the variety of smells at the museum—the mustiness of the library, the antiseptic cleanliness of the planetarium, and the hint of mildew near the reptile displays. In fact, she liked most things about the museum including the research assignments, the analysis and statistics, and the awkward discussions with scientists like Hettie.

Hettie's workstation sat against the far wall under dozens of stuffed birds. A small lamp bathed the top of the desk in a soft glow as she sat in Hettie's chair and hovered her hand over the space bar. She should be home eating slightly burned pizza. She pressed the space bar. With a whirr, computer woke from sleep mode and the screen came to life. She pulled back her hand. Maybe tonight she would go wild and order the artichoke, spinach, and feta slice.

It started with a simple internet search of three key words. *Hettie Van Buren.*

Hettie Van Buren was the great-granddaughter of a formidable figure, the oil magnet Klaus Lowrance. Originally from Germany, Klaus Lowrance had arrived in the United States in 1850 with money to burn. In 1860, he was among the early investors in oil refinery equipment manufacturing in the tiny town Titusville, Pennsylvania. Two years later, after the discovery of oil in Titusville, the population exploded to 10,000, and good ole Klaus made out like a bandit. He became a millionaire almost overnight.

In 1928, Klaus's eldest son, Herbert Lowrance, ascended to the family throne as CEO and Chairman of Frontier Oil, moved the company to Philadelphia, and began the expansion of the empire. Around this period, he broke ground on Titus Hill, the family mansion in a wealthy Philadelphia suburb called Gladwyne. Photos of the property showed the peaked roofs of an enormous home behind a grove of trees and an iron fence. According to press clippings and black-and-white press photos,

Herbert was a thin man with a heavy mustache who had chosen a buxom brunette bride. They produced two offspring, a boy and a girl, but the boy died tragically at the age of five from tuberculosis.

Here the Lowrance story turned feminine. The sole heir of the Lowrance fortune, Yvette Madeline Lowrance, pale blonde with refined features and perfectly big blue eyes, was the darling of the local press throughout her childhood. A skilled equestrian, she graduated from a local all-girls preparatory school and attended Princeton. In 1991, at the age of twenty-four, Yvette appeared in a press photo on the stairs of Gladwyne Episcopal Church arm in arm with her new groom and flanked by both parents. Her groom was a fellow Princeton graduate named Claude Van Buren. A year later, Henrietta (Hettie) Honor Van Buren was baptized. Set against Yvette's beauty, the baby's round head, small, narrow eyes, and chunky cheeks were noticeably unremarkable.

When Herbert Lowrance passed in 1998, Claude took over Frontier Oil at the young age of thirty-one and moved his wife and daughter into Titus Hill. For a number of years, there was no mention in the press of the Van Burens. Hettie attended Baldwin School for Girls where she was an adequate tennis player and then she was accepted to Bryn Mawr College in the Bachelor of Science program with Cal Tech. Claude Van Buren sold Frontier Oil, moved Yvette into a New York City penthouse, and founded Rittenhouse Equity.

The glassy eyes of the dead birds stared down at Mila. How different would Mila's life be if her family had been so illustrious and wealthy? In all probability, Mila would have done exactly what Hettie did—attend the finest schools, get a solid degree, get a low-stress museum job, and enjoy the better side of life. But that cushy life hadn't protected Hettie. What could

Hettie Van Buren have possibly done that had gotten her kidnapped and her boyfriend killed?

Mila's fingers paused on the handle of the desk drawer. Snooping around someone's desk for physical clues felt like crossing a line. She stood and paced the length of the dark lab past a green lampshade askew on a researcher's table, a burned glass vial sitting neatly in a wooden stand, and a white business card spiked in a keyboard. Pausing, she stepped to the desk with the business card and leaned in close. *U.S. Department of Justice, Federal Bureau of Investigation, Domini Walker, Special Agent.* Mila's skin puckered. It was Agent Cool Cucumber assigned to the kidnapping of Hettie that Mila followed through the museum. Domini Walker was no doubt a kidnapping specialist. Like the ones that were assigned to her brother's case. *If she helped find Miss Timid Hettie, would the agent help her open Jimmy's cold case?*

She should be home reading a Leonardo Padura novel in the ratty leather chair by the open window, but instead, Mila spun on her heel, strode to Hettie's desk, sat, and slid open the drawer.

17

IN THE BRIGHT light of the back room of the Port Morris building, Kelvin Pena held his hands over his head, fingers spread wide. The rap music thumped against Dom's skull.

Aiming his gun at Pena's head, Johns snarled, "You Kelvin Pena?"

The bald man at the table nodded mutely.

"You alone?"

Pena nodded again.

Johns motioned his gun to the boom box in front of Pena. "Turn off that music."

Pena unplugged the huge radio and the room plunged into silence.

Johns looked around. "What is this?"

"Just goods, man. Just goods." Pena's voice was high-pitched and desperate.

They knew what it was. Hoodlums got hold of stolen goods and sold it on the black market for prices cheaper than in the stores. It was illegal, but it was low level. The poor didn't have a lot of options. Dom hung her head. They had chased a goose. They lost precious hours tracking down Kelvin Pena and his fucking stolen goods while Hettie was still out there. Hours. They lost hours.

"Look man, just straight-up groceries." Pena waved his arms. "Look, look, man. Detergent. Baby formula. Diapers. Just groceries, man."

To relieve the tension in her legs and arms, Dom stepped to the near wall. As she pivoted back to the room, she glanced down the dark hallway. They were in a brightly lit room with one dark entrance and no windows. In law enforcement this had a name: a funnel trap. Rodriguez noticed her glance, turned, and disappeared back down the hallway.

She circled the perimeter and stopped in front of Pena and his plastic chair. "We got some questions. Put your hands down."

Pena's arms lowered.

"Where were you on Sunday?"

"This Sunday?"

"Yeah."

"I was at my cousin's wedding." His head bobbed to confirm this as truth. "In Maryland. All weekend. Came back yesterday. Lots of witnesses. Stayed with my Auntie. She saw me all weekend."

She tapped the Glock against her thigh. "You know Micah Zapata?"

Confusion crept across his face. "Sure."

"He's dead."

Pena's eyes widened. "What?"

She stepped in close and leaned into his face. "He was killed."

He blinked and squeaked, "What?"

She bored into his eyes.

He swallowed. "Dead?"

She nodded.

"How?"

"He was shot."

"Sunday?" His brow furrowed.

She nodded.

"I was in Maryland. Jesus Christ Almighty. Micah was my friend. I got nothing to do with this."

"Yeah. Okay. Maybe. But do you know anything about it?"

"What? No! I dunno know nothing. Micah a good kid. I dunno know nothing."

"You know anyone who would want to come at him?"

"No. I dunno know...I dunno know nothing."

"You spoke to him last month."

He leaned away as if her words burned. "Yeah. Yeah. I did. But it was nothing."

Again, she tapped the Glock to her thigh. "Oh yeah?"

He fluttered his hands. "Yeah, yeah. It was nothing."

"What did you talk about?"

He glanced left over her shoulder, remembering. "I asked him for money. I want to expand my operations. I was asking him if he knew anybody with money."

"Why were you doing that?"

"He's all rich now. Got rich friends—" Pena clamped his mouth.

"And a rich girlfriend," she said.

Pena nodded slowly. "Yeah. We all know that. His lady is minted." He stretched ten fingers wide. "Listen, I got nothing to do with Micah's ... I got nothing to do with that. I asked the brother to help me out with some capital. He said no. That was it."

"When he said no, what did you do?"

"I guess maybe I pushed a little? But he said no."

"And?"

"I found the cash."

"Where?"

"A friend I know wanted in." He gulped. "I'm giving him a fifty-fifty cut. That's it. End of story."

Dom stepped back. "Tell me what you know about Micah Zapata."

"We were friends from round the way. We hung out. Nothing too bad. Some drugs, you know, like everybody. He was smart. He got into college, left us behind. I get it. Smart guy, had a future, you know? More than most of us up in here. He never looked back. I'm telling you, Micah's clean." His face contorted in pain. "He was…"

Dom glanced at Johns and shook her head. Pena wasn't involved. They were done here.

She turned and took long strides for the dark hallway, crunching over glass. From behind, Johns said, "I know where you live, Kelvin Pena. You want to never see me again, you never saw us tonight. Understood?"

"Sure, man. Dunno nothing. Never saw you."

The outer room seemed darker with the blackened shadows crawling from the corners. Shards of glass in broken windows looked like pointed shark's teeth. A newspaper fluttered with a ghost-like rattle. Through the front door, Rodriguez stood against the night, his silhouette stoic and brave.

Dom stepped into fresh air as her disappointment turned to anger. *A fucking goose chase.* Hettie was somewhere still alone and still terrified. Dom banked right and marched along the building into the darkness. She had made a mistake, had chosen the wrong direction of the investigation, and it had cost hours. *A fucking goose chase that had cost hours.*

Humiliation tore at her chest. An overturned aluminum trash can on the cement glinted in the moon's bluish cast. Reaching the can, Dom arched her right foot back, swung it like a soccer player, and connected with metal. The can careened into the air, soared skyward, and landed with a crash. Her foot carried through the air, useless and inept. Adrenaline surging in her veins ignited the rage. *Her mistake had cost hours.*

Dom spun to the wall and delivered a second full-powered kick against cinder blocks. The agony was immediate as pain exploded through her leg like a firecracker, ripping into the knee, thigh, and hip. She doubled over as vomit climbed to the lower depths of her throat. She spit a mouthful of vomit on the cement. She leaned over and cleared her throat, letting mucus drip from her lips. *Hettie was alone, terrified, and in trouble.*

Out of the gloom, Stewart Walker whispered, *We all make mistakes, my Dom. The key is to stand back up.*

As she breathed in deeply, the rage ebbed away. She stood. Her toe throbbed in agony. *Time to find Hettie.*

Johns and Rodriguez dropped her at the 52nd Precinct. They had exchanged few words on the ride into the Bronx. What was there to say? She used up their day as well. Now they had to get back to their own jobs.

"Thanks. I mean it," she said as she stepped out the car.

Johns leaned out of the window. "It's what we do, Agent. Mm-hmm. It's our job. You don't have to thank us."

"Yeah, but you two were solid today. Thank you. I owe you."

"Just find the girl. That will make us even."

At Lancia, she slowly unholstered the Glock and locked it away in the trunk's safe. She slid into the driver seat, closed the door against the noise of the city, and breathed in deeply of oil and gas. She gripped the wheel at the three and the nine o'clock positions, just as her father had taught her the first time at the track as he explained speed control and wheel rotation.

FBI Special Agent Domini Walker had wasted the precious first six hours of an investigation on the wrong line of pursuit.

She had failed. She felt like a fraud. Fontaine should assign someone else to the case, a more experienced agent, someone who wouldn't chase a tangent or get sidetracked by a lark. He should assign a real agent.

The darkness in the car felt heavy, and she let her head hang on her neck and stared at the rise and fall of her chest. Her toes were smashed, maybe broken. She needed to stop at the drugstore and buy Advil. Through a stream of unstructured thoughts, a calm descended and her father whispered, *Mistakes are important, my Dom. You learn from them.* She picked up her head, clenched her jaw. What had they learned from Kelvin Pena? That Micah Zapata was a good kid. That he was likely not involved in criminal activity. That maybe this case wasn't about Micah Zapata's dodgy past.

She clenched the wheel. Hettie was still out there, alone and terrified. Time to find Hettie.

Her phone rang.

"Walker," she answered.

"Agent Walker?" It was a fearful female voice.

"Yes?"

"It's Yvette Van Buren."

"Mrs. Van Buren, yes?"

"I wonder if you could come by the apartment?"

"I'm on my way." Dom turned the key in the ignition.

18

UNDER THE WALL of dead birds, Mila fingered the contents of Miss Timid Hettie's desk drawer—notepads, pens, paper clips, and loose rubber bands. In the drawer's pen tray, a small square music player rested next to an earplug cord knotted into a ball. She lifted the white slippery cord, unknotted it and, as if on autopilot, settled them in her ears and hit play. She recognized the haunting timbre of a famous female blues singer. With the blues in her ears, Mila skimmed the farthest depth of the drawer. Nothing. In the silence between songs, her nails scratched the bottom of the drawer for a hidden hatch. Nothing.

The opening chord of the next song burst in her ears, but it was the same impassioned song. Her fingers paused. *Had the music player stuck?* She fiddled with the buttons on the player and fast forwarded through the song to the next spat of silence. The opening chord of the third song reverberated in her ears. It was the same song again. Hettie's playlist was a loop of the same haunting song, over and over. *Who does that?*

Mila slid the drawer shut, leaned back in the chair, and let the soulful voice wash over her. The melody and words were at once melancholy and uplifting, as if the singer, having finally been released from captivity, rediscovered the simple joy of freedom. Is Hettie sad? Does this story of breaking free resonate with her?

A shelf of books hovered over the desk. With the music filling her ears, Mila stood, and with a light touch, she traced up and down the spines of each book as she read their titles.

The Most Perfect Thing: Inside (and Outside) a Bird's Egg
Ornithology
Lapwings, Loons and Lousy Jacks: The How and Why of Bird Names
A Dictionary of Scientific Bird Names
ABA Checklist: Birds of the Continental United States and Canada, 7th ed.
Bird Brain: An exploration of Avian Intelligence
Collins Bird Guide
The Genius of Birds
A Sky Full of Birds
Feather Quest
Last of the Curlews

The final book was older. The cloth cover was worn, and the spine was severely cracked. Using one finger, Mila hooked the top edge and angled it out, letting it drop into her hand. The smoothness of the fabric felt like it had been a treasured book. *Last of the Curlews* by Fred Bodsworth. She flipped open the first page and read the date. 1955. The forward read, "*Mr. Bodsworth writes with plain, succinct evocation and beauty of the arctic autumn and the dwindling of the once enormous assemblies of curlews.*"

The song in her ears began the fourth repeat. Hettie read books about the decline of a species and listened to melancholy songs on repeat. Perhaps Hettie Van Buren's soul ran deeper than the rich-girl-with-a-nice-cushy-museum-job impression. *Where are you, Hettie?*

Maybe, just maybe, Mila could help the FBI find Hettie. And to return the favor, maybe the FBI would revisit the cold case of a young boy stolen from the street in broad daylight. Mila was good at chasing down clues, seeing connections, and identifying causal relationships. What if her research skills could significantly increase the odds of Hettie's discovery?

She unplugged the earphones, settled the music player back in the drawer, and slid the drawer closed. At the bottom of the screen, the Facebook icon glowed. With a tap on the mouse, the landing page of Hettie's Facebook account appeared. Mila sat back. Hettie had left her work computer logged into Facebook. She glanced over her shoulder at the white business card propped in a keyboard. Mila should be home with a novel in the chair by the window. But instead, she was in the dark ornithology department snooping into Hettie Van Buren's life to try to help find the missing woman. She took a deep breath against the rising anxiety and turned back to the glow of the screen. She clicked into the Facebook account settings and changed the password. Later, she would log in as Hettie.

She stood, moved to the nearby desk, and snapped a photo of the FBI agent's card. If she found anything of interest, she would call Agent Cool Cucumber. For the first time in a long time, the unpredictable felt exciting.

19

THE MAID'S eyes were puffy and red as she gestured Dom inside. Silk curtains were pulled tight against the night, and the golden glow of a lamp was the only light in the huge living room. Yvette Van Buren sat alone on the tan leather sofa with a large photo album on her lap, gazing into a distant darkness.

Dom approached softly. "Mrs. Van Buren, how are you doing?"

The graceful woman turned with dazed, disoriented eyes. "Agent Walker."

A mother's inability to protect their child must be the worst type of terror. "Is that a photo album?" The leather of the armchair was cool against Dom's jeans.

Yvette stroked the leather book and nodded.

"Does it have photos of Hettie?"

"Yes," Yvette said weakly.

"Do you want to show me?"

Yvette blinked and her gaze slowly settled on Dom. "Will it help?"

Dom nodded and moved to the sofa.

Yvette started at the beginning. From a glossy photo, a tiny

Hettie, enveloped by white lace, stared up from a bassinet stroller with curious blue eyes. "This was her christening. She didn't like our priest. She fussed when he held her." Her finger traced Hettie's chin.

The next photo was taken from the top of a hill, looking down on a rolling green lawn. A crowd of toddlers rambled between balloons and brightly colored games. Pastel napkins littered a long table and encircled a towering princess cake. "This was her second birthday." Yvette's hand smoothed the plastic over the photo. "She loved that cake. Ate two pieces. I thought she would be sick, but she wasn't."

The next photo was taken from the sidelines of a horse ring. Hettie—maybe four or five years old—sat astride a small gray pony, her face beaming from underneath a black riding helmet. "This is Pudgy. She loved him when she was young. After a while she lost interest in riding. I understand. One grows up."

Further into the album, Yvette paused on the image of a teenaged Hettie in a pink lace dress. "Sweet Sixteen. They didn't have that when I was growing up. But her friends, they all had them. She picked out that dress herself. We went to Barneys. It looked lovely on her." In the photo, Hettie smiled with a mixture of pride and bashfulness. "Although it was quite bulky, perhaps not as slimming as it could have been."

Dom eyed the photo closer. Having hit adolescence, Hettie had gained twenty pounds, and the dress was not flattering. Shame her mother still remembered that, but all families had history—unresolved disagreements, sore spots, buried slights. "Where was this photo taken?"

"At the club in Philly."

"Is that a golf club?"

"No, it's the cricket club." Yvette smiled wistfully before turning the page. "Oh, here she is graduating from Baldwin." A slimmer Hettie stood with arms entwined with a friend on the enormous porch of an imposing brick building

"Baldwin?" Dom asked.

"Yes, yes, you don't know Baldwin?"

"No."

"It's one of the best girls schools in the nation."

Apparently pride survived even in despair. "Ah."

"Hettie excelled. She loved her teachers. Her tennis game improved there. I thought it was the best place for her, without the distraction of boys. She was never that interested in boys..." She stared into the distance.

"Did she not like boys?"

"No. It wasn't that. As the other girls blossomed into teens, their figures filled out, and they learned about makeup, what have you. Hettie was at a loss then."

"How so?"

"She was uncomfortable around boys. She would cry about it to me, often. It broke my heart. I kept telling her to bide her time. She did eventually mature and get the right curves during that awkward blossoming. I got her appointments with the best hair dressers. And we went to makeup artists. But I don't think she ever quite recovered from being the one no one wanted. Hasn't ever really had a boyfriend. Until recently."

"You two are close?"

"People used to remark that we behaved more like friends, not mother and daughter." She turned the page. "And here she is graduating from Bryn Mawr." Hettie wore the formal black cap and gown in front of a crowd of similar graduates. Her smile was soft but proud. "You do know Bryn Mawr, Agent Walker?"

She did, thank you very much. Dom simply nodded.

"Another excellent school. Hettie did just fine there. We wished she had studied literature. It's a much better foundation. The classics. Woolf, Bronte, Shelley. That would have suited her disposition much better. And of course Bryn Mawr is exceptional in the arts. But Hettie did a combined degree with Cal Tech. All this science was difficult for her. But she was determined." Yvette's hand flattened gently on the photo with fine manicured nails. "Hettie fought hard for those grades. She studied so diligently. Whenever we spoke she was forever studying. I'm not sure how she ever found time for her friends."

Slowly, Yvette closed the photo album and waited for Dom to lift it off her lap.

Dom placed it on the coffee table and resumed her seat in the armchair.

Yvette clasped her hands in her lap and her body stilled. "I understand Claude has spoken with the FBI."

"Yes. He spoke to our Assistant Director in Charge."

"This boss said Hettie's boyfriend has been found. Killed in his apartment."

"Yes."

Yvette swallowed. "Did you find him?"

"Yes."

"Shot?"

"Yes."

Yvette shook her head, touched her neck. Her face wrinkled in pain. Without the dominating presence of her husband, Yvette was more expressive. "And my Hettie?"

"I believe the two are related."

"Someone has taken her?"

"Yes. That is the assumption we're making."

Yvette closed her eyes. The glow from the lamp painted her skin golden. "Killers have my daughter?" When she eventually opened her eyes, they were clear, focused, as if she had found an untapped reservoir of fortitude. "Is the boyfriend a criminal?"

"We don't have proof of that, no."

"What are you doing to find my daughter?"

After the wasted hours of the failed Kelvin Pena pursuit, the question stung. Dom swallowed. "We are pursuing all lines of inquiry."

"You don't sound confident in your investigation."

"I am confident I will find your daughter, Mrs. Van Buren. In fact, I'd like to reach out to her friends to get more background on Hettie's recent interests and activities."

"Madeline Abbott. That's her dear friend." Yvette looked up a number on her phone, picked up a gold pen off a side table and wrote out a number on a pad of paper before handing the sheet to Dom.

The paper was thick and expensive, and Dom folded it into quarters and slipped it in the pocket of her jeans. "Thank you."

"You will call me when you find something?"

"You and your husband will be the first to know."

"You will call *me*, Agent Walker?"

Interesting. It was another hint of the couple's discord. "I will."

"Thank you for coming," Yvette said softly as she folded her hands and the bewilderment returned to her eyes.

In the elevator, Dom slid out the quartered linen paper from her jeans pocket and unfolded it. She rang Madeline Abbott and was transferred to voicemail. "Madeline. My name is Domini Walker. I'm a special agent with the FBI. Mrs. Van Buren gave me your number. I would like to speak with you about Hettie. Call when you get this." She left her number.

She lost a day chasing down Kelvin Pena. It was time to regroup. There were a few bona fide facts in this case. One, Micah Zapata had been killed, most likely by a professional. Two, Hettie Van Buren had been kidnapped from her apartment. There were also some assumptions. One, Micah Zapata, despite drug use and dodgy friends during his teens, appeared to be a good kid. Two, the two crimes were related. On the face of it, the first day of the investigation hadn't turned up much. When a case hit a dead end, the solution was to march down a different road.

Reaching the ground floor, the elevator doors opened to the expanse of opulent marble. Dom had spent too much time focusing on Micah Zapata. Through the lobby door, the setting sun cast the sky in a bright pink. It was time to dig into Hettie Van Buren. And whatever secrets she was keeping.

THE STREETS CIRCLING Washington Square Park were dark, as if the wealthy didn't need the safety of streetlights. Dom parked at the curb by Hettie's building. It was coming up on midnight, and despite a dose of Advil and eye drops, her toes were throbbing and her eyes felt gritty. In the rearview mirror, a pair of phantom hurricane lanterns glided toward her against an inky night. Rotating tires whining on smooth asphalt went silent as the car came to rest, the high beams lighting up the interior of the Lancia like stage lights. She squinted. *What the crap is this?*

She stretched out of the sports car and walked back toward the lights on a sleek black Mercedes S600. Inside, the dashboard's dim glow illuminated a sweep of gray hair and the face of Claude. *Crap.* Dom flared a flashlight beam across his face as he lowered the window.

She leaned down. "Mr. Van Buren, can you turn on your overhead cabin light?"

He fumbled for the switch and the interior brightened. His face was hard and angry.

She clicked off her flashlight beam. "Sir, what are you doing here?"

"Last I checked, Agent Walker, this was a free country."

"Sir, you should be home."

"I spoke to your boss, Fontaine."

"Yes, he told me."

"I told him we needed a more senior agent."

Dom's father's voice whispered, *Don't let 'em rumble you, my Dom. You're just as good as them.* "He told me."

"My Hettie needs a more senior agent on this. A male agent."

"Sir, you are speaking to an agent of the Federal Bureau of Investigation with over ten years of experience. I'm advising you to show some respect."

He scowled. "You met with my wife. Alone, without me."

"Yes, I did."

"You don't need to do that. She's suffering enough."

"Sir, this is an FBI investigation that involves a homicide and what I believe to be the kidnapping of your daughter. You *want* me to pursue every lead and to learn as much as I can from those who are close to Hettie. There will be plenty of interviews, I assure you. This is how an investigation is done."

Glaring, he said, "I'm glad he's dead."

She shifted on her feet.

"Do you think the murderers have my daughter?"

"I don't know yet," she said. "But that's the assumption."

"What do you know?"

"I know that Hettie's disappearance is related to the murder of Micah Zapata." She tugged the navy jacket down against her shoulders. "I do not know the exact relationship or the motive yet, but I will discover both."

He sneered. "I will crush his family. I will crush them. I will send those dirty brown people back to the third world hell of Honduras that they crawled out from."

Interesting. Earlier he hadn't known the Zapatas' home

country. He must have been doing some homework. "Go home, Mr. Van Buren. You're not doing Hettie any good here. And your wife needs you." She waited until he turned the key in the ignition and the finely built engine purred back into life.

Stepping into the lobby's light, she flashed her badge at Carl the night security guy. He nodded knowingly.

Outside apartment 10E, she glanced to the end of the silent hallway where a red *EXIT* sign glowed. If Hettie had been kidnapped, the perp might have forced her down the back stairs, away from the prying eyes of a security guard. She strode to the *EXIT* door and pushed into a cold, gloomy emergency stairwell. Inside the impenetrable cement walls there was a tomblike silence and the sharp smell of industrial paint. She peered down and around the top of the stairs. *Had the perp pointed a gun at Hettie's head?*

She cornered at the stairs' elbow and descended to the ninth floor. The slap of soft soles echoed above and below, and an elongated shadow preceded her. *Had Hettie protested, maybe screamed?*

Eighth floor.

A film of sweat formed on her neck. *Had Hettie cried or pleaded?*

Fifth floor.

The steel handrail was cold. *Had Hettie been barefoot? Had she felt the cold?*

Second floor.

Had they told Hettie that Micah was dead? Had she been crying?

First floor.

On the landing there were two doors. One read *Lobby*, the other *EXIT*. She pushed into the lobby and the brightness caused her to blink. She nodded to Carl. "Is that rear door alarmed?"

"No. It's only self-locking."

She retreated into the silent landing and pushed the outside door. Fresh air tickled damp skin. The night was loud with city noises: a dump truck wheezed in the distance, a horn honked on a neighboring street, and a breeze rustled leaves. An L-shaped loading platform, ready to receive trucks, faced a short dark driveway.

Hettie had been taken from here. Dom could feel it.

The lights from Washington Square Park beamed across Hettie's white living room like Batman's beacon shining over a sleeping Gotham City. Throughout her years with the Bureau, she had taken advantage of the night. The vacant rooms and shrouded corners allowed her to detach from the logic of an investigation. Alone in silence, her internal dialog ran rampant. Dom moved to the center of the room, closed her eyes, and let the environment permeate her senses. The pungent smell of rotting flowers filled the space.

While her mind looped indiscriminately through disparate thoughts, the smell from the flowers reminded her of burned sugar. I hope Beecher fed the dog. What would happen when the water evaporated from the vase? Was Claude's anger appropriate? What had Hettie and Micah gotten themselves into? How poor do you have to be to buy black market laundry detergent at discounted rates? Did the Honduran soccer shirt mean anything?

She moved slowly down the hallway. In the master bedroom a splash of light from the street on the ceiling resembled the wings of an angel. How long did it take Micah to slide down the wall after being shot? Had Micah had a girlfriend in high school? Years ago, Dom had overheard a conversation in her high school. "Did you know Domini Walker's dad was that cop who hung himself?"

Her flashlight beam circled the bedroom. Lord, my foot is killing me. ERT had taken the overturned dish, its contents, and the smashed photo. Why had Hettie stumbled against the wall? Was it her shoulder that hit the glass? Dom searched each dresser drawer, rifling through underwear, T-shirts, bras, and socks. How much more expensive is nicer underwear? Did Hettie know the abductors?

She glanced at the bottom of the bed. Parents told their kids there weren't monsters under beds, that sharp, dirty fingernails were not grasping for warm bare skin. But parents were wrong. There were monsters. A memory of a cold basement pressed into her mind. She had sliced the ropes from Darlin's ankles, wrapped her in the navy windbreaker with the yellow letters, and pulled her close. "I'm the police. I'm taking you out of here." Would evil's appetite ever be satiated? Of course not. Fidelity, bravery, and integrity. Was Meat Lover's pizza the best?

She knelt and shone the beam across an empty space under the bed. I should get rid of those old sleeping bags under my bed. Why was Hettie's apartment so clean?

She stood and lifted the mattress. Nothing. Had a car pulled up to the dark loading dock?

The shaft of the flashlight drifted over the closet. Clothes hung neatly on hangers. Purses filled the shelf overhead. Dom rarely used a purse. In the corner was a small roller bag. Had Hettie traveled recently? Clasping the flashlight between her chin and shoulder, Dom lifted the roller bag. It was empty. She set the bag in the closet and took a step back. Neither the Van Burens nor the Zapatas had known of any travel.

An imaginary ping, like a distant chime of an elevator car

opening on a lower floor, silenced the mental chatter. Had those five blank days in Hettie's calendar indicated a trip? Was this the project Roberto had mentioned and, when pushed, got angry about? Had Hettie and Micah gone somewhere secretly? What's a good hiding place for travel documents?

She cast the beam across the room, landing it on the top of the single bedside table. Pulling the drawer, she felt it stick. She yanked harder, and reluctantly it slid open. Inside were only a box of tissues and a pair of sunglasses. She bit the flashlight between her lips, pulled the drawer out and off its racks, and peeked into the space. Hidden inside was a thin leather portfolio the size of an envelope. Ping. The imaginary elevator car ascended closer.

She opened the portfolio. Inside were boarding passes, a passport for Hettie Van Buren, and a passport for Micah Zapata. Underneath the passports were eight boarding passes that showed a trip three weeks ago from Newark via Dallas-Fort Worth to Tegucigalpa, Honduras. The stay was five days long.

Ping. The elevator had arrived. Hettie and Micah had taken a secret trip to Honduras. Dom's mind slowed. A mysterious trip wasn't a coincidence, it was a possible motive. Dom's back straightened. The killing of Micah Zapata and the kidnapping of Hettie Van Buren had become a lot more complicated.

She dropped the leather portfolio into a Ziploc bag and sealed it. Back in the living room, a pale and forlorn moonbeam painted the floor. Dom leaned close to one of the photos in the bookshelf and stared into Hettie's pale gray-blue eyes. They looked wise, smart, and reserved. *Don't worry, Hettie. I'm not gonna let the monsters keep you for long. I'm coming.*

The pace of every investigation was different. Some started quickly and braked on a dime. Others simmered before exploding. A wealthy girl and her boyfriend taking a trip to Honduras three weeks before a homicide and a kidnapping hinted of big complicated entanglements. This case would require a very cautious cadence, much like stepping on a frozen lake whose icy surface was unreliable and whose murky depths hid foreboding secrets.

Don't worry, Hettie, dark secrets don't scare me. They're part of my history. I'm coming for you. The monsters don't get to keep you.

WEDNESDAY

An occasional sight record stirs the faint hope that some linger on, but even if a few birds are still alive the species seems doomed.

—Thomas Foster, "Circling to Doom"

21

TEGUCIGALPA, Honduras

Outside the Super El Rey, the big-city nephew had taken Maria Cardona's hand and guided her through the throngs, down a long block lined with hawker stalls, to a second bus terminal where they found a crowded minivan taxi, paid their fare, and climbed aboard. An hour later, the driver yelled their exit.

They found the office on a dusty side street away from the honking taxis. The two rooms had shiny white tiles on the floor and bright pink paint on the walls. An imperious woman in a starched collared shirt brought them two bottles of chilled water. Maria and the nephew carefully cracked the seals and let the cold water wash the city dust from their throats. Where does the dust go? Maria's stomach growled. She had not eaten since breakfast ten hours ago. She had some money, but she didn't risk spending it. Not yet. They had promised her money for transport and food, but she would wait until it was in hand before she ate. She may be from the village, but she wasn't gullible.

The sour woman stared at them from behind thick-framed glasses. Maria smoothed down the coarse dress over her thighs and wondered if glasses made items larger or smaller? A man called out from the back room. The disagreeable woman stood, beckoned Maria to follow, and indicated to the nephew to wait. He smiled broadly in his torn T-shirt and ratty flip-flops, proud to be sitting in an air-conditioned office with a chilled bottle of water. At least his face was clean.

Inside the back office, a large man with a fat neck and greasy hair nodded at a chair. He spoke in Spanish. "You understand what you need to do?"

She understood. She understood a lot of things. She understood the sun would rise regularly over her offspring's offspring far into the future. She understood the rains were coming less so the crops were suffering. She understood some people were more valued than others. And she knew she would get on a flying aluminum can and rush through the clouds. A mother will do many things for a daughter.

Her stomach growled. She would like to get some fruit. Maybe some cheese.

He was asking about her baggage. She had only the one bag that she pointed to on the floor.

"Bring it with you tomorrow," he commanded.

Of course, she thought. What a wasted use of words.

He handed her a slim white envelope with something inside. She accepted it and placed it on her lap.

"Open it," he commanded.

She slid her finger through the flap and ripped it gently before sliding out a stiff shiny passport with gold lettering, *Republica de Honduras Pasaporte*.

He pointed at the passport. "Be careful with that."

More wasted words.

"Where are you staying?" His eyes were suspicious.

Her cousin lived in West Comayagüela. She did not need to

explain to him that it was a poor neighborhood. Everyone knew West Comayagüela.

"How will you get back here tomorrow?" His voice was harsh and his lips were tight.

She was embarrassed. She did not want him to know that she did not have much money and that taking city busses would take a long time and many transfers. She may be a poor person, she may be a small person in the eyes of the world, but she had pride.

He waited.

She said nothing.

He gave her an exasperated look as if she was dense, then called out to the surly woman. "Get her the cash advance."

"We have been told to give you an advance. You will use some of it today to get back to where you are staying and some of it tomorrow to get back to this office. The traffic will be bad tomorrow morning. You must take a taxi. Not a bus. No busses. You cannot be late tomorrow morning. Do you understand?" He stared at her with disdain.

She may be from a village, but she wasn't stupid. She nodded.

The ill-tempered woman handed him an oblong brown envelope, just like the ones the market ladies save from the bank. It was thick with cash. Her stomach growled.

His fat hand waggled the envelope as only the rich can, simultaneously reluctant to offer it yet indifferent to the amount. "Don't use it for anything other than transport or food. You understand? This is for your transport and your food. Only those two things."

Always the insult. That poor people were somehow irresponsible or thieves. She was neither. She was just poor.

22

AT FOUR AM Dom was staring at the bedroom ceiling as possible scenarios looped through her mind. Hettie was being held by a gang who had lashed her to a bed with duct-tape. Hettie was locked in a basement with music blaring from overhead. Hettie was drugged in a crack house, her mind spaced out on meth. Dom threw back the sheet, sat up, ground her heels into carpet, and checked her phone. Madeline Abbott had left a voice mail: She was available first thing in the morning. A tiny Chihuahua, its pink tongue extended, raised its head off a pillow.

Two years ago, Tinks & Tongue had been relegated to a high-kill shelter. "It's okay, Tinks. I'll put you in with Beecher."

Dom got dressed by the dim light of a bedside lamp. Scooping up the dog, she padded down the hall and rapped on Beecher's door.

A sleepy voice mumbled, "Yo. Come on in."

The room smelled of sour breath and the tangy sweat of male sleep. She gently set Tinks on the bed. "You got her? I gotta run out."

Beecher pulled the dog to his chest and rolled toward the wall. "We got this. Me and Tinks. Good luck with the case."

The Javits Building's eighth floor was one long field of cubicles like tiny farming plots under a fluorescent sun. At this time of the morning, huge ceiling vents ruffled papers on empty desks.

Dom set down a large coffee on Lea Peck's desk in the center of the space. "As promised."

Lea's hundred tight braids were pulled back into a neat ponytail, and her eyes were teenager-lack-of-sleep puffy. "Guardian angel, you." She sipped from the plastic lid's slit. "Did you sleep at all?"

Dom eased into a chair. The throbbing in her toes had softened but it had not disappeared. "I got a bit."

"There was nobody out this early. I dominated the streets." Lea's head wobbled. "Even the idiot Uber drivers got outta my way."

It was good to be working with Lea's sass again. "How you been?"

"Oh, yeah, all good. My last assignment after St. Chris was Italian mob. That shit is no joke. Fatty Fingers this, Uncle Gumbo that, Cousin Two-Shits the other thing. I mean, holy shit, can them old boys talk when they think nobody is listening. But we were up in there with electronic surveillance, consensual monitoring, what have you. It was fascinating."

"Out of organized crime?"

"Yup. And, hey, thanks for asking Fontaine for me. My boss ain't overly impressed, but then again, I ain't overly impressed by my boss." She eyed Dom. "You ever seen my boss's ass? That man has a dozen Dunkin Donuts for butt cheeks."

Dom grinned. "Don't worry. I got your back." During St. Chris a number of older agents tried to dominate Lea because she was a triple threat: young, black, and a woman. Dom would have none of it. Women stuck together.

"Hell, I know you do." Lea peered over the cup's lip. "How are you doing?"

"I'm okay."

Lea's inspection was steady. "Three months away is a long time."

"Absolutely."

"So you're good?"

It was a loaded question. *Good* in this building meant courageous, tough, and confident. Dom didn't feel any of those yet. But to be fair, this was only the second day back on the job. "Sure. I'm good." Stewart Walker's ghost grinned at the bravado.

"How's that tall-glass-of-fine-blonde water you call a brother? Yum, yum." She sounded like a fifty-year-old sexpot.

Dom grinned. "He's good."

"He still living with you?"

Dom nodded.

"Can you invite me round for dinner?"

Dom chuckled.

"I mean, he's still divorcing that bitch, right?"

"Yup, yup. Paperwork is going through. He'll be rid of her soon."

Lea's mood turned somber. "What's the word from the internal investigation?"

Dom's stomach crunched. "It's gonna be what it's gonna be."

"What swinging dicks. You gonna play it straight?"

Dom shrugged.

"I mean, for fuck's sake, you saved a crap ton of kids. I'm about to go all up in their shit, if they come interview me. But they haven't come at me yet. They need to be giving you a medal instead of prying open everybody's ass cheeks and staring at brown rings with proctology scopes." Lea's coffee was kicking in.

"Is there actually something called a proctology scope?"

"I think it may be called a proctoscope, but it's early morning still."

"If they do come interview you, just play it straight."

"Maybe I'll take the initiative and call 'em and offer my testimony as to your personal character." She shook her head and set down the coffee cup. "When we find Hettie Van Buren, we can wave that in front of their faces. Am I right?" Her face softened. "I'm sorry about the Kelvin Pena chase."

"Time to regroup." Dom fished out the Ziploc bag containing the travel documents. "There's been a turn of events." She described the search and the odd secrecy around Hettie and Micah's Honduran trip.

"What do you think that's all about?"

"I don't know but we're going to find out. You ready?"

"Fuck right, I am." Lea cracked her knuckles and settled fingers on the keyboard. "Hit me, Ruth the Moabite. Where you go, I go."

Dom ignored the arcane biblical reference. "Let's start at the beginning. What have you found in the phone records?"

Like frenetic spider legs, Lea's fingers rattled on keys. Her eyes glanced between twin computer screens. "First the landline for the Van Burens. Nada. No calls in or out in the last week."

"Go back a few months, before the Honduras trip."

Lea scanned the screen. "Nope. Nobody used it. I mean, who uses landlines anymore?"

"Okay. Next. Micah's phone logs."

"Sunday morning at 11:05, Micah had a call with Hettie that lasted twenty-three minutes. Later that afternoon he received three texts and a ten-minute call from numbers that appear to be friends or family—frequent numbers. His evening and night were quiet. Nothing looks unusual in the final hours of his life. The last time his phone pinged off his tower was 23:48."

Micah's phone stopped working at approximately midnight on Sunday, forty-eight hours earlier.

Lea clicked over to Hettie's phone log. "She made two connections on Sunday. The first was that 11:05 call to Micah. That was their last connected call. She connected with her mother at 13:26 for five minutes. Her phone last pinged against the local cell tower at 02:00 Monday morning."

"So, given that window of time, the perp hits Micah some-time before midnight then heads over to Washington Square Park some time before two am."

Lea nodded.

Lea's fingers tapped. "Now, let me check the five days they were in Honduras. Nope, Micah didn't use his phone. And nope, Hettie didn't use her phone while they were there."

"That's gotta be intentional." This secret trip was smelling increasingly hinky.

The brightly lit floor was silent except for the blasts from the air vents.

"Now, let me check their credit card records." Lea scanned a new document on the screen. "They didn't use their credit cards while they were in Honduras. They must have used cash."

"This trip smells really fishy. Why turn off their phones? Why use only cash? Why hide it from both sets of parents? Why hide the travel documents in her bedside table? There are too many questions and not enough answers." She stood and stretched her back. Her toes throbbed.

"What did that gangsta brother say?"

Dom relayed the story of the chase in the alley and Roberto ready to strike with the steel pipe.

Lea whistled.

"But I don't think he's involved. He had very genuine shock reactions. He did mention a project. I'm guessing it was this trip." Dom cracked her neck. "What did ERT find at the two apartments?"

Lea glanced at her notepad. "Micah's door lock was blown off with force. The perp would have jackbooted his way in. At which point Micah ran into the bedroom. The perp followed him down the hall and shot him from the bedroom door. Quick and dirty."

"I can't believe our perp tossed a gun with prints. Nothing back on the prints yet?"

Lea shook her head.

"What did ERT find at Hettie's?"

"Nothing. Literally nothing. No forced entry. No residuals. No blood. No prints. Other than the overturned dish in the bedroom, there was nothing."

"That's really odd. At Micah's, the perp slammed his way in —it would have been noisy—blew Micah away—that would have been noisy—and then threw the gun in the bushes with prints all over it. But at Hettie's, there's no noise, nobody saw anything, and he leaves absolutely no prints?"

"Maybe he was being more careful at Hettie's, considering the neighborhood?"

"Yeah, maybe." Dom paced to the window on throbbing toes. The sun had not risen. When it did it would bring the third day Hettie Van Buren was being held by a monster.

Lea said, "I'm going to start digging into Hettie's computer. They just brought it up."

"Okay, I've got someone I need to meet."

23

MADELINE ABBOT'S bloodshot eyes stood out against translucent skin on her pixie face. "Would you like some coffee?" She sniffed back tears.

"Yes, please." Dom took coffee where she could get it.

Madeline's refurbished SoHo unit was on the second floor of a walk-up on Sullivan Street. Through a window, the sky was blushing pink.

"Cream?"

"Black is fine. Thanks."

The space was more loft than apartment, with a big entertaining area, an open kitchen, and a bedroom behind a sliding barn door. Exposed bricks were painted white, and the unit had lots of glam. *Did everyone in this crowd use a designer?* Under a low-hanging chrome chandelier, a round silver bean of a coffee table was littered with used tissues.

A long time ago Dom had learned to soothe her tension by sitting. She settled on one side of an L-shaped velveteen couch.

Five minutes later, Madeline handed her a warm mug, sat on the sectional, and wiped her nose with a crushed tissue. "How can I help ... Agent?"

"Please call me Dom." Younger women had issues with using the word *Agent*. She wanted Madeline as comfortable as possible, given the circumstances. "Thanks for seeing me so early."

The tears dropped from Madeline's eyes, and she smashed the tissue against her cheek.

"Did the Van Burens tell you what's happening?"

Madeline nodded.

"So you know that Hettie is still missing?"

The tears streamed and she nodded again.

"I'm sorry to be here under these circumstances." Best friends are slightly easier than families. But not by much.

"Her mom said Micah is dead." Tears flowed freely and her shoulders slouched.

"Yes, that's right."

"I can't believe it." She crossed her arms over her chest, and both hands rubbed upper arms.

Madeline's body language was 100 percent sadness. Dom nodded.

"He's such a good guy."

"Was he?"

"Oh yeah. A lovely, lovely guy. Smart, funny. And boy, did he treat her well."

"How's that?"

"I dunno, just reliable, caring, called her, checked in with her. They laughed all the time. Really well suited. They both have the same energy: optimistic, upbeat. They see the good things in life." Her eyes widened as tears rolled. "Oh, God. They both *saw* the good things in life."

"What kind of stuff do they do?"

"Uh, dinners. Walking around town. Movies. Drinks with friends."

Madeline showed no signs of anxiety on this subject. Madeline believed Micah and Hettie were an authentic loving couple. "Anything special? Unique?"

"Uh, they like comedy clubs."

"Okay."

"They find newcomers, comics on the rise. They go to the small clubs down in the East Village, over on Bleecker. I've been with them. It's fun."

"Big drinkers?"

"No, not really. Normal."

"Drugs."

"No. Hettie's pretty straightlaced."

"Sports?"

"Hettie used to play tennis and ride horses. She doesn't do either anymore. Her mom made her take lessons. It became slightly too demanding. She skis. She used to go with her family out to Tahoe, but she hasn't done that in a long time." Madeline frowned.

"Why not?

Madeline touched her neck. "You know, family stuff."

Was the family a sore subject? "Like what?"

"Who do you think did it?"

Madeline avoided the topic of the family. Perhaps the family *was* a sensitive subject. "We're looking into a number of leads. Tell me more about Hettie."

"Oh, my God. She's my best friend. We've been like sisters since college." She wiped her nose, then decided to blow it. "She's funny, she's happy, she's loyal, she's honest. She loves nature, and the planet, and birds. I mean, she's my best friend. She and I go shopping. We watch movies. We cook. We laugh. She's not uppity or shallow. She thinks about the world and its problems. She's using her standing in society to do something for the planet. Gosh, she's just the greatest." Madeline grinned through the tears. "She's obsessed with this whitefish salad from Russ & Daughters—"

"Over on Houston?"

"Yeah. She'll go buy like two pounds of it. She'll buy bagels and carrots and whatever, but I've seen her eat it with a spoon right out of the container."

"Is she an extrovert or an introvert?"

"Oh, she's really quiet."

"Can you explain her personality?"

"I'd say shy. She doesn't dominate conversations. Very thoughtful. Deliberate. She will go to parties with me even though she's not really in her element. She stands in the corner, will find someone to chat with one-on-one. Not into crowds."

"Boys?"

"You mean before Micah?"

Dom nodded.

"I mean, nothing to speak of. Before Micah." One side of Madeline's lips pulled down and she glanced at Dom with a small shrug.

It was enough of a signal. Hettie didn't get a lot of male attention. Dom nodded understandingly. "Was she fearful?"

"Uh. She doesn't stick up for herself. But I wouldn't say afraid of things. No."

"Any sadness?"

"Uh, you know. Maybe." Madeline touched her neck again.

Was this a cluster of tells around the topic of the family? "Madeline, is there sadness around the family? Maybe some unpleasant dynamics?"

Madeline closed her eyes.

Yes, it was a clear eye block.

She opened them and nodded.

"Like what?"

"I knew you were gonna ask about this. Uh, Hettie and her parents ... are uh ... not on the greatest of terms." She glanced out the window. "Her parents ... are not great parents, in the kinda normal sense of the word."

Families were always complicated. "How so?"

"They all don't get along."

"Can you explain that?"

"Her dad...I feel bad saying—" she squeezed her face.

"It may help me find Hettie."

Her eyes widened. "If I talk about her parents?"

"Not necessarily about her parents, but it helps me understand how Hettie works."

"Uh, her dad is this rich banker. My brother is a stockbroker. I know their kind. They're not always nice people."

It was an interesting choice of words. "How do you mean, not nice?"

"I mean they can be abrupt, tough, tell-it-like-it-is kind of people. Really into winning and making money."

Dom asked softly, "As in a bully?"

"Yeah. A bully. My brother is like that. And I am pretty sure Mr. Van Buren is like that. I mean, I don't want to say it, but he's kinda an asshole."

This confirmed Dom's suspicions. "Any physical bullying?"

Madeline quickly shook her head. "No, nothing like that. Nothing I've ever seen. Nothing Hettie ever told me. And to be honest, she would have told me. It's just, she's not a huge fan of them. They think they own the world. They don't care about anything of any depth. Just super entitled, I guess."

During the visits to the Central Park apartment, the father was definitely bullish and domineering, and Yvette was subdued. *Was there discord with the mother too?* "And Hettie's mom?"

"She's okay, I guess. They aren't super close."

Interesting. That's not what Yvette told her. "As in they don't spend a lot of time together?"

"As in, they don't talk about stuff. It's a pretty ... distant relationship."

"Got it." Dom sipped the coffee. "Anything else about the family?"

"I mean, they do love her, just in their own way, I'm sure. I mean, it's just that they had fights about stuff, and then Hettie would take a break from them."

"Was Hettie taking a break from them currently?"

"Yes." Madeline nodded.

Funny that neither Claude nor Yvette ever mentioned this break, a serious omission when your daughter had been kidnapped. "How long was this recent break?"

"A few months?"

"More like two, or more like six?"

"More like three?" She nodded. "Yeah, it was around July fourth."

Under the surface of the frozen lake, the water turned a whole lot murkier. What happened three months ago? Was there some kind of provocation for the fight between them? Was the Sunday shopping date with Yvette an olive branch between the mother and daughter? "Do you know if Hettie saw her mother recently?"

"I don't know."

"Did Hettie tell you about any trips she had taken recently?"

Madeline glanced away. "What do you mean?"

Was that avoidance? "Did she travel anywhere recently?"

"Do you think that's important?" Madeline picked at her cuticles.

"Yes," Dom said curtly.

Madeline glanced up, eyes wide and lips quivering. "Oh."

"What do you know, Madeline?"

Madeline swallowed. "She and Micah went to Honduras."

"It was a secret?"

"Yes. She told me that I was the only one who knew, and nobody else could know."

"Why was it a secret?"

"She didn't tell me."

"Tell me what you know about the trip."

"Not much. I assumed it was research on some rare birds that she didn't want anyone else to know about. Like maybe she had a scoop or something—for an ornithologist—you know, like a work scoop. She and Micah went for a week or something."

The trip was work-related? "What else did she tell you about this trip?"

"Uh, I didn't see her right away. When I did, she said they had a good time."

"That's it?"

Madeline's face froze, and her eyes glanced left as she remembered the conversation. "Yeah, you know ... she did act a bit different after they got back."

"How different?

"Maybe quieter?"

Had something happened on the trip? "But she didn't tell you anything that stood out?"

"No. Oh, God, do you think something happened while they were in Honduras? Something that has to do with all this now?"

"It's a possibility." Dom watched her closely.

"Micah and his family are from Honduras. Micah told me about his brother. That the brother is in gangs and drugs and whatever. That he's been to jail. For drugs."

Dom nodded.

"Oh, God. Do you think Hettie has gotten wrapped up in that? In Honduras?"

"We have no proof of that. But is there anything else you can tell me about their trip?"

"Oh, God. No. I don't know anything." Madeline sat up. "Wait! When she got back she sent me pictures from the trip. Will that help?"

"Absolutely."

Madeline picked up a cell phone off the coffee table, tapped the screen, and flipped through messages. With a sad smile she paused to read one before her face broke and she sobbed. "Oh, God. Hettie."

These were the worst moments. Dom waited, head bowed.

Madeline recovered and handed the phone to Dom. "Scroll down. There are five photos."

Dom set her coffee mug on the bean. The first photo was a selfie of Hettie and Micah laughing outside in the sun with a huge sign above their heads that read *Toncontín International Airport.* The second was of Micah in a jeep, the windows down, the cityscape out the window, his dark hair blowing in the wind and his smile wide and white. In the third, the two stood before a stark white modern building set against a green jungle. The photographer was standing at a distance. The fourth photo was a landscape, a lake with mountains in the distance. The final fifth photo was of a dry, dusty, and empty field with a similar mountain range in the background.

Dom looked up, "Can I send these to myself, to make a copy?"

"Of course!"

As Dom forwarded the photos to herself, a ray of morning sunlight shifted across the room. It was officially the third day Hettie was missing.

Dom rose. "I'll find her, Madeline. I'll bring her home."

Madeline's lips trembled as she nodded.

"Stay strong. Hettie's going to need you when she gets back."

24

MILA'S favorite place in the museum was the Milstein Hall of Ocean Life where overhead a 94-foot-long, 21,000-pound fiberglass model of a female blue whale rode a downward deep ocean current. During a recent gala, spotlights had saturated the room in magical shimmering azure, transporting the guests thousands of feet below the ocean's surface. Today Mila sat on a bench under the whale's tail fin and waited out the break forced upon her by the 100-year-old librarian. She tested her memory of various plaques. Life had first emerged over 3.5 billion years ago, oceans held 96 percent of all water, less than 5 percent of the deep ocean had been explored, killer whales were actually dolphins. After thirty minutes, she made her way back to the library, passed the visitors researching in the main room, moved quietly down an aisle between stuffed shelves, and unlocked a slatted wood door. Inside, a tiny room—really, more like a large closet—was jammed with two rolling book carts and a large battered desk with a pale green rotary phone and a Dell computer. A slim window overlooked the museum grounds along Columbus Avenue. The room had been the interns' *office* for over fifty years.

Mila slid herself to the desk and pulled up Miss Timid Hettie's Facebook account. Last night she spent two hours on the page. It was a time-consuming process, and she hadn't learned much. Hettie had 102 friends, which was average for a socially normal girl. But, to be fair, Mila didn't have a Facebook account or any kind of reference point. She was not a very social girl. Instead, she kept her head down, focused on studying, and spent hours in the NYU libraries. While other kids were in the bars, she and her friend Roz made pizzas and watched old movies. Sometimes at night they walked the city talking about the universe.

Hettie's newsfeed was littered with environmental posts from Greenpeace and World Wildlife Fund and political messages from liberal news sites like MotherJones. There were photos of her with Handsome Boyfriend including a selfie in a candlelit restaurant, the couple smiling in Central Park, and the boyfriend outside a comedy club. An article from Cornell Lab noted a new breeding ground for the long-billed curlew. Rolling Stone wrote a long article on beauty pageants. An ad for Writers World scrolled past. A friend named Madeline posted a funny cartoon about the difference between men and women.

On the mouse, Mila's finger paused. Why did Facebook show Hettie an ad for writers?

Hovering over the top right corner of the ad, Mila noticed a message. *"Why are you getting this?"* She clicked on the question and the answer was supplied by Facebook in a very reasonable, concise manner. *"The reason you're seeing this ad is that Writers World wants to reach people who are part of an audience called "writers." This is based on your activity on Facebook and other apps and websites, as well as where you connect to the internet."* Did Hettie consider herself a writer? That didn't make sense for a bird scientist. What would she write about?

Mila searched the internet for *Hettie Van Buren* and *writer*. There were no relevant results.

What does a bird scientist write about? Clearly, Hettie was into curlews. In a new search, Mila typed in *curlew* and *Van Buren*. One result read *Hettie Van Buren, Nest Survival of Eskimo Curlews in the 1900s, in the Journal of Avian Ecology*, September 2012. Mila clicked to the article and skimmed it. Hettie did write. Scientific stuff. Is that why Facebook was feeding her that ad?

Mila pulled up a new search and typed in *curlew* and *writer*. One result popped up. It was a post on Wattpad.com by someone using the pen name @LastCurlew.

Clicking over, Wattpad appeared to be a site where amateur writers posted their work and connected with readers. The profile for @LastCurlew had begun posting five years ago, had built up a following of over 200, and had last posted most recently a month ago. Was this Hettie Van Buren?

The postings were not in any order. Nor were they dated. Mila skimmed the first few. The fourth had the tone of a young girl living in a marbled penthouse with rich parents. It could have been written by Hettie. Mila reread it slowly.

Caged
@LastCurlew

1.
Silence of tombs
crushes. In penthouses also.
An ear glued to a door,
veins pumping wildly
as voices explode from a distance.
Stop this, you shiver.
Tonight, please be the last.

2.

Certain you are the subject
of the skirmish. A mistake.
His octave jarring,
flying arrows strike warm humanity
from a cold quiver.
Her response, I never treasured
in all that time,
only lonely and forlorn.
She threatens departure.
She will never go.

3.

The faces of envy,
eyes of green. Across marble floors.
Parties of opulent silk and pearls
where she faded to beige.
Nowhere to disappear,
bruised by a smile
stiff with counterfeit.

4.

Ahead is only lament.
Neither door opens to release.
Clotted veins. Stagnant.
Break out!
Daybreak delivers more misery.

Mila sat back. The poem was heavy on emotion and awkwardly personal. Had Mila stumbled onto the privately published poems of Hettie Van Buren? How uncomfortable.

Her finger scrolled further into the Wattpad posts.

Love and Strength
@LastCurlew

Together, silence is loud
with meaning.

A hand, soft
and assuring, pulls

strength from the fear of the night.
The world is lighter.

The sun rises
a golden mist

with hope and
and expectation. Her song

is fanciful, fresh
after years of injustice,

transformed into protest
weighted with sincerity.

The moment has become
one of many,

no longer an endurance
but a path of joy

stretching.

Had Hettie been writing about her handsome boyfriend?

Mila's fingers tingled. The odds felt decidedly in favor that Miss Timid Hettie was using a pen name to write deeply passionate poems about her family, her loneliness, and her new boyfriend. But did the odds warrant a tip to the FBI? When she got home tonight, Mila would do a bit more snooping around on the Wattpad account to determine if she should call Agent Cool Cucumber.

25

THE JIFFY LUBE looked more decrepit. During the night, wind had tossed litter into the air and it now hung limply on the perimeter fence like white flags of surrender. Dust speckled the dirty broken glass of the office window. Her toes throbbed as she crossed the lot.

Roberto met her at the door in dirty coveralls and an angry face. "Yo, you went after Toro. I told you that guy was a punk."

She stood outside the door and angled herself at the street with one eye on the foot traffic. "It was a lead I had to explore." She wasn't in the mood for a verbal duel with a gangbanger.

"I told you, I got ears in Micah's neighborhood."

"And?"

"It wasn't local."

"Meaning what?"

"Micah was clean. He ain't working with any gangs. No local crews. Nothing"

"Your contacts would know if your brother was wrapped up with local drugs or gangs?"

"That's what I'm sayin'. He wasn't doing nothin' in New York."

"Okay, what else?"

"It's weird. But this is what I got: there was a dude in his apartment late Sunday night."

The time frame worked. Micah was shot early in the morning on Monday. "Someone saw this guy?"

"Yeah. A neighbor."

"And the neighbor said it was only one guy?"

He nodded.

"A neighbor told your contacts this? Was the neighbor under duress?"

He glared at her. "Yo, we're talkin' my brother. You want the info or not?"

She held up her hands. "You're right. What did they say about this man?"

"He wore cowboy boots."

Dom's mind stumbled. "What do you mean?"

"Jesus." He clicked the inside of his cheek. "If you see hombres wearing cowboy boots in New York City, they from somewhere else."

"As in not from New York?"

"As in not from America. I'm saying he's not from America. I'm saying the killer is from Central America. Them hombres wear cowboy boots."

She took a tiny step ahead, inching into his personal space. "Funny you should say that, Roberto. What were Micah and Hettie doing in Honduras three weeks ago?"

He squinted and his lips pursed, but he held his ground. Tough guys were not easily surprised.

"You knew they went, right? This is the project you mentioned to me yesterday, right?"

He glared at her.

"Roberto, you knew they went to Honduras. Now you're telling me an hombre—potentially from Central America—

broke into Micah's apartment and shot him. I think it's time you tell me what you know about the Honduras trip."

He took a step back.

She cocked her head and raised her eyebrows

He straightened. "Micah asked for help. I told him no. He wanted to take Hettie to Honduras. They wanted to go hiking in the boonies. I told him he was loco. We got out of that shithole, no need to ever go back. He pushed me, asked if I knew people. I told him he was crazy and I wasn't helping him."

"Why didn't you tell me this yesterday?"

"I didn't think it mattered. I wasn't sure." He shrugged.

"Okay. Tell me what you know about this trip."

"Like I said, when I saw him last at my parents, he said he and Hettie were going. He said Hettie wanted to do some research or some shit. Then he asked me to connect him to someone. Some kind of guide that could show them around."

"He wanted you to connect him to someone in Honduras to be a guide?"

"Yeah. That's what he asked. I said no." He shook his head. "I ain't got nothin' to do with Honduras. For people like us, that's only trouble."

Dom pulled up the photos from Madeline and stepped closer to him. The coveralls smelled of mildew and the neckline released the sour stench of greasy skin. "Do you know where this is?"

He watched the screen as she scrolled the photos. "No. Some dirt town like everywhere else. Lots'a land. No roads. Just dirt. And poor people."

"Are there drugs in the country?"

"Sure. Same as everywhere. But Micah ain't into drugs. I told you, he said something about research."

"Did Micah find a guide?"

Roberto looked away.

"Did Micah find a guide?"

His jaw stiffened. "I dunno."

"But you could find out?"

"This got nothing to do with me. I ain't into shit outta Honduras."

"Roberto, your brother is dead, and his girlfriend is missing. Believe me when I say I am not looking into your drug or gang affiliations. I don't care who you know in Honduras. I just want to find Hettie. Now call whomever you need to call to find out if Micah found a guide."

Roberto sucked his teeth before pulling out his phone, calling someone, and dropping into rapid-fire Spanish. He hung up and called a second person. On the third call, he listened intently before putting his hand over the phone. "Micah found someone. They put him in touch with a guy named Darcel."

"Is that Darcel on the phone?"

"Nah, it's Darcel's cousin. Darcel is in Honduras."

"This Darcel into drugs?"

"Everybody I know is into drugs. But I'm telling you, Micah's trip wasn't about drugs."

"What did Darcel say about where they went?"

Roberto spoke Spanish into the phone then translated the response. "They went up to the northwest. Hiking. Hettie had binoculars and maps. Books with notes. Like I said, sounds like some kind of research."

"Tell me where." She pulled up a map of Honduras on her phone.

Using a pinching motion, he expanded the map, his finger circling an area in the northwest. "They went hiking for three days in this area, north of San Jerónimo, out into the village. It's part of the departmento called Copán. Darcel took them there, took them back to the capital. That's it. That's all the cousin knew."

A secret research trip. San Jerónimo. Honduras. Investigatory leads were lighting up like coordinates on a GPS map.

26

THE ORNITHOLOGY DEPARTMENT, bright in the after-noon sun, smelled thickly of formaldehyde. Hands stilled with curiosity and the eyes of a dozen researchers watched as Dom passed lab tables, bookshelves, and purring machines.

Jonathan's shoulders sagged as she approached his desk. "I heard about Micah. I mean, he's dead. I just don't ... I can't even ... and Hettie?"

"Hi, Jonathan."

His lips quivered. "You're gonna find her, right? She's gonna be okay, right?"

Monsters do exist. An image of red thumbtacks caused her chest to tighten. "Don't worry. I'm going to find Hettie and I'm going to bring her home."

"You promise?"

But you can defeat monsters. Fidelity, bravery, and integrity. "Yes. I'm going to bring her home."

"Okay." Jonathan wiped his face with open hands.

Settling into a nearby chair, the pressure on her toes eased. "We've gotten into Hettie's desktop. On it we found a research proposal. It looks like a proposal for funding for a trip to Honduras. I need your help understanding it."

He nodded.

"First, can you explain to me what Hettie does?"

"She studies North American migratory birds. Mostly the Eskimo curlew." He looked up at the wall and pointed to a brown seagull with a long, curved beak. "It looks a lot like that bird. The Eskimo curlew is the smallest of all the curlews in the Western Hemisphere. The original population was in the hundreds of thousands. In the winter, they flew from Alaska to South America—Southern Brazil, Uruguay and Chile, and maybe even to Patagonia. In the spring, they returned through Central America to Alaska to breed." He frowned. "The Eskimo curlews' story is sad. They were wiped out around the turn of the century. Man destroyed their natural habitats with fire and land conversion. Then the hunters ... shot them all down ... for the meat markets in the city. The Eskimo curlew had a very tragic species-typical behavior. When one of the flock was shot down, the Eskimo curlew circled overhead, keeping an eye on the fallen bird. The hunters would just pick them off." He shook his head.

"This Eskimo curlew is Hettie's primary subject of research?"

"Yes. It's her obsession."

"They're extinct?"

"Assumed extinct. She's been tracing their former paths."

"So. Let me get this straight. Hettie is chasing an extinct bird along its migratory path?"

Jonathan held up a finger. "Assumed extinct."

"As in, there may be some out there?"

He sat back. "If Hettie finds an Eskimo curlew there are a ton of implications. The Migratory Bird Treaty Act and the Endangered Species Act both protect the actual bird, so the

Eskimo curlew would be protected. But more importantly—if she finds one—their grounds would also be protected under the 1940 Convention on Nature Protection and Wildlife Preservation in the Western Hemisphere. It would protect the actual land they use. It would be an amazing coup for conservation."

Dom raised her eyebrows.

"Human encroachment on protected lands is a global issue. Being able to declare some land protected, that would be a coup."

"Do you know anything about a trip Hettie took recently?"

He rubbed his face. "I mean, not really. Four years ago she went to Patagonia, then three years ago she studied in Costa Rica. Then Nicaragua." He shrugged. "I thought she was planning on Panama this year, but she decided against it. I don't know why."

In Dom's ear, the soft ping of an elevator sounded. This year, Hettie originally planned to go to Panama, but changed the destination to Honduras? *Why the switch?* She handed Jonathan the research proposal Lea had printed. "What can you tell me about this?"

He scanned the pages. "It's a research prospectus outlining her research." He returned back to the first page. "Let's see, background on the Eskimo curlew ... by 1900 there were very few sightings ... last photo was in Texas in 1962 ... history of ornithology in Honduras ... Mayans had sacred birds like the scarlet macaw." He pointed to a hand drawn image of a colorful bird. "Osbert Salvin was the first naturalist in Honduras. Hettie is carrying on in his honor." He flipped more pages and pointed at a map. It was the same area Roberto identified. "The best odds are up here, in this area, she thinks." He looked up. "This is a standard proposal for funding for the trip."

On the wall, stuffed birds stared into space, trapped in time.

"Okay. Let me get this straight. Hettie's passionate about

this bird. Every year, she is doing research along its migratory path and looking for one remaining bird?"

"Yes, that's Hettie."

"As far as you knew, she was planning on going to Panama this year, but changed her mind."

He frowned. "Yup."

In an investigation, dates often proved important—a pivotal moment a motive was hatched. "Do you remember when she changed her mind?"

"No, but—" He flipped to the front page of the proposal. "Looks like she wrote this in three months ago."

"Do you know of anything of significance that happened three, or maybe even four, months ago?"

He shook his head.

"You sure?"

"Sure."

Jonathan may not know of any significant event, but Dom was sure something—some sort of provocation event—had happened three months ago or earlier that set into motion the ill-fated Honduras trip.

27

AT SUNSET, Mila coasted through Nolita on Mott Street, braked in front of a four-floor mid-century walk-up, and carried her bike up the front steps. The foyer smelled of garlic. Ignoring the scruffy mailboxes—she rarely got mail—she headed to the shared back closet and arranged the Kryptonite lock on the bike's back wheel. She trailed her fingers on the thick ancient banister as she trudged up four floors and let herself into the back unit.

She clicked on the dimmed overhead light, dropped keys on a small bookshelf while the other hand rummaged through a pocket, pulled out a shiny penny and dropped it in a mason jar full of pennies. This was her sanctuary, quiet and uncluttered. She moved along a stained laminate kitchen counter, pulled an apple from an ancient refrigerator, and settled into a weathered leather armchair by four tall, slender windows.

Outside, Elizabeth Street Park was shadowed in the setting sun. The size of a basketball court sandwiched between buildings, the park was a disheveled conglomeration of bushes, overgrown flower beds, patches of green lawn, and haphazard statues. Mila loved the park. It was one of the few unruly things she savored.

Crunching into the cold green apple with the perfectly crisp skin, she slid her laptop from her bag, rested her feet on the windowsill, settled the laptop on her lap and lifted the lid. She logged into Wattpad, found @LastCurlew, and began slowly reading.

Rapoosa
@LastCurlew

The fight in the distance
is not to be won,
images pulse,
then everything's gone.

The generals from afar,
safe in a glass tower,
watch with dispassion
as the pawns cower.

The blood and the earth,
have nothing but time,
the body decays,
it will never be fine.

Silence is illicit,
the voice of complicit.

A door to release
a peal of a mind's bleat,
set me free once more,
when this war is complete.

Wow, this poem sounded sinister. Mila crunched thought-fully. If these poems were written by Hettie, maybe now was a good time to get in touch with that FBI agent.

Mila set the apple core on the floor and opened a new search. *Domini Walker*. She clicked through on an image of a young teenage girl holding the hand of a younger blond-haired brother. Both heads were turned down against a crowd of paparazzi as they descended wide courthouse steps. Trailing behind, a frail blonde woman stared over the crowd with a dazed look. The caption read, *"Domini Walker, Beecher Walker, and Esther Walker leaving the court house the day Stewart Walker, NYPD, is sentenced to ten years for police corruption in the Filthy Five case."*

Oh, my. Agent Cool Cucumber had a personal history. Mila magnified the photo. The girl had a resemblance to the FBI agent from the museum lobby.

Next, Mila typed in a search for *Filthy Five.* She clicked over to the Wikipedia page and skimmed the contents. In 1999, five NYPD officers from Precinct 9 were arrested on charges of corruption and illegal conduct. Based on a year of NYPD Internal Affairs surveillance, the five were arrested through a sting operation involving a fake crime scene and planted evidence—$2M in drugs and a duffel bag of $250,000 in rolled cash. The trial took place six months later. Three officers were exonerated—Robert Gessen, Art Dyson, and Mike Turner. Two officers, Stewart R. Walker and John Belafonte, were indicted on civil rights conspiracy, perjury, extortion, grand larceny, and the possession and distribution of narcotics. Stewart Walker was identified as the ring leader and was sentenced to ten years. A month into his sentence, Stewart Walker hung himself in his cell. In a newspaper photo taken the previous year, Stewart Walker was wearing a dark blue dress uniform with shiny brass buttons. His smile was broad under gentle hazel eyes that winked at the camera. *He didn't look crooked.*

This was a really poignant history. What happened to the three remaining Walker family members? Did they recover from the stigma of a corrupt father who committed suicide? Did the mom remarry? Did the son enter law enforcement like his older sister?

Mila wondered about the three exonerated officers. She searched *Robert Gessen.* He continued at the NYPD, serving out of Precinct 59 in the Bronx. Interestingly, two years ago he was transferred back to the 9th Precinct. They brought him back to the scene of the original sin? She typed in *Art Dyson.* He too was transferred back to the 9th Precinct two years ago. Quickly, her fingers tapped, *Mike Turner.* He too was transferred back to the original precinct. Why was the gang getting back together?

Outside in the park, a cricket struck up a melancholy song. Mila's mind spun rapidly.

She next searched *corrupt police NYPD.* Hidden among the many search results was a link to the Center for Research in Crime and Justice of the New York University Law School's Police Records Project. The project had recently won a Freedom of Information Act request and were the proud new owners of a database of all complaints filed against the NYPD since 2006. The project had its own website with login and access for NYU students. Bingo. She logged in.

The project's data was overwhelming and apparently not in any kind of order. Over 30,000 records listed incidents of NYPD misconduct: the officer's name, the complainant's name, the alleged misconduct—coerced false confession, false arrest, police perjury, witness tampering, police brutality—and the resulting internal investigation. She quickly sorted the data into neat categories and scanned the results. Of the roughly 34,000

NYPD police officers, only a small fraction—less than 10 percent—were repeat offenders. These 10 percent had received 34 percent of the complaints in the last five years. A few bad apples were responsible for a significant number of complaints. A few bad ones in a whole truck load of apples.

She searched for *Robert Gessen*. Fifteen complaints returned. They all occurred since Gessen returned to Precinct 9 two years ago. Fifteen in just two years. Mila's fingers flew on the keyboard. Art Dyson had a similar profile. Upon his return to Precinct 9, six complaints had been logged. Mike Turner's record was similar. In fact, of the NYPD officers with the most complaints, Robert Gessen, Art Dyson, and Mike Turner were among the top ten.

Outside the park was dark, and a dog barked in the distance.

Did Special Agent Domini Walker know that her father's co-conspirators were returning to Precinct 9? Would she even care? Mila stared at her screen. Come to think of it, who *should* care that the few bad apples had all gotten back in the same basket?

She googled Precinct 9, tracked down the name of the Chief and surmised his email. Surely this guy deserved to know. The Hotmail account she opened five years ago used an anonymous name, anon204948@hotmail.com. She hit compose, entered the Chief's email, and typed a brief message. *Was researching in the Police Records Project at NYU Law School. Noticed three of the ten officers with the most complaints are back in your precinct and were part of the Filthy Five.* She hit send.

She smiled at herself with a smug nod. Mila Pascale was nothing if not civic-minded. Speaking of, tomorrow she would call the Agent Cool Cucumber and tell her about @LastCurlew.

28

A BREEZE off Central Park kissed Dom's face as she stared up at the Van Burens' building, one of the most exclusive addresses in the city. When it opened in 2007, it reportedly cost $950 billion dollars to build. Celebrities and banking *masters of the universe* resided here. The tower loomed in front of colossal puffed clouds backlit by bright moonlight. A question tickled her consciousness. Could this case be about money?

Dom pulled her phone and dialed a familiar number. The building's polished limestone appeared elegant and impenetrable.

Beecher answered on the second ring. "Hey. What's up?"

"I've got a question for an economist that used to work at a bank." A sleek gray awning extended from the lobby door to protect residents from bad weather as they caught curbside taxis.

"Shoot."

"People who run private equity firms can be really rich, right?"

"Oh yeah. Top of their game."

She raised her foot to ease the pain. "How does a private equity fund actually work?"

"Right. Well, first off, there are a lot of regulations that govern traditional banks—the Goldmans and JPMorgans of the world. These regulations restrict the where they can invest. But there are investors—the wealthier individuals who are savvier—that want more flexibility with their investments. Into this gap stepped private equity firms. They are less regulated so can invest in stuff the big banks can't."

"Why aren't private equity firms more regulated?"

"Only the rich, the savvier, can get in."

She scratched her scalp. "So the government doesn't care, since rich people are the ones losing money?"

"Exactly." He laughed. "In my opinion, the government looks out for fraud against the larger population—your average Joes. If the wealthy want to risk their money, the government lets them. Each private equity firm has its own investment strategy. Some invest in venture capital. Others only in growth capital, mezzanine financing, or leveraged or distressed buyouts. The KKRs, Blackrocks, Carlyle Group, they all have their own strategies."

"I did not follow all of that, but keep going."

"The partners in the firm will raise funds. With this they will buy equity in companies. They often hold the ownership in a company for four to seven years, at which point they sell, hopefully for a profit. That's why they're called private equity firms."

A doorman held the door for an exiting nanny pushing a stroller. "How do they find companies to invest in?"

"Their investment team will go looking. A lot of private equity firms try to get in early on deals. They like to find their own companies. Then, the management team will keep an eye on the overall portfolio of investments. Some like to get really involved in the companies they buy. Others are more passive." He paused. "Most firms make a 2 percent annual fee plus 20 percent on gross profits when they sell the equity. The partners split the profit. For example, Blackrock's annual revenue is in the billions. And profits are split among their management team—"

Her mouth dropped open. "Billions a year?" It was a staggering, almost unimaginable number.

"Yeah, I think Blackrock is like $300 billion assets under management now."

"Holy crapsicle."

"Yup. If you give me the name of the private equity firm, I may be able to help you."

She couldn't think of any harm in Beecher doing a search on Claude Van Buren's firm. He knew nothing about the case. "Rittenhouse Equity."

The tapping of Beecher's fingers on a keyboard resonated through the phone. "There's one in New York, over on Park Avenue above Grand Central Station."

"Yes. That's it."

"Okay. Let's see. According to some coverage in the financial news, looks like Rittenhouse requires a minimum of $500,000 from their investors. Their current assets under management—the pot of money they use to invest—is at $2 billion."

"With a B?" She whistled. Greed was the basest of human interests. Was it possible this case was about money?

"Yup. Let me see here, I'm clicking over to their website. It's private. They don't list of what they invest in. That's not unusual."

"So at a 2 percent straight management fee, the firm's partners make money even if their investments lose for the client?"

"Yup. 2 percent on 2 billion is $40 million. A year."

"How many ultra-high net worth individuals in the world?"

"I think less than one percent."

Fontaine had used the 1 percent reference. Not only was Claude legitimately rich, he was the 1 percent rich. Was this case about money? It was a long shot, but a good investigator considered all possibilities. In fact, a good investigator would have thought of this before. She should have thought of this before. Damn it, why hadn't she explored this angle before now? Her father whispered, *Don't do that, my Dom. Don't beat yourself up.*

Beecher's sniff broke her train of thought.

She pushed the phone tighter against her ear. "Sorry, how are you?"

He cleared his throat.

The familiar noise grabbed her attention. "What?"

He hesitated. "Nothing."

"What?"

"Nothing, you're in the middle of a case. It can wait."

"Don't do that. What is it?"

"Dom, it's nothing."

"Do. Not. Do. That."

"We got a letter. From Florida."

Their mother. Dom's jaw locked, as if ice had grazed an exposed nerve.

"I haven't opened it," he said.

Esther. A chill slithered into Dom's chest and frost crept into her lungs.

"I haven't opened it."

Their disappearing mother. A cold snaked through Dom's hairline. "Don't open it."

"Okay."

"She's not allowed to just come back. All these years later."

"Dom, I agree. You know we're in this together."

"She's not allowed. Not now. Not ever."

"I heard you."

She snapped, "Throw it out."

"Are you sure?"

"Yes. Throw it out."

29

YVETTE WAITED for Dom on the couch, luminous pools of gold cast by table lamps gleamed on the wood at her feet. Reading glasses were pushed into sleek hair, and her eyes were worried as she held out her hand. "Special Agent Walker. We've heard nothing. There has been no phone call. Nothing." Her clutch was desperately strong.

"Yes, I understand that." From the eleventh floor perspective, Central Park had been transformed into a grim fairy-tale forest complete with lighted pathways twisting through shadows.

Yvette did not release Dom's hand. "There has been no request for payment."

Claude stormed in. "Agent Walker, what have you found?"

Breaking loose from Yvette, Dom turned. "Mr. Van Buren, how are you holding up?"

"I'd be a lot fucking better if I had my daughter."

"Yes, sir. I understand how you feel."

"Do you?" His face twisted in anger. "Do you know what it's like to be in this situation?"

"Please, Mr. Van Buren, Mrs. Van Buren, let's sit and I'll give you the latest."

He bellowed, "I'm not happy about the progress of this investigation. Apparently you have very few leads. Have we been assigned FBI bush league here or what? I've complained loudly to your Director Fontaine."

In her ear, Stewart Walker whispered, *To be successful, you don't always have to know the answers, my Dom. Believe in yourself.* "Yes, Mr. Van Buren, I understand your anger. This is a terrible situation. Why don't we sit, and I'll bring you up to speed?"

Claude grunted and stomped to the couch. Yvette moved to a position a few feet from her husband, her back stiff against the cushions.

Dom sat across from them. "This is what we know. It appears the assailant entered Micah's apartment sometime around midnight on Sunday, and Micah died shortly thereafter. We believe the assailant proceeded to Hettie's. At Hettie's apartment there was no forced entry, so it appears Hettie opened the door—"

"Goddamn it!" Claude growled. "They have doormen at her building. What the hell was she doing opening up the door in the middle of the night?"

Yvette's hands clasped tightly on her lap.

Dom remained calm. "I believe there was a struggle in Hettie's bedroom. I believe the assailant forced her down the back stairwell and into a getaway car."

Yvette stifled a gasp.

Claude glared.

"I think in both locations the strikes were premeditated. The assailant moved quickly, there are few witnesses, and nothing was stolen. He had clear intent, murder and kidnapping."

Both sets of eyes were glued to Dom.

"There is nothing to indicate that either Micah or your daughter were fearful leading up to the assaults, so I do not think either of them saw this coming. Your daughter had meetings and dinner dates planned." She pressed her lips together. "We have a possible sighting of a foreign suspect entering Micah's house.

"Goddamn it!" he exploded. "I knew it was those goddamned Spics from that god-damned third world fucking country."

"We are now digging into motive." She let the idea hang in the air.

Claude clamped his mouth shut.

Yvette clasped hands tighter in her lap as she blinked rapidly.

"I've come across some new information." Dom took a deep breath and focused on their body and facial movements. "Are either of you aware that Micah and Hettie traveled to Honduras three weeks ago?"

Claude's face froze. Yvette Van stared directly at Dom. Claude stood and marched from the room.

It was a shocking action, and Dom eyed Yvette curiously.

Yvette sat like a statue.

"Mrs. Van Buren, I take it you and your husband didn't approve of the Honduras trip?"

Yvette stared at her mutely.

"Did you know about the trip?"

Yvette shook her head slowly.

"Did your husband know about the trip?"

Yvette whispered, "I don't know."

Dom raised one eyebrow at her.

"We have not been on good terms with Hettie the last few

months. I'm sure there are things that our daughter did not tell either of us. Perhaps important things."

"Can you explain that for me, the not-good terms?"

Yvette's knuckles turned white. "We do not always see eye to eye. As a family, we do not always communicate frequently."

"Mrs. Van Buren, when you and I first spoke, you mentioned that you had not spoken to Hettie on Monday as you had expected. Can you explain that to me?"

Yvette's eyes narrowed. She never anticipated that Dom would remember exact words. "I had seen her Sunday. We agreed to speak the next day. We agreed to speak on Monday."

"Before Sunday, when was the last time you saw her?"

Yvette touched her neck. "Four months before that."

A distant ping chimed in Dom's ear. Three months ago, Hettie had changed her research destination from Panama to Honduras. "What happened four months ago?"

"We had a fight."

"About what?"

"Her research."

Here it comes. "What about it?"

"We did not want her going to developing countries anymore."

"And?"

"We threatened to cut her off if she continued to travel to dangerous places."

Claude returned and sat heavily on the sofa with a puffed chest.

"Mrs. Van Buren, I can imagine that threatening to cut her off didn't go over well with Hettie?"

"As you can imagine, no."

"I imagine that was an extreme threat for your daughter."

"She was endangering herself inappropriately. We decided, as her parents, we needed to step in."

The doorbell rang. *Who the crap was this?* Dom turned to the entrance. All eyes followed the maid scurrying to the front door.

The door opened to a huge bear of a man. He bounded in, hand raised in salutation, salt-and-pepper hair swept back from a jowly face and thick black-framed glasses over buggy eyes. "Yes, hi, hi. Yvette. Claude. Yes, yes," He strode across the room.

Who the crap is this?

"Well, hello, Special Agent." He approached with an outstretched enormous hand. "You are Special Agent Walker?" The blue suit looked expensive, and the perfectly worn leather shoes had been recently polished.

"I am."

"My name is Oslo Bockel," he said with a bobbing head. He flashed a big toothy smile at full wattage. "As in the city in Norway. My parents went there on honeymoon." He nodded to the Van Burens. "I represent the family."

Crap wrapped in a lawyer's envelope. The family was closing ranks. How did he get here so quickly? Ah, right. Claude's odd exit. "I was just briefing the Van Burens."

"Yes, yes, well don't let me intrude, please go ahead." He fell into a big armchair.

Dom wasn't afraid of lawyers. They worked for the paycheck too, but they had never been on a freezing overnight Quantico training course or fired a live round at monsters. Further, Claude called the lawyer for a reason. It indicated something about the investigation hit close to home. *That's right, Dom,* Stewart Walker whispered. *Lawyers are a sign you're near the mark.*

Dom sat and turned her gaze to Claude. "I was just asking Mr. Van Buren if he could give me some background on a disagreement Hettie had with her parents about four months ago. As I understand, the family has not been in much communication since that time."

Claude glowered. "We disagreed on her travel."

"Yes, what travel in particular?"

"Her fucking travel to banana republics chasing fucking birds. It was dangerous. We have had enough of the worry, the anxiety."

"You told her no more travel or you'd cut her off?"

"Yes."

"What did she say?"

"She didn't. She left."

"As in she walked out of the room?

"Yes," he said through tight lips.

"Mr. Van Buren, when we met yesterday, you said Hettie had come to your office last week."

Both Mr. and Mrs. Van Buren frowned. Dom's memory was surprising.

He nodded slowly.

"Was that the first time you had seen her in four months since the disagreement?

He nodded again.

"What did you discuss last week when she came to your office?"

"She started to tell me about some fucking bird. I told her that I didn't have time."

"You hadn't seen your daughter in four months and when she shows up at your office, you don't have time for her?"

Yvette scowled at her husband.

His chest swelled and his chin retracted. "It was a hectic day at work. I told her that I would speak with her outside the office. Hettie knew better than to come to our office in the middle of the day."

Was this case about money? Dom spoke slowly and deliberately, "Hettie came to your office, at Rittenhouse Equity?"

Claude watched her cautiously. "Yes."

"Rittenhouse Equity. Over on Park Avenue, north of Grand Central?"

"Yes."

She tilted her head. "I'm afraid I don't know much about finance. Can you explain what Rittenhouse Equity does?"

"What does this have to do with Hettie?" he asked tightly.

"Most likely nothing. Can you explain what you do?"

Oslo Bockel straightened. "I'm sure there is no relation between Hettie and Rittenhouse Equity, Special Agent Walker."

"That may be absolutely true, but it would be helpful for me to understand what Mr. Van Buren does."

Claude's voice was curt. "We invest in companies where we see potential."

It sounded like a brochure. "What kind of things do you invest in?"

"I'm afraid that information isn't publicly available."

"I'm not the public."

Yvette, still as a rock, trained her eyes on her husband.

Claude said, "Our portfolio is strictly private, Agent."

Here we go. Fontaine was going to be pissed. Like really pissed. "Any chance, Mr. Van Buren, that Rittenhouse Equity has invested in companies based in Honduras?"

All three froze.

Claude blinked first. "How dare you."

Ping.

Oslo Bockel jumped to his feet.

Claude pointed at Dom. "How dare you!"

Ping.

Oslo Bockel was standing over Dom. "Special Agent

Walker, I think it's best if we leave now. Return to it tomorrow. Let the family get some rest."

Claude rose and wagged his finger at Dom. "How dare you! How dare you imply in any way—"

Dom stood. "I am following leads to find your daughter—"

"How dare you!" He bellowed.

Yvette's eyes were wide and fearful.

Oslo Bockel cupped Dom's elbow and held up a calming hand to Claude. "Just calm down, Claude. The agent here is doing her job." Oslo Bockel turned Dom toward the elevator. "We'll give this a rest for tonight."

Claude yelled, "How dare you!"

"All horrible stuff, poor Hettie, now the FBI—" Oslo Bockel said over his shoulder to Claude as he led Dom to the elevator. "She's just doing her law enforcement job here, Claude. Truly horrible. Let's reconvene tomorrow, shall we?"

Claude roared, "That's my daughter we're talking about!"

The sinister frozen lake had gotten deeper.

As the gold elevator doors chimed shut on the eleventh floor, Oslo Bockel smiled. "My, my. Well that was something."

"Mr. Bockel," Dom asked softly. "Which part of the Van Buren family do you represent?"

He maintained the smile. "I represent the family, Special Agent."

"Yes, but which side—Mr. Van Buren or Mrs. Van Buren?"

"I'm not sure that's relevant."

"Yes, well, many things are relevant when the FBI is investigating a missing persons case."

His nodded. "Yes, I can see that. I can see that."

"So, which is it? Mr. Van Buren or Mrs. Van Buren?"

"I have been with the Lowrance family most of my career."

So Yvette paid his bills. "When push comes to shove, you represent Mrs. Van Buren?"

"Push has never come to shove, Agent."

"Any thoughts on what may have happened to Hettie?"

He faked a look of alarm. "I'm sure I have no idea."

"I'm sure you must have some thoughts, even if they are immaterial."

His body stilled, giving the appearance of calm. Good lawyers were careful with body language. Oslo Bockel struck her as a good lawyer. "Well, you're right there, Special Agent. I have thought about it."

The elevator slid smoothly down. She waited.

"As a lawyer, I often suspect the worst. I suspect she may have gotten involved with the wrong people."

"Is that right?" She cocked her head. "But it's odd timing."

"How's that?"

"The family had a disagreement four months ago, and a month later Hettie revised her research plans. Instead of going to Panama as planned, she redirected that research to Honduras."

"Is that right? Perhaps it's just a coincidence?"

"Maybe."

"Your questions upstairs implied you think this may have something to do with Rittenhouse Equity."

"Just a line of questioning. One of many."

"Well, as an FBI agent I'm sure you know what you're doing," he said soberly.

The seriousness of his tone piqued her interest. "Do you support my line of questioning into Rittenhouse's involvement, Mr. Bockel?"

His eyes widened dramatically. "I'm sure I have no opinion one way or the other."

But he did. His chin had moved toward her, and his head

had tilted. *Had the wife's lawyer just thrown the husband under the bus?*

"Do you think there is a connection with Rittenhouse Equity?"

A big paw hand covered his mouth. "I certainly did not say that."

"But you are not disavowing me of the idea that somehow Hettie could have gotten caught up in a conflict with Rittenhouse?"

"I certainly didn't want to give that impression."

But he had. Everything about his body language—his lawyerly trained, intentional body language—told Dom to pursue the connection between the Honduras trip and Rittenhouse Equity. The ping in her ear was deafening.

The elevator reached the ground floor and Oslo Bockel stepped out while handing his card to her. "Please, please, I'm here to help." He retreated across the lobby's polished marble, his shiny shoes tapping.

Conclusions scrolled through Dom's mind like film credits. First, whatever instigated the disagreement four months ago had changed the course of Hettie's research and set off the malevolent chain of events surrounding the Honduras trip. Second, Claude was extremely touchy about a connection between the Honduras trip and his firm. Third, Yvette's lawyer had just encouraged Dom to probe that connection.

The icy surface of the lake lurched beneath her feet.

THURSDAY

He knew this new curlew was smaller and slightly browner, like himself, than the others had been. But these thoughts were fleeting, barely formed. It was a combination of voice, posture, the movements of the other bird, and not her appearance, which signaled instantly that the mate had come.

—Fred Bodsworth, "Last of the Curlews"

30

TEGUCIGALPA, Honduras

Earlier in the morning, she had arrived at the office to find the disagreeable woman, pink pumps clean of the city grime, waiting for her. They traveled by taxi to the government building and followed the sweeping stone stairs into a huge hall. Down a long hallway they found the passport department and the disagreeable woman instructed Maria to sit and to wait her turn before the disagreeable woman left.

The queue was long. Maria calculated four hours before her name would be called. She gazed out the window at the bustling street below. It was the first time she had been on a second floor, but the view was less exciting than she had imagined. It was just a day in a big city. The roiling river of humanity—all colors, shapes, and sizes—was neither intimidating or exhilarating. Funny what you get used to.

Inside the thick walls of the government building no one would even hear the sound of rain. There had been a thunderstorm a month ago in the village. A dark bank of clouds had rolled in over the lake, slowly blanking out the sky and the clouds. Night had fallen as the dark clouds reached the shore. Inside the hut, Maria had counted the time between the lightning flashes and the thunder cracks. In time, thick rain pelted the tin roof. Blasts crashed and the wind wheezed through the window frames. The waves on the lake rumbled against the shore.

From her bed, Ines had whimpered, "Mama?"

Maria had soothed her with a whispered response. She did not go to comfort her daughter with a hug. She wanted Ines to be brave. There were plenty of real dangers to be afraid of.

Later, Maria and the disagreeable woman stood outside the airport. The sour woman asked, "Do you know what an airplane is?"

Maria shrugged. Of course she did. There were televisions in the village. For the previous month the villagers talked of almost nothing other than Maria's trip, scaring each other with talk of aluminum cans falling from the sky. Two days ago, they said a prayer for her.

"Just follow the crowd," said the sour woman. "Stand in line with your ticket, and then follow the crowd. Give your ticket to the ladies in uniform. They will show you to your seat. Then you sit. Then at the end, you will come out again. You will get in a line and wait, then you will hand the official your passport. Someone will be waiting for you at the other side. Don't look around, don't look scared. Just act like you know what you're doing. Understand?"

Maria nodded.

"You have the money for food?"

She nodded. Of course she had the money.

"Any questions?"

Sometimes there were too many questions. Maria shook her head no.

.   .   .

She stepped into the chilled air of the Toncontín International Airport. The entrance queue was long. Like all poor people, she waited patiently. Finally, the security officer in the blue uniform with the gun on his hip waved her to approach. She handed him her bag, and he rummaged through it. He was satisfied and pushed the bag past the beeping archway. She walked through. There were no beeps. The next security officer waved her on.

She stopped at a Kentucky Fried Chicken stand and stared at the menu. She ordered a chicken sandwich with a bottle of water, and the young man in the restaurant uniform handed her a bag. Following the gate number on her ticket, she sat by a window and watched as the lights of planes landed on the huge runways with the deep rumbling like a thunderstorm. She slowly unwrapped the sandwich. It was the first fast food she had ever eaten, and she wondered if she should find some fruit to balance her meal. She would need strength for this journey.

She had learned about balanced meals from the aid workers that had come to the village. They had shown them charts and pictures. A plate divided into four, they explained with gentle smiles. Your child must have all these groups balanced on their plate. Protein, grains, vegetables, and fruit. Do you understand, they asked with their gentle smiles while standing under the tree in their clean shoes.

Of course, the villagers said. We understand. We are not dumb, we are just poor. We understand that our children misbehave because their stomachs hurt as they squeeze in on emptiness. Our problem is not that we don't know what it takes to feed a child properly. Our ancestors were very good at providing their families with chickens and pigs and cows and maize and greens. We used to grow fruit here too. But the dry season is lasting longer, and there is not enough water. The government workers come and tell us that our boundaries are changing, that our fields are smaller. They do this without asking us. Now we have less land to grow food on. Now we must buy our foodstuffs in the market where fruit and vegetables are more expensive. We buy less. We go hungry for our children, but they are still hungry.

She chewed on the sandwich dully. She would have liked to save it for Ines. Ines had never had a Kentucky Fried Chicken sandwich either.

In the darkness above the runways, the city's halo of light stretched into the sky. In the village, the night sky was truly black and close enough to graze your skin. Over the roar and lights of the planes, the Tegucigalpa sky seemed terribly distant, as if it had been shoved away by humans.

31

IT WAS four am when Dom shuffled across the analysts floor of the Javits building with two Starbucks coffees in a cardboard tray and a crinkled white bakery bag. She set the offerings on the corner of Lea Peck's desk, shrugged out of her windbreaker, hung it on the back of the side chair, and sat. Her toes ached, her eyes stung, and her stomach growled.

Lea's fingers danced with gleeful energy. "The savior returns."

Did young people never get tired?

Lea had tacked two photos on the side of her screen. The first was the bright selfie of Hettie and Micah outside the Toncontín International Airport, the sun glimmering on their cheeks. Hettie had the radiant smile of a young woman intoxicated with adventure and love. The second image was a grainy black-and-white newspaper photo of the Van Buren family at a black-tie affair. The photograph had captured Yvette's tight face and Hettie's enigmatic pained expression. What a trio. A brash father with dominating tendencies, a distant mother with gentile polish, and a quiet daughter with a defiant love. Discord, like cold currents, swirled around this family.

Lea rummaged in the bag. "Oooh, paninis. Nice work, Miss Domini. And they're hot!"

"We're gonna need sustenance and caffeine." The coffee's tang soothed her throat as she looked over the coffee lid at Lea. *Fontaine was gonna be helluva pissed.* "What we're about to do is off-the-record."

Lea's eyebrows rose as she munched. "I'm liking the sound of this."

"As in, on the down low."

"I'm with you."

"We've got some research to do...into the financial industry."

Lea's eyebrows shot skyward and she whispered, "Are we looking into the Van Burens?"

Dom nodded once. "We are."

"And we're not supposed to be."

"And we're not supposed to be. Because somebody doesn't want us looking into the parents."

Lea slowly mouthed the word, Fontaine?

Boy was Fontaine gonna be pissed. Dom nodded.

Lea grinned wickedly. "Takin' on the big folks. Aiming for their ankles. Me like it."

For the first time since this investigation started, Dom felt lighter. She and Lea were a small, but powerful team built on a history of trust.

Lea took a huge bite and mumbled, "Already feeling stronger." Setting the sandwich aside, she placed her fingers on the keyboard.

"Okay." Dom sipped on her coffee. "Let's start with Señor Claude."

Lea typed into a search bar *Claude Van Buren*. Articles filled the screen. They both leaned in.

Forbes, 2012 — Claude Van Buren takes a hit on his investment in Argentina.

New Yorker, 2013 — Claude Van Buren's wife, the Lowrance heir, joins American Museum of Natural History Board.

CNBC, 2014 — New York Attorney General looking into Claude Van Buren's stakes in Brazil.

Bloomberg, 2015 — Claude Van Buren narrowly cleared, despite losing big this year.

Bloomberg, 2015 — Claude Van Buren finally sees a turn around.

Vanity Fair, 2016 — Claude Van Buren is riding high after troubled times.

New York Times, 2016 — Claude Van Buren is making himself a name as a smart crusader.

"Hmm … " Dom said. "Seems our man Van Buren wasn't always so successful. That can't feel good for a guy whose wife was born with a silver spoon. That probably weighs heavily on him. Failure can't be fun."

"And only recently turned his fortunes around."

"Okay, let's check out Rittenhouse Equity."

Lea pulled up a black homepage with small, clean font in silver that read *Rittenhouse Equity.* Her mouse clicked on the site, but there was only one hot link that read *Shareholders Login.* Her voice took on a German accent. "So sleek and fancy. And secretive." She clicked over to an internet search and typed in *Rittenhouse Equity.* The search delivered only the link back to the home page. The German accent returned. "So super sneaky." She turned to Dom and spoke normally. "They must hire someone to scrub the internet. I hate that. A bit of a stymie in our research."

Dom whistled a little tune.

"What?" Lea cocked her head. "You got some insider intel?"

"I may have pulled in a favor."

"With who?"

"I know a certain someone who used to work in banking. He still has friends there. He's a good guy. People like him."

Lea grinned widely. "That Beecher is a righteous temptation."

Dom rubbed the crumbs from her lips as she pulled up her phone and with a clean pinky, opened the email program, and forwarded an email to Lea. "Delete that when we're done."

"It will be lost like Moses' tablets from the Mount Sinai."

Wait, what? "Moses lost the tablets?"

"Well, technically they were supposed to have been shattered. And are now in the Ark of the Covenant. You know, like Indiana Jones..." Lea pulled up the email and opened the attachment, an Excel spreadsheet. "Don't worry about it—leave it to us Bible thumpers. Now what have we here?"

"Those are positions Rittenhouse has exited in the past seven years. It's everything they've sold off. You and I are gonna try to figure out what they invest in. What is their business strategy? It may give us some clues."

Lea grinned.

"Print this all out, I'll take half, you take half."

Lea's grin broadened. This was right up her alley.

An hour later, Dom set down her pen. "What did you find?"

"Lots of mining." Lea stretched her back.

"Yeah, me too. Looks like they are heavily slanted to the extractives. Overseas mining companies. Mining, drilling, quarries, pits. Supply companies that provide to bigger extractive companies."

"Yup. Exactly the same on my list. Yvette Van Buren's family made their wealth in oil. She would have encouraged her husband to invest in extractives to carry on the family tradition, blah, blah, blah."

Dom stood on throbbing toes and walked slowly to the dark window. Hettie was a well-trained, highly specialized environmentalist to whom extractives would surely be objectionable. "They're on opposite sides."

The air conditioning unit thrummed.

She turned and drifted back to the desk. "The father and the daughter are on opposite sides. She wants to find this extinct bird and protect the land. He wants to get rich digging up the land."

The fluorescent lights above the desks blinked brighter.

Lea said, "I mean, the conflict has to be over land in Honduras, am I right?"

"Yes. It's gotta be Honduras." She pointed to the list of Rittenhouse investments. "Did you see anything in Honduras?"

Lea shook her head. "Nope."

"Me neither."

The fan in the desktop computer whined.

"But wait." Lea pointed at the papers. "These lists are the investments they *exited* in the last seven years, right?"

"Yes." Dom smiled. "And if they're still invested in Honduras it wouldn't be in those lists."

"They could have current investments in Honduras." Lea reached for the keyboard.

Dom pulled out her cellphone, opened the map of Honduras. "The brother said Hettie and Micah went up to the northwest, to a province called Copán."

Lea skimmed a list of sites registered with the Honduran Government. "There's only one extractive company with activity in Copán. A company named Phalanx." She clicked to a second window and opened the Phalanx site. "It's a listed company. Registered in Tegucigalpa in 1995. Holds exploration concessions for over 10,500 hectares. Mostly extracts zinc deposits. Five sites are operational." She turned to Dom. "It's gotta be Phalanx. Rittenhouse has got to be invested in Phalanx."

"I think you may be right. Okay, let's review. We know four months ago something significant happened. The provocation event. Let's assume Hettie finds out her father is invested in Phalanx. As a result of this, three months ago she plans a trip to Honduras. Her parents forbid the travel—they threaten to cut her off. She defies them, and three weeks ago she and Micah go to Copán, to the Phalanx site to try to spot an Eskimo curlew. When she returns, she confronts her father with the discovery of her beloved Eskimo curlew and threatens to shut down the Phalanx operation."

Outside on the street, a car honked.

Lea whispered, "If that theory is correct, we're saying Claude Van Buren may be involved in these crimes."

Across the office space, the air conditioner cranked up a notch.

"Dom, did we just find the motive?"

Dom whistled. "Does this boil down to simple greed as the motive? Is that even possible? That Phalanx site has to be worth a ton to have instigated this whole thing and be the motive."

Lea clicked through the Phalanx website, slid over a calculator, and entered numbers. "For the sake of estimating, let's divide Phalanx's total production across their five sites evenly... which puts...a return from one site...at 23,000 tons of zinc a year." She looked up the price of zinc online. "Looks like zinc is $1.50 per pound which means...they make $76 million from one site in a year." She sat back and said, "$76 million. A year."

It was a significant amount. Was it a big enough amount to have caused these crimes? Dom turned and trudged back to the window.

From the desk, Lea asked, "Is $76 million a year enough of a motive to kill Micah and kidnap his own daughter?"

The frozen lake was suddenly much darker and infinitely more sinister. Dom blew warm breath against the chilled glass and whispered, "I better go find out."

32

THE RITTENHOUSE EQUITY offices were in a towering, glass-and-steel building north of Grand Central Station and nestled among opulent buildings where deferential wealth managers silently transferred millions for high-end clients. The early morning traffic on Park Avenue was hushed and well-mannered. Dom sat in the Lancia sipping a coffee and watching bankers in blue pin-striped suits cross the glass enclosed lobby. Her eyes felt gritty from the sleepless night, as if someone had pried open the lids and salted the pupils.

Money was a textbook motive. In this case, it had become—by a mile—her most compelling lead. But was a $76 million per year loss from the Phalanx site enough to trigger the chain of events that led to the murder of Micah Zapata and the kidnapping of Hettie Van Buren?

She took another sip. Through the early morning hours, she considered calling Fontaine. His instructions two days ago had been explicit. *If this case gets anywhere near the family, you clear any actions with me first. Is that English plain enough, Walker?* Eventually she had decided against calling him. She needed the spontaneous, authentic reactions of the principles of Rittenhouse Equity when confronted, and she didn't trust Fontaine to not warn Claude Van Buren.

She took the last hit of caffeine and unwound from the car. Later, she would take the lumps from Fontaine. Now she needed to find Hettie.

The lobby on the twenty-fifth floor was an artful palette of ivory marble, glass, and stainless steel. A brushed silver plaque on the glass door read, *Rittenhouse Equity*. Dom pushed through. Two colossal steel pots held white and pink orchids on either side of a glass reception desk where a pretty chestnut-haired receptionist smiled.

Dom flashed her badge. "I'm with the FBI. Special Agent Domini Walker. I would like to speak with Claude Van Buren."

To her credit, the smile didn't falter. "Of course. Just a moment." She whispered into her headset before saying, "His assistant will be right up."

A second young woman in a smart suit, heels clacking on marble, led Dom down a hallway of sparkling glass walls and rows of stark modern offices. Young men in shirts and ties stared at screens or spoke on phones. They probably drove expensive leased cars and lived on the Upper East Side. Their parents probably paid their Ivy League tuitions up front. Dom tugged on the navy windbreaker. Fidelity, bravery, and integrity.

The assistant led her to a conference room with a long glass table flanked by twenty white-leather roller chairs. A wall of windows opened to the city below.

"Coffee, water?" the assistant asked.

"No, I'm fine, thank you."

"Mr. Van Buren will be right with you."

Outside, cotton clouds, still and lonely, hovered against a

blue sky while the contrail of a departed plane cleaved the vista like a suspended stain of modernity. In the far distance, the horizon was tinted gray as if a legion of dark clouds was assembling.

The rat-a-tat-tat of footfalls grew stronger as a small troop of people pounded down a hallway.

In her ear, Stewart Walker whispered, *You are enough, my Dom. Don't ever doubt yourself.*

Claude was the first to enter. He led with a puffed chest and a dark anger. "Agent Walker, after your antics last night, I'm surprised you're here."

Adrenaline rippled under her skin and her shoulder blades tightened. "Yes, cases move quickly and we can't always give proper notice."

He scowled at her as three people filed into the room behind him. The first was a gaunt man of medium height with the tightly grooved face of a runner. He was followed by a tall horsey woman with shiny black hair. Pulling up the rear was a heavyset jowly white man with a 1980s mustache. Claude made quick introductions: the runner was Roger Atkins, Head of Security; the horsey woman was Patricia Coll, General Counsel; and the mustache was Chase Craig, Partner.

"Well, let's get to it, Agent," Claude said with a tight voice, indicating the table. "Please sit."

Dom waved a dismissal. "I am better when I stand, actually."

Heavy silence hung in the air as the four hesitated before turning, circling the table, taking positions, and squinting into the sun. They sat stiffly, poised for an offensive.

She wondered if they already knew they were suspects. "Mr. Van Buren, are you comfortable with me sharing information about Hettie's case with your colleagues?"

He shot her an annoyed look. "Yes, of course. That's why they are here, Agent."

She turned to the window, her back to the foursome. The contrail lingered against deep blue. "I was going to tell you about the forensic evidence we've compiled. How Micah Zapata was shot at point-blank range. How he would have slammed against the wall, then how he would have slid down, slowly, onto his haunches. I could tell you that the initial impact would have felt like a sledgehammer, swung against his chest, just over his heart. I could tell you, that as the blood rushed in a torrent from the wound, it would have felt as if a blowtorch was fanning his chest." She turned to face them with steely eyes.

Claude glanced at the glass table, his face ashen. The images Dom described were new to him. He had not witnessed them himself.

The three other sets of eyes were frozen wide.

"I can tell you this, because I'm FBI, and we deal in violent crime every day. We know how it goes. We know Micah would have felt the heat pouring down over his torso and legs."

In disgust, Horsey pulled her chin, a white-glove lawyer shocked by death's dirty details. Again, the micro expressions represented shock. Dom doubted Horsey had witnessed Micah's death either.

"For fifteen minutes, Micah would have sat against his bedroom wall, surrounded by his belongings, feeling his heartbeat weakening and his breathing diminishing."

Mustache the partner sat like a wide-eyed statue, stunned into stillness. The concept of death was new to him also.

"He would have felt numbness climb up his limbs to the core of his body."

Dom turned to watch Runner. He was eyeing her unflinchingly. Death didn't shock this one. He must have served somewhere, maybe Afghanistan, maybe all over. *Interesting.*

"Micah would have watched the killer walk back down the hallway. He would have sat alone in the silence of his bedroom. When that numbness reached his chest, he may have known he had only moments left on earth.

Runner watched her. He gave away no expression of having witnessed Micah Zapata's death.

"We'll never know what he thought about in those last moments of his life. Maybe he thought of Hettie."

Dom made a rapid assessment. None of these four had witnessed the killing. The sun beamed around her as she walked to the conference table, closing in on them. But had they ordered it?

"I won't go into more details of the killing of Micah Zapata because they don't speak to motive."

As one, all four faces blanked. Mentally, they were readying for the assault.

"I'm here this morning to speak to motive. Because if I can identify a motive... " Dom placed her fingertips on the glass table like a prosecutor in a courtroom. "I can find Hettie."

Four sets of eyes widened.

"Which leads me to a story about your daughter, Mr. Van Buren. You see, Hettie has been chasing a very elusive bird. It's called the Eskimo curlew. Every year it migrates across a path from Alaska to the southern tip of South America. She's been trying to spot this particular bird along this path for the last four years. She started in Patagonia, moved on to Costa Rica, and then Nicaragua. This year she was planning research in Panama, then she changed her mind. Instead of Panama, she decided to chase this bird—this likely extinct bird—in Honduras."

Was it possible that four blank faces became blanker? This was not news to them.

"The extinct part is a key issue because if Hettie can

confirm a sighting of this bird in Honduras, she can get land declared protected."

Four frozen statues.

You are enough, my Dom. Never doubt that. "It turns out that three weeks ago she and Micah traveled to the northwest province of Honduras."

None of them blinked. None of their eyes moved. The trip to Honduras was not news to them.

Fontaine was gonna be super pissed. "Does Rittenhouse Equity own shares in a Honduran mining company named Phalanx Incorporated?"

Across the frozen surface of the lake, hairline fractures shot out like a spider's web. Horsey jumped from her seat. Mustache vigorously wobbled his head. Runner rose smoothly. Claude hissed, "We had nothing to do with this!"

"It's a simple question."

Runner closed his arms across his chest like a soldier in a squad.

Claude snarled, "We had nothing to do with this. How dare you—"

Horsey placed a hand on Claude's shoulder. "That's enough, Agent Walker. I believe we are done here."

Claude growled, "How dare you suggest we had something to do with this!"

Horsey repeated, "We're done here, Agent."

"Are we done? Because we're talking about saving Hettie. Mr. Van Buren, we're talking about saving your daughter."

Horsey's voice was strong. "This interview is over. We are instructing you to leave now, Agent."

The three men clamped mouths shut.

"I'll put these here." Dom placed four business cards on the table. "When one of you remembers your investments in

Phalanx, please use that number to get in touch. In the mean-time, I'll be looking for Hettie."

The four watched as she strode from the room.

The new cracks across the lake's frozen surface had held fast, but Dom wasn't worried. This was only the first incursion.

33

IN MIDTOWN EAST, Dom parked the Lancia on Lexington Avenue near the MetLife Building. The morning traffic had picked up, bringing with it the intermittent blasts of taxi horns and the thundering grumbles of bus airbrakes. Her eyes stung, and her toes throbbed. She dialed Lea Peck. "It's Dom."

"How'd the meeting go?"

"Claude got fired up. They kicked me out."

"What?"

A pedestrian passed by the windshield. "Their reactions were inappropriate. They should have been focused on finding Hettie. They should have heard me out."

"I'll never understand rich people."

Dom described the meeting at Rittenhouse. "They are a tight-knit group. They held together. Nobody broke."

"And Claude?"

"He may have been the angriest."

Lea snorted. "Guilty like Jephthat offering up his virgin daughter so he could be king. Unbelievable. So, which ones do you think are involved?"

"I don't know. They all have motive, because they all stand

to lose money. We need one of them to turn. We need someone to rat the others out." Dom squeezed the steering wheel. "What have you got?"

"I'm watching all of Claude's calls. Nothing yet. On the others—Roger Atkins, Patricia Coll, and Chase Craig—I am scouring their call logs for unusual patterns." Distant fingers tapped a keyboard. "I've put in requests for ongoing surveillance on all three."

"Chase the surveillance requests. We need that up and running. They're gonna break today. And when Fontaine hears about this he's gonna come at me." *Find Hettie now, take the lumps later.* "I give him two hours."

"Roger that. Also, I'm working up phone taps on Roberto Zapata and that lawyer Oslo Bockel. By the way, who names their kid Oslo?"

"Apparently he was conceived there."

Silence. "I will seriously never understand rich people. Thank the Blessed Mary that my mother, who is from Pole Cat Hollow, West Virginia, wasn't rich or I'd be named Tajikistan." A keyboard clacked again. "What next?"

"I'm going to try a pincer move on the other half." Across the street, a plaque on the wall of a small building read *Skatten Hammersol, Lawyers.* "I'm gonna see if the mother's side will break. I'm going to see her lawyer."

Lea chuckled. "Inception in Norway!"

Oslo Bockel stepped into the hushed wood-paneled lobby of the family law firm with the smile of a long-lost friend. "Special Agent Walker, how nice to see you. I did not expect to see you so soon after last night's meeting." The bear paw handshake was energetic. "Despite the circumstances, it's very nice to see you. Please, please do come in."

It took a clever man to use amiability to disarm.

He led her to a small library with mahogany leather seats, framed oil paintings of sailboats, and shelves of antique books. The room smelled of chamomile tea and cologne. "Would you like some coffee?"

"Yes, please. Black." The leather chair was cold against her jeans.

Handing her a cup of swirling black liquid, his face was full of compassion. "I bet that isn't your first of the day, now is it, Agent?"

Yup, Oslo Bockel was smart. And confident. "You are correct, Oslo."

"And how does our coffee stand up?"

The caffeine hit her veins immediately. "It's good."

"I am always telling our office manager that our coffee is tops, just tops. I can't replicate it at home. I have one of those machines that foams and sprays and whistles. There's just no telling the whims of physics. Or why the coffee maker in a law firm would choose on its own accord to make some of the best coffee in New York City. Odd that. But then, things are odd often." He raised eyebrows in a contemplative look. "So, Special Agent Walker, to what do I owe this visit?"

After his innuendos last night of a possible connection between the trip, the crimes, and Rittenhouse Equity, Dom needed to know what else Yvette had instructed him to reveal. "I have some questions, if you don't mind."

"Please, proceed." He leaned back with hands clasped across the top of his belly.

Start slow, go easy, let the subject feel they have control of the interview. "I'm trying to fill in some pretty straightforward blanks I still have. What can you tell me about Hettie? What type of person is she?" Oslo Bockel wasn't the only smart one in the room.

"Well, let's see. She's quiet. Very studious. Certainly not your typical socialite from a wealthy family."

"Reserved?"

"Yes, I'd say that. Quite a world view, what with her environmental work, bird research, whatnot. She's always concerned with some cause. She would often ask me to donate to this fundraiser or that."

"Mostly environmental?"

"Yes."

"What else about Hettie?"

"She was very competent. She didn't rely too much on her parents from what I understand. Never too much trouble. I never had to bail her out of jail or write a note to a newspaper. Very contained. She had friends, of course."

Dom sipped encouragingly.

"She had her work, that boyfriend, a life of a young professional in the city. She was happy."

"Anything else?"

"Nothing overly remarkable, no."

Now let's get to the meaty stuff. What has Yvette instructed him to say? "And the Van Burens? Anything remarkable there?"

"No, not really." He shrugged. "A wealthy couple, social, philanthropists. Yvette's work, at the museum and with other charities, is very well regarded. I understand they attend events quite often. I do keep an eye on their press. Nothing too bad on a personal level."

"Have they always lived on Central Park?"

"No, no. Yvette is from Philadelphia, from a very wealthy family. They only moved up to the city after they were married."

"How did they meet?"

"It was through friends at a Princeton party. They were

both in their early twenties. She married him despite her parents' misgivings."

A soft ping sounded in her ear. "What misgivings?"

"Well, that he wasn't exactly from the right family. You know how it is with these old families. It's all about pedigree and appearances. Yvette Lowrance would have been quite a prize for someone like Claude Van Buren."

Was he purposefully demeaning Claude Van Buren? "And?"

"After they married, as expected, Claude went into business with Yvette's father. Oil. Quite lucrative. I think he was fine there. Not promoted as much as he should have been. Remained a director when he should have been vice president. Sat around as a vice president when he should have been executive vice president. I think Claude wasn't really up to it. He's not as ambitious as folks would have preferred. When old Mr. Lowrance passed, Claude took over. He lasted a few years but couldn't really make the company run well. He sold the company and moved the family to New York."

The second ping was louder. Yvette's lawyer was definitely trash-talking Claude. "And then?"

"Claude got set up over at Rittenhouse."

Ping. Yvette's lawyer had turned the focus to Rittenhouse Equity. "What should I know about Rittenhouse?"

"Funny you ask that. These private equity firms can be so secretive. In fact, despite the fact that Yvette has put in capital, she has no control whatsoever over what Rittenhouse does. We've tried to look into their investments, but they are literally a black box." Oslo threw up his hands helplessly.

In Dom's mind, the elevator arrived with a loud ping. As a good lawyer, Oslo had smoothly demeaned Claude, turned the conversation toward Rittenhouse, and distanced Yvette from both. "Do you think Claude is related to the crimes?"

"Good Lord, Agent Walker. Is Claude a suspect?" He rose with a dramatic grab at his lapels. "I'm sure it's no longer appropriate to have this discussion."

"Yes, I do believe I understand." Dom rose.

She understood very well. Out of fear for her daughter, Yvette had sent a message through her lawyer. Claude and Rittenhouse Equity were involved in the crimes.

The cracks on the frozen lake were weakening.

Outside the sun was shining. Dom's phone pinged with a message from Fontaine. *Meet me at Hong Kong Garden. Now!*

Time to take the lumps. The confrontation with her boss had arrived sooner than expected.

34

IN THE TINY intern alcove in the museum library, Mila enlarged a photo of the Van Buren family in a *New Yorker* article. In the center, Yvette Van Buren, in a cream silk gown, smiled prettily for the camera. To her right, a black-clad Claude Van Buren glared at the photographer. Dressed in a pale pink gown, Miss Timid Hettie stood at a distance from her mother with an expression that was hard to read. Mila enlarged the focus on Hettie's face. Was that a look of resignation or sadness? What a mysterious young woman. Despite being born into great wealth and elite society, Hettie had chosen a quiet research career and wrote anonymously of sadness, self-consciousness, and displacement. What secrets did this young woman keep?

Resizing the image, Mila realized the photo had been taken in the Milstein Hall of Ocean Life. She quickly toggled to the museum's home page and typed *events* in the search tab. She found an image of Yvette Van Buren in the pale dress in the gallery of photos from a gala that had taken place three months ago. There were no other pictures of the Van Buren family at that event. Grabbing the rotary phone, she dialed the main number.

A peppy female voice answered the line. "American Museum of Natural History."

"Museum Events, please."

"Just one moment."

A scratchy voice answered, "Museum Events, Val speaking."

Mila had met Val, a heavyset woman who rarely smiled. "Hey, Val. It's Mila."

"What's up, Mila?"

"Did you work the gala three months ago? The one in February?"

"Yup. Why? What's up?"

"Was there video?"

"Yup."

"Can I see the footage?"

"Why?"

Mila glanced at Hettie's sad face. "No reason, just curious."

"Sure. It was a good party. Decent food. They had those Cajun crab balls. The band wasn't great. And that protest was weird."

Mila pressed the receiver against her ear. "Protest?"

"Yeah. There were protestors outside."

"What?"

"Some crazy guys protested on the red carpet. Everybody was already in the party."

"I hadn't heard about that."

"The board talked about it for a week. But I didn't see it. Nobody really saw it. Anyway, I've got all the party footage on a hard drive down here if you want to come borrow it."

Mila stood. "Thanks, Val. I'm on my way."

Back in the alcove, Mila locked the door, pulled up Val's hard drive, and plunged into the first of six video files. On the screen, the Milstein Hall of Ocean Life was ablaze with candelabras and chandeliers. Tall magenta flower arrangements and shimmering crystal glasses dotted white tables. Screening the first video, she spotted Claude Van Buren talking to a crowd of men and later getting a drink from a bar. In one sequence, Yvette Van Buren laughed with similarly gowned and bejeweled women. Hettie had not been captured in the first video. How much of the party had she attended?

The next footage was of a wide-angle view from the top of the red carpeted grand stairs. It was late in the day, and cars passed cautiously on icy Central Park West. In the park, barren tree branches were whitened with snow. Tiny snowflakes wafted like winter fairies past the camera lens.

The first ten minutes of the video showed only the slow traffic. At the eleven-minute timestamp, a black SUV pulled to the valet stand. Two men stepped out and made their way up the stairs. Four minutes later, three taxis dropped off six guests. Soon a line of cars snaked along the curb. Valets ran to open doors, accept keys, and slip into driver seats. As the sky darkened, the golden beam of a spotlight blazed across the scene, glittering across diamond earrings and catching ethereal snowflakes dancing on invisible currents.

Cars and taxis arrived faster, and the line for the valet reached twenty deep. The shaft of headlights flickered across the lower right corner of the screen where the dark forms of three people appeared. Mila leaned closer to the screen. Bundled in unremarkable parkas, the three made their way to the shadows near the bottom of the stairs and crossed their arms. Had anyone noticed these ominous onlookers at the time? It didn't appear so. Women in furs and men in black overcoats laughed their way up the stairs, valets ran to open car doors, and hundreds made their way to the brightly lit museum entrance.

Fifty minutes later, the line of cars had become a trickle as late guests hurried up the stairs. Central Park resembled a dark forest hiding wolves and witches. A wet snowflake landed on the camera lens, and a gloved finger wiped it. In the dark shadows, the three figures stood as motionless as statues.

The headlights of a large sedan pulled to the curb. As a valet ran to the driver side of the black Mercedes, one of the figures nodded. A second protestor reached into a backpack, pulled out a tall cylinder that resembled a thermos, and held it with a crooked arm.

Mila leaned even closer to the screen.

On the passenger side, a second valet opened the door, and Yvette Van Buren emerged in a long pale fur coat. Claude Van Buren made his way around the car, offered his arm to her, and they began a slow, careful walk past the shadows.

The small protestor slashed his arm. Had he just thrown something? Mila's hand slapped the keyboard to pause the video. She rewound the footage. In slow motion, a long ghost-like cloud moved through the air and splattered across Yvette Van Buren's fur. Oh shit, he *had* thrown something. Some kind of liquid.

Yvette Van Buren dropped her hand from her husband's arm and turned abruptly to the shadows. Claude Van Buren, unaware, continued to the stairs. Yvette Van Buren peered into the darkness. The statues stood their ground. Realizing his wife wasn't at his side, Claude Van Buren turned, hurried back, and followed his wife's gaze. He raised his hand and yelled. For two minutes, there was a standoff.

Claude Van Buren gently took his wife's elbow, turned her, and led her up to the top of the stairs where he stopped to inspect a long brown stain that ran the length of her fur coat. With a tight hold, Yvette Van Buren yanked the coat from his grasp and they exchanged heated words.

Miss Timid Hettie emerged at the entrance, her blond hair angelic in the back light. Yvette Van Buren brushed past her daughter and strode into the party. Eyes wide, Hettie said something to her father, but he shook her off and escorted her into the brightness.

Mila released a breath. What was that all about? She grabbed the rotary phone and rang the main number. "Tours, please."

A male voice picked up. "Museum Tours."

"Ralph?" Ralph did all the tours for the elementary schools.

"Yes?"

"It's Mila from the library."

"Hi, Mila. What can I do for you?"

"Does anyone on your team read lips?"

"Sure. Mike Hampton does."

"Is he there?"

"He's on a tour."

"When's he back?"

"Not till late. Seven pm."

Seven pm was well past Mila's regularly scheduled departure. Only a few select things were worth an impromptu change of plans to one's daily schedule. The hunt for Miss Timid Hettie was definitely one of those things. "Can you tell him I'll meet him then?"

35

"WHAT THE EVER-LOVING fuck are you doing?" roared Yves Fontaine in the quiet Hong Kong Garden restaurant. He was camped out in a private booth in the back amid the potent aroma of greasy fried meat, sweet soy sauce, and clammy boiled rice.

She slid into the booth's opposite seat.

He growled, "What about 'check with me first' did you not hear? Last night Van Buren tells me you were at their apartment dropping bombs about the daughter traveling."

"I can explain."

"I'm not ready for your fucking explanation yet, Walker," he snarled. "Then *this morning* I get a call from Claude Van Buren's corporate lawyer, chewing out my ear, honking on about you up in their office with guns blazing." Two hands slammed the table. "What. The. Fuck. Are you doing?"

Behind them, the kitchen door clattered.

I'm coming, Hettie. No matter what, no matter the lumps, I'm coming to get you. She said, "My job."

"Do *not* give me that bullshit about doing your job! I've

heard that a million times before." He pointed at her nose. "Your job was to check in with me before going half-cocked on the family."

She sat straighter. "Sir, I was overtaken by events."

"No, you fucking weren't," he roared. "You *created* events."

In the kitchen, a Chinese chef snapped orders.

She blinked.

"You decided on your own to sweat this family. Goddamn it, Walker. I told you to notify me."

"Sir, we got a new lead. In the middle of last night."

"This had better be fucking solid." He sat back.

"We discovered it at four am. I think Hettie's research may have threatened one of Rittenhouse Equity's investments. I think Hettie, as an environmentalist, discovered Rittenhouse is involved in a mining site on land of a protected bird—"

"Jesus H Christ, Walker!"

I'm coming, Hettie. She held up a hand. "I know it sounds crazy, but if this bird was seen on this site in Honduras, it would shut down the mine. That would cost Rittenhouse a lot of money."

He laid both hands on the laminate table and breathed through his nose.

"I think the Rittenhouse investment in the site may be worth $76 million."

His eyes narrowed.

"A year. $76 million *a year*."

His right hand signaled for her to continue.

I'm coming, Hettie. I'm putting the pieces together and I'm coming to find you. "Micah and Hettie took a trip to Honduras three weeks ago. She did not tell her parents. Last night at the Van Buren residence, I explained these facts, and Mr. Van Buren exploded."

Fontaine glared.

"He didn't want us near this topic. Why was the topic of Hettie and Honduras so upsetting? Of course, his resistance sent us digging. We dug into Rittenhouse's finances."

He crossed his arms over his chest.

"At four am, we discovered that Rittenhouse Equity may have a financial investment in a Honduran mining company. If Hettie can prove this bird is there, the land will be protected. I went to Rittenhouse this morning and confronted them with this theory. Their response was very off. Overly defensive. In fact, they kicked me out. Then an hour ago, Yvette Van Buren's lawyer threw Claude Van Buren and Rittenhouse under the bus. The wife is distancing herself from the husband and Rittenhouse. I think she knows something."

He spoke with a softer voice. "You think this is all about money?"

She nodded.

"Why didn't you notify me this morning of your plans?"

"Plausible deniability."

His lips tightened. "I did not instruct you to protect me."

Find Hettie now, take the lumps later. She sat mutely.

"I'll tell you what I think." He squinted at her. "I think you didn't trust me not to call them. To warn them."

"You're right."

The stark honesty succeeded in replacing Fountain's anger with fatigue. He rubbed his eyes and blew out his lips. "You think someone at Rittenhouse teed up these two crimes? To protect $76 million?"

"A year. $76 million *a year*."

"You think someone at Rittenhouse set up these crimes—got rid of the boyfriend and kidnapped Hettie—over money?"

He was right to question the motive. It was a niggling question. "It's our most compelling lead. But no, I'm not a hundred percent sure. It's still a working theory."

"Okay. Who? Who do you think did it?"

"I'm not sure yet. There are four principles in Rittenhouse Equity. I think it may be one of them or a combination of them."

"You went in this morning with guns blazing to try to divide them?"

"Yes. We're watching their phones now."

Silence descended between them. In the kitchen, a waiter barked. Out on the street, a car honked.

Fontaine rubbed his face. "The call from the lawyer wasn't the only one I got about your investigation this morning."

This was news. Who else would be interested so quickly? "Who's coming at you?"

"The Mayor and the AG."

This was *big* news. Two of the most powerful men in town were showing an interest in the case.

"Claude is throwing his weight around," Fontaine said. "They want you off the case."

"What did you say?"

"I told them that I had a good agent on the case. I told them that I had a rock-solid agent on the case. Because I do."

She glanced at the table. "I'm sorry." She looked up. "I should have trusted you."

"Yes, you should have."

She shifted in the booth.

Fontaine rubbed his lips. "A private equity fund is essentially other people's money. There are heavy, heavy hitters in this town who have a lot of money tied up in Rittenhouse Equity. You start sniffing around Rittenhouse and they get squirrelly. They get really squirrelly."

"Crap on a duck."

"Yeah. And I'm the duck." He shut his eyes, dropped his

chin, and asked gingerly. "You truly think Rittenhouse is involved?

"I'm saying it's my prime lead right now. The money is just too strong a motive. Their reactions are not right."

"Jesus."

"It's gonna crack it today."

He snorted.

"Hettie's been gone three days. Everybody knows that. The Rittenhouse guys are in a pressure cooker, and I just turned the heat up a notch." She pushed her shoulders back. "One of them is gonna break today."

He nodded slowly. "Well, get on with it."

Bravo, Boss. Hettie, I'm still coming! She slid to the edge of the booth. "Thank you, sir. Thank you."

He nodded again, but the lines in his face had softened and his eyes had turned gentle. "If you solve this soon, that would be good. I mean, not just because you'll get the girl back."

She paused halfway across the booth. "Why? What do you mean?"

"Walker, Office of Professional Responsibility is ready to interview you."

It had been six months since the OPR investigation into St. Chris had begun. They must be reaching the end of the inquiry. Her heartbeat spiked. "When?"

"Monday."

That was three days away. For a kidnapping case it was a lifetime. She had plenty of time to worry about OPR later. Now, she had to find Hettie. She nodded and resumed sliding from the booth.

"You're going to be fine." He clasped both hands and placed them on the table.

She stood and shrugged. "I did what I did."

"For a very good reason."

"I'm not proud of it."

"You're also not the first agent to break. We all see shit, sleep shit, live shit, breathe shit. You see enough shit, it gets to you. It has to come out sideways." He watched her. "I saw the notes from Darlin's interview."

Her heartbeat spiked higher. She wouldn't allow him to distract her. *Hettie, I'm coming.* Later, she would deal with OPR. She turned to go.

Fontaine leaned back, unclasped his hands and laid them flat on the table like a professor speaking to a student. "That little girl didn't give you up. That's one tough cookie. She told them all about what happened to her. Her story ... in black and white ... it breaks you a little." He shook his head. "But that little girl didn't give you up. They asked her point-blank if she saw you do anything. Anything. And that little girl just said no each time. They asked her five times and five times she said no."

Dom didn't have time for this. *Hettie, I'm coming.* She took a step to the front of the restaurant.

"Walker, do not give yourself up to OPR."

He had been telling her the same thing for months: Don't admit anything. Her phone rang. It was an unregistered number. "Special Agent Walker."

"Agent Walker, this is Yvette Van Buren." Yvette's voice cracked.

Dom's eyes flashed to Fontaine. "Yes, Mrs. Van Buren, how are you?"

Fontaine's eyes widened.

Yvette said softly, "I was wondering if perhaps you could give me an update. About my daughter. Perhaps just you and me?"

"Yes, Mrs. Van Buren. Of course, I'd be happy to come meet with you."

Fontaine hooked a thumb to the door.

Hettie, I'm coming. Nothing is going to stop me. Not OPR, not the Mayor, not the AG, not Rittenhouse, not your father. I'm coming to get you back from the monsters. She strode to the front of the restaurant, the phone pressed to her ear. "Mrs. Van Buren, I'm on my way."

Deceit
@LastCurlew

the years of deceit materialize out of dusty drifts
like howls of banshees trapped in secrecy—
culprits—of my own tribe—caught, entangled, enmeshed,
images pierce virtuous skin like acetic darts
and shoot inward at kidney, liver, heart lancing
serene domestic memories created in happier times—
liars—declaring, announcing to all the admirers
of a gentile world, claiming a fortune of honor,
please continue you dissimulating perjurers, frauds,
because a reckoning is converging.

DESPITE THE HEAVY beige curtains drawn against the windows on the eleventh Floor of Central Park West, a sliver of sun intruded and flickered across the polished floor. Yvette drifted into the room in an ivory cashmere sweater with matching ivory slacks, an oddly warm outfit for a summer day. Her gray hair had been pulled back into a sleek, tight knot above a thin neck. She appeared to have lost weight since yesterday. Light makeup couldn't distract from the red rims around her eyes.

The maid in the white dress followed closely behind.

"Agent Walker," Yvette said in a tremulous voice, "thank you for coming. Please, let's take a seat." She turned to the maid. "Marla, will you make us two Manhattans please?" To no one in particular, she whispered, "Fortitude in the face of adversity."

It wasn't a good sign that Yvette was drinking at noon. But coping mechanisms came in all different hues. The two women sat.

"What news do you have of my daughter?" Yvette's eyes appeared glassy.

Had she already been drinking this morning? "We are following a very compelling lead at the moment."

"I see."

"Mrs. Van Buren, have you spoken with your husband today?"

"No, I can't say that I have."

This was a bit of luck. "I was at his office this morning."

"I see," she whispered.

"He was, how shall I say ... not terribly happy to see me."

"What happened?"

The maid padded to the seating area, set down a silver tray with crystal glasses of dark cocktails, and disappeared again.

Dom said, "I was surprised to be honest, about your husband's reaction."

Leaning over to pick up a drink, Yvette squinted at the crystal glasses and frowned. She picked up a silver bell and gave it a quick shake that sent a peel through the apartment. The maid rushed through the door and scurried over.

Yvette said, "Patrice, please do match the glasses. It's the least we can do for our guest."

She grabbed the platter and disappeared quickly from the room.

Yvette turned to Dom. "I'm sorry for that. What was it you were saying about my husband?"

"He was quite angry this morning."

"Was he?" she said flatly.

"Yes, quite. His temper flared. Quickly."

"Let me choose my words carefully, Agent Walker, because I don't want to give you the wrong impression." Her hands clasped each other. "Claude's manners sometimes are not what they should be."

"So you know this temper?"

The maid returned with a new tray and retreated. Yvette grasped a glass and took a long thirsty slug.

It was not the first drink of the day.

"Yes, of course," Yvette said. "Wives know their husbands. Mine runs testy."

"Well, his anger got the better of him. He kicked me out before we discussed the details of the case and the search for your daughter. It was a highly unusual turn of events."

"Pardon me?"

"Yes, before I could explain my latest findings, he kicked me out."

Both hands held the glass. "Why? Did you, in some way, imply that he or his firm had something to do with my daughter's disappearance?"

There. The theory was out in the open. Adrenaline hit Dom's neck. Would Yvette implicate her husband? "Yes. I suggested that Hettie's research may risk a Rittenhouse investment." Would the cracks in the lake's frozen surface finally give way?

Yvette pushed back against the sofa. "How ... how ... What is the connection?"

"A possible sighting of an endangered bird on the site of a mine. In Honduras. I believe your husband's firm is invested in this mine."

Yvette's eyes blinked rapidly. "Honduras?"

"Yes."

"You think there is something ... nefarious ... about the trip to Honduras?"

"Yes."

"You think Hettie discovered this ... a bird ... at a mining site owned by my husband? That she informed ... confronted Claude?"

"Yes."

Yvette took a long sip, and her eyelids fluttered. "And that somehow...he..."

The alcohol was having an impact, and disquiet was descending around her like a fog. Dom didn't have much time. "Is there something you want to tell me about your husband and Hettic?"

Yvette stared off into the distance.

"Mrs. Van Buren, is there something you can tell me?"

"Reputation is important in this town, Agent. It's everything."

"Excuse me? How do you mean, Mrs. Van Buren?"

"It keeps your friends close and your enemies at bay. It keeps the family moving into the future. It ensures progress. It takes lifetimes to build a reputation. A family name. Then one false move and it's gone."

She was rambling. "Did Mr. Van Buren ever bully you, Mrs. Van Buren?"

Yvette's eyes focused on Dom. "Define bully, please, Agent."

"Used his power or strength to coerce or intimidate you ... perhaps to do things you didn't want to do? It often takes the form of aggression."

"Yes."

Dom's adrenaline surged. "How?"

"Many ways. Small and large."

"Regularly?"

"Yes."

"Habitually?"

"Yes."

"Have you told anyone?"

"No." Her brow furrowed. "The lies we tell."

"Can you describe the ways your husband bullies you?"

She took another deep sip. "I think the topic that is far more pertinent—after your discovery this morning—is how this relates to Hettie."

Dom's heart spiked. "Does your husband bully Hettie?"

"Oh yes."

"Regularly, small and large?"

"Oh yes. And my Hettie is very quiet—she's not able to stand up to him."

I'm coming, Hettie, I'm getting close. "Did he ever hurt either of you?"

"Physically? No. That's not his style." She finished the drink in a final gulp.

"Mrs. Van Buren, do you think your husband may be involved in Hettie's disappearance?"

Yvette's gray eyes glazed over. She set the empty glass on the silver tray and with a tiny voice whispered, "I'm sure I can't answer that."

"Mrs. Van Buren, if it would help find your daughter, I believe you must answer it."

Yvette stared into the distance.

She was mentally shutting down. "Mrs. Van Buren, is there something you should be telling me?"

Yvette closed her eyes.

"Mrs. Van Buren, I can protect you. If you are afraid, I can protect you."

Cloudy eyes looked past Dom. "Our world is different. You do not understand our world." Then Yvette stood and, as if in a trance, crossed the huge living room and disappeared through a door.

Outside, Dom stared across Central Park. The blue sky was being pushed aside by a bank of gray. A storm was coming. The night was going to be long. There was much to do. She dialed Beecher.

"Yo," he said.

"Listen, it's going to be late again."

"Don't worry, I got Tinks."

"Thanks. How's your day?"

He cleared his throat.

It was never a good sign. "What?"

"Nothing," he said.

"Seriously? What?"

"It's nothing."

"I'm one hundred percent not doing this with you. Tell me."

"Esther's letter."

A chill rose through her body. "What about it?"

"I read it."

He read the letter without her. As if pushed from an air lock, Dom was suddenly unmoored, floating in dark space as a crushing weight pressed down on her chest.

"I read it."

Esther had abandoned them. Esther hadn't wanted them, hadn't loved them. Dom and Beecher were unwanted, unlovable.

"Dom, I read the letter."

With a huge breath she filled her lungs, trying to push against the pressure. "You agreed you would throw it out."

"I know. But she wants to meet us."

The pressure pushed back on her chest. "No."

"She says there's more to the story."

In an instant, white hot anger surged. "Fuck that. We don't need to know her side of the story. Fuck that. No way. Her side of the story can go fuck itself."

"That's not what she wrote. She said more to the story. Not her story. Maybe there's more about Dad than we know."

"Dad killed himself. Our mother left us. That's the fucking story."

He remained silent.

Anger tightened her voice. "We agreed you'd throw it out."

"Yes, we did," he said slowly. "But the situation has changed. I changed my mind."

"You're not allowed to do that."

"Dom, it's human nature. People change their minds."

"No. No they don't. Not about this." Esther didn't love them. Esther hadn't wanted them.

"Dom, what can it hurt to talk to her?"

"You don't know. You don't know about her. You don't know how it went down."

"Dom, I do know. I was there. We both lived through it—"

"You were ten."

"I was still a sentient being. Just because I was ten doesn't mean I didn't live through it just like you did."

As if he had blown on a lit candle, the gust extinguished the anger. Gentle, soft, Beecher. He had feelings too.

"Just because you were older, and in charge, doesn't mean I don't have opinions on this."

Beecher. His voice sounded so vulnerable.

"You can't be in charge of everything," he said.

"Throw it out," was all she could muster.

"We'll talk about it later."

"Please throw it out."

"Go back to your investigation. We'll talk about it later." He was gone.

38

LEA PECK GLANCED out the window where gray, angry clouds gathered in the distance and stretched her neck. A ping from the computer announced the arrival of an email with the results from match for the fingerprints on the gun. The email message had only one word: *NON-IDENTIFICATION*. *Dammit*. It meant the murderer's prints did not match any in the Integrated Automated Fingerprint Identification System, known as IAFIS. It was unexpected that someone who had executed a clean shot into Micah Zapata's chest did not match anyone in the national databases of over 70 million crime-related prints, 31 million civilian prints, or 73,000 known suspected terrorists. *My pretty wants to hide from me.*

She stood, strode to the far end of the room, and jacked her knees to her chest in two sets. Except for the three hours of sleep grabbed on a cot in the basement locker room, she had been going strong for thirty-six hours. The first few days of a kidnapping required it. She completed ten jumps onto the chair and felt the oxygen buzz her brain. She had tried to use IAFIS to narrow in on the killer. What if she reversed the search? *You can't hide from me, my pretty little killer.*

She strode back to the desk and sat. She cracked her knuckles and scanned piles of documents on the desk. What if she started narrow, at the core of the crimes, and worked out? She mentally reviewed all the computer files on this case—the phone logs, the credit card charges, the photos. All of them were related. They all intersected. Micah Zapata. Bronx. Hettie Van Buren. Greenwich Village. Rittenhouse Equity. Honduras. Hiking. Dusty field. Mining. Phalanx. Her head snapped up. What if the killer had come to Honduras to do the dirty deeds? *My fury upon this place, and it is not quenched.*

What was at the core of the crimes? She pulled up the five photos taken on vacation to trigger her brain to make connections. The selfie outside an airport. Micah driving a Jeep. The dusty field. On the mouse, her finger paused. She clicked back to the airport image. She hit the back button and stared at the two outside the airport. *You can't hide from me, my pretty little motherfucking international killer.* She grinned and dialed a number.

A deep voice answered, "Detective Johns."

"Detective Johns?"

"Yup. The one and only."

"My name is Lea Peck. I provide support to Special Agent Domini Walker here at the FBI."

"Mm-hmm. You find the missing girl?"

"Not yet."

"Sorry to hear that. Girl's been missing what, going on four days now?"

"Yes, sir."

"Dang." Law enforcement types never said too much about a case, no need to belabor the extraordinarily poor odds. "How's Walker's foot?"

"I'm sorry? What?" Lea asked.

"Uh, oh. Nothing," he said. "What can I do for you, Ms. Peck?"

"Thank you for your assistance on the case, Detective."

"Of course."

"I wondered if I could ask a large favor?"

"Hit me."

"I have some unmatched prints from the throwaway gun left at the scene. I'm thinking the perp may be a foreigner, possibly from Central America, maybe even Honduras. I'm wondering if he came through any of the New York airports would his prints be in their systems?"

"Yup, indeed. If your shooter came through an airport, they would have printed him. We know some guys out at JFK and Newark. Send 'em my way."

She shot a fist into the air. *Not from me, my pretty little killer. You can't hide from me.* "Thank you, Detective Johns! I'm sending you the prints now."

Five minutes later, she leaned back and toggled between the five photos. Had Hettie found her beloved Eskimo curlew in *Copán* province? On the screen was the dusty field, and in the far distance the pristine lake, a peaked mountain range, and a blue sky with white downy clouds. She straightened in her chair. Dom and Lea hadn't been able to determine the exact location of the Phalanx site, but had Hettie? If Lea could prove Hettie's photos were taken near the mining site, they would have one more piece of solid evidence.

Lea's fingers flew across the keyboard, and her mouse worked magic across the internet. Soon she was staring at satellite photos taken of a wide square area in northwest Honduras. Twenty small towns dotted the map. When she tinted the coloring on the screen, three large swathes appeared. She cross-referenced the dark areas and determined they were national parks. *Parque Nacional Celaque, Reserva de Vida Silvestre*

Erapuca, and *Reserva Biológica Volcán Pacayita.* Time to find this mountain range.

She settled in for the tedious work of comparing park photos against Hettie's peaked mountain.

An hour later, Lea hit pay dirt. Hettie's mountain range was located in *Reserva Biológica Volcán Pacayita* in *Copán* province. Hettie and Micah had been in *Copán.* Lea snapped her fingers. Getting closer. Now, was the mountain range in the *Reserva Biológica Volcán Pacayita* near the Phalanx site? On the map, she zoomed in tight to an area east of the park. There were four villages there: *Cornet, San Marcos de Caiquin, Arcomon,* and *Rapoosa.* One of them had to be the site of the Phalanx mine. Getting closer.

Lea pulled up the third image of Hettie and Micah standing in front of a white modern building, the walls stark and glossy with no stains or cracks. Behind the building, a jungle was thick with foliage, vines, and dark underbrush. Was this a hotel in one of the four villages? She snapped her fingers. Getting closer. She typed an internet search for *hotels near Reserva Biológica Volcán Pacayita.* Four websites were returned.

It was the third website that sent her heart racing. *Villa Paradiso's,* a four-star hotel, had a professional home page with high-definition images of a pristine, modern white structure surrounded by jungle. It was the same glossy building in Hettie's photos. The contacts listed on the hotel's website were *Rapoosa, Copán, Honduras.* Lea shot out of her chair. *Gotcha!* One hundred bucks says the Phalanx mining site was near *Rapoosa.*

39

AGAINST THE GRAY sky peeking through the skyscrapers on Park Avenue, a dark bank of clouds roiled as if readying for a storm. In the driver's seat of the Lancia, sleep deprivation—dry mouth, aching shoulders, and burning eyes—battled for attention against aching toes. Dom's mind spun with a smoldering anger. That bastard bully Claude Van Buren and his soulless Rittenhouse Equity partners were going to pay for having Micah Zapata killed and Hettie kidnapped.

Lea rang on her cellphone. "I used Hettie's photos to confirm where they went. We were right, they went up to the province of Copán. During the day they searched for the bird in an area east of a national park. At night they stayed at a hotel called the Villa Paradiso. It's the only four-star place in the whole North West sector."

This was good news. "Nice work."

"It gets better. I called the hotel. They have records of Hettie and Micah staying there three weeks ago. Dom, it's coming together."

Traffic was picking up with the arrival of rush hour. A taxi at high speed narrowly missed the Lancia's side-view mirror.

They were filling in the jigsaw puzzle, and their suspicions were correct. "Really good work, Lea." These goddamned bastards were going to pay.

"Also, I've got the surveillance up and running on the Rittenhouse foursome. They haven't called each other in the last two days. In fact, none of them—not Van Buren, Chase, Coll, or Atkins—have used their cell since your meeting this morning."

The bastards were going dark. They were circling the wagons, trying to figure out their next play. "Keep me posted."

"Copy that. Where are you?"

In the stark lobby of the office building, Chase Craig, aka Mustache and Rittenhouse Equity's jowly partner, scurried across the marble on stubby legs. A blue tailored suit couldn't hide a pear shape.

Red-hot anger shot through Dom's veins. "I'm about to turn up the heat on the Rittenhouse foursome."

"Fucking righteous warrior! You go, girl."

Dom turned the ignition key and the Lancia growled.

Forty minutes later, Dom flashed her badge at the maitre d' of an expensive Italian restaurant on Sullivan Street in Soho. The air was thick with garlic, herbs, and sirloin as she made her way past candles and small talk toward a table in the back. Mustache sniffed a cork offered by a sommelier and smiled greedily at a slender woman twenty years his junior but froze when he recognized Dom.

She stopped within a foot of the table. "Hello, Chase."

"What do you want?" he asked flatly.

"Just a quick question."

He blinked.

"How well do you know Claude Van Buren?"

He squinted.

"Do you know him well enough to go to jail for him?"

His eyes widened, and his lips clamped.

"Today I'm offering a deal." She gently laid her card by his fork. "To one of you. Only one. I need to know about the crimes against Micah Zapata and Hettie Van Buren." She leaned into his ear, catching the hint of briny sweat. "Chase, you don't want one of your cronies taking my offer first."

Out on the street, Dom's phone rang.

It was Lea. "Your two NYPD detectives found a match on the prints out at JFK. The guy who killed Micah entered the States in Miami on early Sunday morning. His name is Jose Onofre. From Honduras. I'm chasing him down with help from the US Embassy in Honduras."

The jigsaw puzzle was fitting together quickly now. "Nice work. Keep me posted."

Thirty minutes later, Dom waited in the bright lobby of a residential building on the Upper East Side as suited professionals strode briskly across black and white tiles, briefcases and handbags swinging. Dom stood as the horsey Patricia Coll, General Counsel of Rittenhouse Equity, strode through the front door. "Ms. Coll."

Startled, Horsey faltered. "What are you doing?"

"Have you got a minute?" Dom indicated the gray flannel couch she had been using.

Horsey shook her head. "No. As a matter of fact, I don't. This is highly unusual."

"Actually, it's not."

"You can meet me in our offices."

"Or here."

Horsey checked for onlookers before sitting on the couch and placing her large satchel purse by an ankle.

Dom sat close. "You seem anxious."

"I am."

"Why is that?"

"My colleague's daughter is missing, a man has been murdered, and an FBI agent is questioning me at my residence. It is stressful."

"Yeah. I get that."

Horsey stared ahead.

"So," Dom said. "You know why I'm here."

Horsey remained still.

"How well do you know Claude Van Buren?"

"Well enough. I've worked closely with him for ten years."

"And what is your impression of Claude Van Buren?"

"Is he suspect?"

Dom grinned. "Yes."

Horsey blinked, yanked her purse, and stood quickly. "I will require the presence of a lawyer to discuss this case any further with you. I'll have the office send you my lawyer's name."

"Yeah." Dom stood. "I thought you'd say that. But being a lawyer, you know how this goes." She held out her card. "Today, I'm offering a deal for information about the crimes against Micah Zapata and Hettie Van Buren. I only need one of you to tell the story. The rest of you will be hung out to dry."

Horsey gaped but a manicured hand snatched the card.

An hour later, dusk had settled, shadows had lengthened, and street lights had flickered on. The sports car was parked in the gloom across from a red brick townhouse in Vinegar Hill, Brooklyn. Double black doors topped an impressive front stair. The blood in Dom's veins pumped forcefully from a mix of anger and caffeine. Five minutes earlier she had sunk eye drops into her scratchy eyes. It hadn't helped.

The phone rang. "Nothing," Lea said. "Total silence. Not a single one of the Rittenhouse four has made a call."

Dom's eyes were trained on the black doors. "It's coming. It will happen tonight."

"I've tracked down Jose Onofre. He has a record. A long sheet. Dom, you're not going to believe this next bit. Onofre works for the one and only Phalanx."

The blood in her veins clanged. "Goddamn it. Bastards."

Their theory was proving accurate. The jigsaw puzzle was filling in. One, four months ago, the Van Burens forbade Hettie to travel to developing countries. Two, in an act of vindication, Hettie identified a Rittenhouse investment in Copán Province, Honduras that was a possible habitat of the beloved Eskimo curlew. Three, together Hettie and Micah had planned the trip, found a tour guide, traveled to Copán, and spotted the Eskimo curlew. Four, upon their return, Hettie informed Rittenhouse that the land was to be protected. Five, standing to lose $76 million, Rittenhouse called Phalanx. Six, Phalanx sent Onofre to get rid of the problem.

Dom hissed, "Goddamned bastards."

"I mean what were they thinking to call in Phalanx?"

"They didn't expect us to connect them to the Honduras mining site."

The photo of Hettie and Micah smiling outside the Honduran airport flashed in front of Dom's burning eyes, and the anger in her veins turned to lava. These bastards were not going to get away with it. She wanted one of these four to break tonight. "Keep an eye on those phones."

"Roger that." Lea rang off.

The black doors of the townhouse opened, and Roger Atkins, aka Runner, appeared at the top of the stairs in a T-shirt and running tights. Dom set her coffee cup in the cup holder, reached for the door handle, and unwound from the car. Runner clocked her immediately. It was no surprise that the head of security of a billion-dollar private equity fund was smart and attentive. She leaned back against the car and slowly crossed her arms, resisting the urge to walk over and punch his smug face.

Runner jogged down the stairs and paused on the sidewalk. There was no fear behind the intense eyes. He was smart, attentive, and tough.

"I'm going to find Hettie," she said. "We're connecting the dots already. I'm going to bring her back." She held out her card. "If you were involved in any way in these crimes, I will make it my lifelong mission to put you in jail for a very long time. But today, I'm offering one of you a deal."

With a final cold stare, Runner turned and jogged down the street. Smart, attentive, tough and potentially dangerous.

But it didn't matter. She was closing in. She and Lea were 90 percent there. *I'm coming, Hettie. Hold on just a little bit longer.*

Watching his figure move into the shadows, she lowered the business card.

40

A Charlatan King in Rapoosa
@LastCurlew

Five hours of stillness
and the roar of the plane's engines.
There will be heat,
vapor and foreign tongues
awaiting their touch down.

Red soil greets tires
birthing dust clouds
that obscure hungry eyes
and empty stalls.

Hours later
the white Hotel of Paradise
inside a waterfall's murmur
within a thundering jungle.

A candlelit terrace

with silent waiters
and white tablecloths.
Beyond the foliage,
radiates a blood red sky.

A charlatan king's gleaming eyes.
A bright red sky!
Heralds tomorrow, Father crows,
to Rapoosa did Kubla Khan
send our quest.

The morning cracks the whip
as the squad prepares.
A mission beckons
with treasures of gold and silver
for corrupt men.

41

THE TOUR OFFICE was located just off the museum's Roosevelt Rotunda. Pushing through the swing door, Mila stepped into the swampy outer office. Framed photos of the various exhibits cluttered all four walls. A single phone was ringing in the back office. At the reception desk, a pimply high schooler in a blue uniform pushed pamphlets into plexiglass holders.

"Mike Hampton here?" Mila asked.

The teenager pointed at the back office.

Five minutes later, she and the bony Mike Hampton were watching the scene taking place outside the winter gala. Mila reached over and paused the image on the moment the Van Burens stepped into the light at the top of the stairs. "Here, just here. I want to know what they say to each other."

Twerpy Mike whined, "That's totally not okay, Mila."

She said nothing.

"It's an invasion of privacy," he squeaked.

"It's two minutes of dialog."

"What are you after?"

Cold sweat pinged across her skin. She would have to lie.

"Listen, totally off the record, these guys made a donation to the museum library, specifically to our library. I want to know why the protestors targeted them." The delivery had been cumbersome. She held her breath.

"Mila, I know these are the Van Burens. You're full of crap. This is about Hettie, isn't it?"

Her heart rate spiked, and her face flushed. She had never been good on the social skills. Getting caught by Twerpy Mike was excruciating, and she cringed.

"Whatever." Twerpy Mike shook his head. "I'll do it, but I'll deny it if anyone asks."

"Deal. I was never here. We never spoke."

"When I hold up my right hand, it's Mr. Van Buren talking. When I hold up my left hand, it's the wife talking."

Mila nodded.

On the screen, Claude Van Buren inspected his wife's stained coat before turning to the protestors and yelling.

On the screen, Yvette Van Buren's face was tight with anger.

Claude Van Buren turned back to his wife and reached to touch her but she recoiled.

Twerpy Mike raised his hand as Claude Van Buren's lips moved. "It's fake blood. Those bastards."

"They are here, in the city." Yvette Van Buren was livid.

"Yes."

"This is can, isn't it?"

"Yes... "

Twerpy Mike tapped the space bar to pause the video. "I think they said, 'Can' but I can't be sure. My lip reading isn't exact, and it's complicated by the fact that they aren't facing me. Lots of words look the same. You kinda have to know the context."

"Can? As in C-A-N?" Mila asked.

"Yeah."

Mila nodded.

Twerpy Mike hit play, and Claude Van Buren's lips moved. "Yes... I think it probably is."

"Damn you, Claude." Yvette Van Buren appeared to hiss.

"I'll take care of it."

"My home, Claude. They're attacking me here in my city, my home. Do something."

Behind her parents, Miss Timid Hettie appeared in the light.

Yvette Van Buren brushed past both.

Hettie asked her father, "What's that all about?"

"Nothing." It was the only word Claude Van Buren spoke as he turned toward the party.

Mila raced back to the intern alcove and hurtled into the chair. Pulling up the internet, she searched for environmental groups in New York. The search returned fifteen names including the Climate Action Network, whose nickname was CAN and who had been mentioned in a recent article, *NEW YORK CITY >> This Wednesday members from a local environmental group, the Climate Action Network (CAN), were arrested at 9 pm outside an event at the New York Fashion Week.*

What were the odds that there was more than one organization that protested red carpet events and had a similar or same acronym as CAN? Infinitesimal. The odds were literally infinitesimal. Why was CAN throwing fake blood on Yvette Van Buren? Goosebumps puckered along Mila's arms. How had the Van Burens known which organization it was? Boy, oh boy, this sure felt like some kind of mystery. Mila looked up the contact information for CAN. Their office was located on 2nd

Avenue by Gramercy Park. That wasn't far by bike. She would confirm CAN and call Agent Cool Cucumber.

Five minutes later, fresh air hit Mila's face as she raced into the underground driveway. She clicked the bike helmet's chin strap and adjusted the backpack. Reaching her bike, she clipped her pants legs, unlocked the Kryptonite claw, and slipped it in the holder. In the dark, a bus heading uptown chugged acrid exhaust. With one foot on a pedal, she pushed the bike out onto the sidewalk and threw her right leg over in an ingrained movement. For the millionth time she wondered if that action would build up her right butt muscles oddly, like the rollerbladers.

The quickest route was straight down 7th Avenue. It was a new route for her, and the thought of departure from the regular route caused her heart to thump. All in the name of Miss Timid Hettie. She sped out onto West Central Park drive, merged into the headlights of heavy traffic, hooked a left at West 84th Street, weaved through cars, and hooked a left southbound on Columbus Avenue. Her feet spun as she shifted into a high gear. Streetlights rushed past.

Fifteen minutes later, she slowed on 2nd Avenue and stopped by a signpost. She dismounted and locked the bike. Slipping in earphones, she pulled out her cell phone and pretended to listen to music while she got her bearings. Across the street, CAN's office was a tall townhouse with a large green door and a brass nameplate. A nearby streetlight threw down a white circle across tall stairs. With her cell phone, she snapped photos from various angles of the front door, just in case the FBI agent needed them. She moved up the street, turned and passed the green door again. Now what?

She had stopped by the entrance to a coffee shop with a large window on the street. It might be a good look out and place to regroup. Inside, the empty space was a homage to raw pale wood and handmade chalk signs. The air smelled of sugar and tangy, burned-earth coffee.

Mila ordered a drip coffee at the counter from a diffident red-headed girl who didn't smile much. By the front window, she poured in sugar and half-and-half into her cup.

She turned back to the counter and Diffident Girl. "Can I ask you a question?"

Diffident Girl nodded.

"You work here very long?"

Diffident Girl gave her a funny look. "Yeah, about a year."

Mila glanced out the front windows at the CAN entrance. It was a long shot, but what the hell? She pulled out her phone, found a photo of Hettie, and handed it to Diffident Girl. "This woman ever come in here?"

"Yeah. Actually yeah. A few times."

What were the odds that this was not related to the gala and the video? Infinitesimal. "Recently?"

"Yeah, like a few months ago, maybe?"

"You remember what she did?"

Diffident Girl shrugged. "She got coffee."

Mila smiled awkwardly. Small talk was not in her wheelhouse.

"Yo, she sat by the window."

Bingo. Hettie was casing CAN. "How many times has she come here?"

"I dunno."

"But she sat by the window?"

"That's what I said."

"Thanks." Mila chose a table by the window and stared at the green door of CAN. The coffee tasted sour. After a long moment, she pulled up the photo of the FBI card with Domini Walker's phone number and slowly pressed the eleven numbers. Some things were worth spontaneity. Scratch that.

Only a very few things were worth spontaneity. Helping to find Hettie was one of those rare things.

The agent answered on the second ring. "Walker."

Mila cleared her throat. "My name is Mila Pascale."

"Yes?"

Mila swallowed. "I think I may have something for you."

"Okay?"

Across the street, the green of the CAN door stood out brightly against the streetlight. The skin behind Mila's ears tingled. "The odds just really speak for themselves. The odds are ... uh ... overwhelming."

"I'm listening."

"It's about Hettie Van Buren."

"I'm definitely listening."

"I'm friends with Hettie at work. I know you're looking for her. I've done some snooping on her social media. I found out she writes. She writes on the side, under a pen name. She posts on Wattpad under the pen name @ LastCurlew."

Silence.

"But that's not as important as something else I've found."

Silence.

Through the coffee shop window, the CAN green door was mesmerizing. "Four months ago an environmental group named CAN protested a museum gala. They threw fake blood on Hettie's mom."

Silence.

"CAN is located near Gramercy Park. There's a coffee shop across the street. After the gala, Hettie came here, to the coffee shop. I think she came here, sat by the window, to stake out CAN."

"Where are you now, Ms. Pascale?"

"At the coffee shop. By the window."

"What's the address of the coffee shop?"

Mila gave it to her.

"Don't move, Ms. Pascale. I'm coming to you."

"Okay."

"Don't move," the agent insisted. "Stand like a statue."

When things were unpredictable, when everything had been turned upside down, when life had kicked you out of safe routines, it was important to get the small things right. "I'm sitting."

"Then stay seated, Miss Pascale. But by all things honorable and necessary, you stay right there."

Agent Cool Cucumber was gone.

THE OFFICES of CAN were in a converted townhouse in Gramercy Park. The front reception area was covered in brightly colored posters displaying natural resources: a huge canopy of tropical trees reached towering heights, a crashing waterfall misted over rocks, and the gentle black eyes of an orangutan peered out from behind green leaves. Even at eight pm, open doors along the first floor released the ringing of phones and the peal of laughter. The overall vibe was of proud optimism.

Dom flashed her FBI shield at an unimpressed millennial receptionist. "I'd like to speak with your Executive Director. My name is Special Agent Domini Walker. Tell him—"

"It's a woman," she interrupted.

"Tell her that I'd just like ten minutes of her time please."

The millennial picked up the phone and dialed three numbers, watching Dom with a fearless gaze, and said, "There is an FBI agent here who would like to meet with Eileen please." She listened. "Yes, okay." She hung up the phone. "Our Executive Director is not here, but our Deputy ED is." She indicated a short hallway behind her desk. "He'll meet you in the conference room down on the left."

The conference room, painted a warm orange and covered in more posters, had one slim window with a view of brick wall.

A tall Asian man in his thirties with smooth skin and a confident air, strode in with an outstretched hand. His eyes were clear and gentle, as if he had no secrets. "George Gao. I'm the Deputy Executive Director of CAN."

"FBI Special Agent Domini Walker," she said as they shook hands. "I wonder if I can have a few moments of your time?"

"Of course." He indicated the scarred conference table.

As they sat, Dom said, "I am investigating a case that I believe may have something to do with your organization."

"Okay?"

"George, do you know Claude and Yvette Van Buren?"

He tensed. "Personally? No."

"But you know of them?"

He squinted. "Of course."

Mila Pascale, the odd little mouse of a museum researcher, had divulged some very interesting information. In fact, odd little Mila may have stumbled on the provocation event that triggered this whole saga. Time to put that theory to the test. "Three months ago the Van Burens attended a gala at the Natural History Museum. On their way in, I believe one of your colleagues threw fake blood on them."

He straightened. "Yes."

"You know about this?"

"Yes. We have paid the fines."

"Why were the Van Burens targeted?"

"Because Claude Van Buren runs a private equity firm called Rittenhouse." He chose his words slowly. "We at CAN are aware of him because he makes investments in extractive companies."

"And that is relevant to CAN?"

"Agent Walker, we are an environmental activist group. We keep an eye on all things that damage our planet. I'm not sure how informed you are about climate change ..."

"Enough."

"Earth is on—currently—a trajectory with ruinous consequences. Overwhelming environmental disruption, massive economic instability. Man-made climate change is potentially catastrophic. We believe that unless this trajectory is changed, we are all in for a future we won't recognize." None of his micro tells indicated misrepresentation. His gaze was direct and sincere. "Not enough people are taking it seriously. Bankers, in particular, are not taking it seriously. Their interest is very much on the short term. Selfishly. Tragically. For the rest of us."

"As in, they want to make short-term profits?"

"Yes. At the expense of the planet's future. Their behavior is in fact, illogical if they have children, because the damage they are reaping will be left behind. But people behave irrationally often. Particularly when greed is involved." He crossed his arms. "We keep a sharp, focused eye on those actors in the financial sector who negatively influence climate change."

"Like Claude Van Buren?"

"Rittenhouse Equity enables extractive companies to flourish despite their tenuous economic shelf life."

"So you monitor his firm?"

George shrugged. "As much as we can. Rittenhouse's investments—most private equity firms—are not public, so we glean what we can. Much of the financial sector is opaque. Unfortunately for the humans and fauna of the planet."

"Why protest Claude or Yvette Van Buren? That seems extreme."

"To you, I'm sure it does. But there are very few opportunities we have as citizens to voice our concerns."

"I'm not sure throwing fake blood made the point."

"With respect, Agent, I'm not sure it didn't."

She leaned in. "George, Hettie Van Buren is missing."

He froze. Eyes widened, pupils dilated, and nostrils flared. This was news to him and it caused immediate stress. "Do you know Hettie Van Buren?"

He glanced left and nodded.

"Have you ever met Hettie Van Buren?"

His voice was soft. "She's missing?"

"Yes."

"Since when?"

"Late Sunday night, as far as we can tell."

He blew out his cheeks. "She came here."

"When?"

"After the protest at the gala. A few months back."

Dom's heart rate picked up a beat. "What were your impressions?"

"She was quiet."

"What did she want?"

"She wanted to know why we targeted her parents. She wanted to know why we were protesting them, why we threw the blood on her mother."

Dom's nerves fired and her skin hummed. "The Eskimo curlew," she said it as a statement, not a question.

His brow furrowed.

"The Eskimo curlew in Honduras. Hettie spotted one and was going to shut down a mining site."

"What?" Shaking his head, he said, "No. That's not what we discussed with Hettie Van Buren."

Wait. What? Confusion braked Dom's thoughts. "This isn't about the Eskimo curlew in Honduras?"

"No. It's about Honduras, but not the Eskimo curlew. It's a long story, so let me start at the beginning." He settled against the chair. "Five years ago, Rittenhouse Equity bought into a Honduran mining company named Phalanx. With the investment they were able to develop a new silver mine near a small village named Rapoosa—"

"Yes, we know that. Hettie found an Eskimo curlew in Rapoosa—" Dom's mind was stuttering.

"No, Special Agent. That is what I am telling you. This has nothing to do with a bird."

This had nothing to do with Eskimo curlews? Dom leaned back in her chair.

"The villagers of Rapoosa did not want Phalanx mining near their homes. They had seen and heard about the environmental damage of other mines. They did not want the site. So they protested. They went to the capital city and marched outside Phalanx's office. They put up roadblocks on the dirt road leading to the planned site. But it didn't matter. The local law enforcement and government were on Phalanx's side." He clasped his hands in his lap and his face fell. "This is where the story turns tragic. Five years ago, on November eighth, the night before the groundbreaking at the site was to commence, Phalanx sent thugs to clear out the village. All the villagers were evicted and their houses were burned to the ground. Special Agent, there are very credible allegations of serious human rights abuses that occurred that night. By morning, the village of Rapoosa had been leveled and the construction of the mine began."

What George Gao was telling her was an entirely new story that didn't yet add up. How did this relate to Hettie? Dom stumbled to put the new jigsaw pieces into place.

"What we don't know is if Rittenhouse Equity knew about the events on November eighth or about the abuses. To be clear, mining is a very dirty industry. What happens in far flung, under-developed countries with limited or corrupted law enforcement can be horrendous."

"Why did you protest them at the gala four months ago?"

He raised his eyebrows. "Well, clearly, Claude Van Buren attending an event at a natural history museum is overwhelming in its hypocrisy." He unclasped his hands. "But we wanted to send him a message."

"What was that?"

"We wanted to let Claude Van Buren know that we were on to him, that we suspected Rittenhouse knew about the abuses in Rapoosa."

"And that message was heard by Hettie. She came here to figure out why CAN protested her parents?"

"Yes, she did. I told her the truth. I told her that I didn't know if Rittenhouse knew. We don't know if her father knew what happened at Rapoosa. We assume he knew but we don't know for sure."

Oh lord. Hettie and Micah went to Rapoosa three weeks ago to dig up dirt on Claude. They went to investigate how much Claude knew about the abuses. "Did you know that Hettie went to Rapoosa three weeks ago?"

He nodded sadly.

"It's not only Hettie missing. Her boyfriend traveled with her to Rapoosa and he has been murdered."

George reared back. "What?"

She nodded.

"Jesus." He cleared his throat. "What Rittenhouse Equity, what Claude Van Buren knew and when, matters now as part of a much bigger story ..."

Oh lord, this gets bigger?

"A month after the events of November eighth, a huge Canadian mining conglomerate bought Phalanx for an astronomical price—"

"Did they know about the abuses?"

"Again, we don't know what the Canadian firm knew. Many of the big mining conglomerates, mostly based in Canada, deal with these issues all the time." He placed his hands on the table and hung his head. "Her missing, the boyfriend, it all makes sense."

Chills coursed through her veins. "Why?"

"Because of the court case."

Dom's heart pumped frozen slush. "What court case?"

He spoke to the table top. "That Canadian mining conglomerate ..."

"Yes?"

"That bought Phalanx?"

"Yes."

"They are going on trial. For human rights abuses. To answer questions about how much they knew about the human rights abuses in Rapoosa. In Toronto. On Monday."

Slush froze to ice. She leaned in. "Will this trial examine what Rittenhouse knew?"

"Yes."

"Was Hettie going to testify?"

"It is a closely guarded secret, but yes, Hettie is going to testify."

From across the table, George seemed very far, as if, in the last millisecond, her perspective had changed completely, and the blurry missing pieces of the jigsaw puzzle sharpened into focus as they drifted into view. The crimes weren't committed to save $76 million a year. The threat was much larger than that. This was now a threat to mining conglomerate. "If Claude Van Buren knew about the abuses, it would be very damaging to Rittenhouse and this Canadian behemoth?"

George nodded.

"Both their reputations could be devastated. At a bare minimum it could destroy Rittenhouse?"

He continued to nod.

Instead of killing Hettie, as they had done Micah, Rittenhouse Equity had kidnapped her to prevent her from testifying. "If Hettie had proof that her father knew about the abuses, she could present this at trial?"

He nodded.

From the earlier meeting in the apartment overlooking Central Park, Yvette's strange words repeated themselves, *"Reputation is important in this town, Agent. It's everything."* Hettie and Micah had proof that could bring down Rittenhouse Equity. "If Claude knew about the abuses, this could put Rittenhouse Equity out of business. It would destroy his firm and his reputation."

The corners of George's lips turned up in an ironic smile. "Indeed. It's what we're hoping."

With an enormous crashing sound, the surface of the frozen lake broke and a million icebergs ricocheted apart.

THURSDAY NIGHT

Then the thunder burst a second time and a violent but invisible blow blasted two of the biggest feathers from one of his extended wings. The impact twisted him completely over in midair and he thudded into the earth at the female's side. Terrified and bewildered at a foe that could strike without visible form.

    —Fred Bodsworth, "Last of the Curlews"

43

30,000 FEET over South Carolina

Before the plane left Honduras, while they were still on the runway, the pilot had spoken in Spanish through a tinny intercom. She thought he had explained the rituals of preparation for flight, but she wasn't sure because he spoke very quickly and her Spanish was not good since she had left school when she was ten years old to help her aging parents. Then the pilot had spoken in English and she became very nervous. Was she missing key information about the flight? About how to prepare? She glanced left, but the older gentleman had closed his eyes. On her right, the teen boy with spiked hair stared absently out the window at the runway's lights. No one appeared nervous. A woman in a uniform was making her way down the center aisle checking people's seat belts with a smile. The smile made Maria feel a bit better.

That was two hours ago. Now the stiff seat between the two men felt confining. She couldn't move her arms. She hadn't been confined in years and she wanted to get up and run down the aisle. Was no one else in this flying aluminum can, pried into these uncomfortable, narrow seats quietly suffering like a goat with a tether wound tightly around an ankle? The cold wormed through the woven threads of the big sweater and ate at her skin. She had not imagined the blue sky that housed the beaming sun would be so cold.

One aisle forward a mother tried to soothe a fussy infant. The baby was small, only a few weeks old, with dazed eyes trying to focus on the lights in the ceiling and a tender cry. The baby was not as small as Ines was at that age. The midwife had warned her that Ines may not survive she was so little, that such tiny lungs may not be capable of filling the blood with oxygen. Old village grandmothers that came to visit had warned about holding baby Ines' head, don't let it roll or it may break the neck. She had been so sure that Ines' round head would tumble and break her thin neck before the lungs had time to grow that for weeks she had been filled with fear to pick up her daughter. But every day tiny Ines had sucked the milk greedily, had burped with a sigh, had fisted long hair in a tiny hand, and had transferred strength to her mother, building a fierce mother wolf. It was not the only thing that had taught her strength.

It occurred to her that having survived Tegucigalpa, she had now also conquered a big city. She had stared down its belching cars, thunderous market places, teeming sidewalks, and superior, well-dressed dwellers. It no longer felt as threatening as before. Funny how that worked. When the unknown becomes known, it is no longer a threat.

Maybe she should take Ines to the city. Let it be known and understood. She did not want her daughter to be afraid.

Funny what you realize while freezing in a flying can.

44

"HETTIE DISCOVERED INFORMATION"— Dom gasped, leaning on her knees to catch her breath, —"that could bring down Rittenhouse Equity."

Raindrops slapped against the windows of Fontaine's office. Light from streetlights flickered against quivering rivulets. Behind his desk, Fontaine's hard eyes were inscrutable.

Ten minutes earlier, Dom had sprinted out of the CAN office, gunned the Lancia through traffic, squealed into an illegal spot by the security post, and raced through the halls of the Javits building.

"The information"— she panted—"that Hettie discovered will destroy Claude Van Buren's reputation. It will destroy Rittenhouse Equity's reputation. They will go out of business."

Fontaine steepled fingers against his lips with impenetrable thoughtfulness.

Hettie, I'm coming. I'm so close now. "Five years ago, a Honduran mining company cleared a village for a new mine. Rittenhouse was an investor. The company evicted the residents, burned the homes to the ground, and physically abused the villagers. Later, Rittenhouse sold their shares of the mining company to a Canadian conglomerate. Now the Canadian conglomerate is on trial for the crimes." She stood and placed hands on her head to open her chest. "We think Hettie confirmed Claude knew of the crimes."

He stared at her.

She dropped her arms. "It's all about the trial. It starts on Monday. They killed Micah and stole Hettie to prevent their testimony."

"How confident are you?"

Hettie, I'm coming. No matter what, I'm coming. "Very. Everything fits together. Hettie and Micah went to Honduras. They found out about the crimes. Hettie threatened Claude and Rittenhouse. It pushed them over the edge."

"Them?" He held up a finger, his eyes locking in on her face. "Do you know who orchestrated the crimes?"

She shook her head. "Not yet, I don't."

"Do you have admissible evidence linking Rittenhouse directly to the crimes?"

"Not yet. No. But all the clues are adding up."

He squinted. "What *is* the status of the investigation?"

"I've made the offer of a deal to all four. One of them will break. Tonight."

It was a moment of truth. Would Fontaine bow to political pressure and pull her off the case? *The monsters don't get to keep you, Hettie.* She would continue the search no matter what Fontaine or the Bureau instructed. *Fidelity, bravery, and integrity.*

He turned to the window and watched the rain.

"Sir, one of them will break. I'll get her back. I'll get Hettie back."

His nod was sharp and definitive. "Okay, agreed. We wait

for one of them to break. You get her back. Make sure you have something admissible for court."

I'm coming, Hettie! She bounded from the room.

As Dom rushed across the cubicle floor, Lea shook her head.

Dom slowed as she reached the desk. "Nothing? None of them have made any calls?" She was sure the Rittenhouse principals would have broken while she was in with George Gao at CAN and Fontaine upstairs.

"Nothing," Lea said softly. "None of them have used their cell phones since this morning. Even fools are thought wise if they keep silent. Proverbs."

"You're watching them?"

Lea pointed to the left screen. "Fuck, yes, I am!"

"Okay, now it's a waiting game." Dom settled into the seat. It was instant relief on her throbbing toes. In the photo taped to the computer screen, Hettie's smile was full of happiness, confidence, and love. "Damn it. I thought at least one of them would have panicked by now. There should at least be lawyers."

"Maybe they need more time?"

Dom pressed her palms into aching eyes. "Still. Now we know that at least one of them is guilty as sin.

"I found an article that confirms CAN's story about the trial."

Dom squinted at the screen and the article in Canada Today with the title, *Orion Extractives Faces The Music.* Lea had highlighted the last paragraph.

"The defendants will argue that the Canadian company, Orion Extractives, has a responsibility for environmental and human rights abuses perpetrated by foreign subsidiaries. The trial will attempt to uncover who knew what and when. The defendants will argue that those who knew about these crimes are

responsible under Canadian—not Honduran—law. For perhaps the first time in the tragic history of the world's mining sector, someone will be held accountable. Orion Extractives is an enormous corporate entity with annual revenues of $41 billion. The trial is expected to be explosive."

Dom shook her head. "So much sloshing money, so much motive."

"Your riches are corrupted," Lea intoned, "and your garments are moth eaten. James. So what do you think Hettie and Micah found? What evidence?"

"It has to do with her father knowing about the crimes in the village. It's got to be." Dom cracked her neck.

"Who is this museum chick that called you?"

"Her name is Mila Pascale. She knows Hettie from work. An odd little duck. A research intern at the museum. She made the connection to CAN. She found a video from a gala three months ago. It's what provoked this whole thing. I haven't seen it yet. Have you watched it?"

"Not yet. I've just pulled it up." Lea clicked the video open.

They both watched as snowflakes swirled in a light breeze against the backdrop of a muted sunset. Along Central Park West, a line of thirty cars dropped off guests. Women in long coats and gowns laughed with men in tuxedos as they proceeded up the grand stairs carpeted in red. Bright spotlights blinked on, illuminating the festivities as the sky darkened.

In the lower right corner of the screen three individuals appeared. Dom whispered, "The CAN protestors."

Blinking coronas of light hovered around streetlights in the distance. The three were dressed in dark colors and walking slowly but determinedly toward the stairs. They positioned themselves in the shadows by the base of the stairs. Cars thinned against the blackness of the night. A snowflake settled on the camera lens and a gloved finger wiped it off. Throughout, the three dark figures stood like statues in the shadows. Eventually there were no more cars. But the figures remained.

A dark Mercedes appeared at the end of the block, pulled slowly to the curb, and a valet ran to open the driver side door. Claude emerged. Dom straightened.

Claude walked around the sedan and collected his wife dressed in a long fur coat against the cold.

As the Van Burens reached the shadows, a protestor stepped forward with a downward slice of an arm. Liquid splattered across Yvette's fur coat. Claude, oblivious, strolled toward the steps. Yvette paused and turned toward the shadows.

Dom whispered, "Pause that."

Lea clicked the mouse.

"Rewind and play in slow."

On the screen, the movements crawled. The protestor's arm swung in slow motion. A wavering dark clump sailed through the air. Yvette jerked as she felt the liquid hit her coat. Startled, Yvette turned toward the shadows, peering into the dark. She said something before she took a step toward the shadows.

"Stop," Dom whispered. "Rewind."

The wavering liquid splattered across Yvette's fur coat. She turned toward the shadows. She peered into the darkness. She said something. She took a step off the red carpet toward the darkness. Yvette had taken a step toward unknown assailants hidden in shadows.

Dom bolted from the chair as adrenaline punched against the dull, thick thinking of exhaustion.

Yvette had stepped toward dark shadows where an unknown assailant had thrown something at her.

Intuition whispered into the fog of Dom's fatigue. She walked slowly to the dark window. Rain hit the glass with a *spat-spat-spat*. From deep inside her eardrum, a faint hiss emerged. The gears in Dom's mind nudged into motion. Yvette had stepped toward an assailant. The hiss grew louder. Yvette's fearlessness was out of character, the audacity in the video did not correspond to the emotionally broken woman from earlier today.

Dom's eyes ricocheted across the room noticing the indentations in the white painted bricks as craters on a moon, the dried drips of paint as tears trapped in time. Mothers were capable of many things. What had Yvette said? *Reputation is important in this town, Agent. It's everything.* What had she said next? *It keeps your friends close and your enemies at bay. It keeps the family moving into the future. It ensures progress.*

The hair at the nape of Dom's neck quivered. Three days ago, Hettie had opened the door to her kidnapper—there had been no sign of forced entry because she had known her kidnapper. Was a mother capable of such a thing?

The hiss blew through Dom's mind like a train entering a subway station.

Yes. A mother is capable of many things. The dog-eared memory of the barren Brooklyn apartment flooded Dom's senses. In the memory, Aunt Lucille straightened a white shirt over a flat chest. *Your mother is not coming back.*

Dom turned from the window and shouted to Lea. "Are you watching Yvette's phone?"

The bottom half of Lea's mouth dropped open.

"Pull up her phone."

Lea whispered, "Oh shit." Her fingers flew across the keyboard as her eyes scanned the screen. "For the last twenty-four hours she was up by Central Park. But—" Lea's eyes widened to saucers. "She's moved."

Dom strode to the desk, her mind clear and focused. "Where is she?"

"Philadelphia. Looks like a suburb of Philly called Gladwyne."

Dom bolted across the floor. "Search Yvette's calls going back a month."

"You think it was Yvette? You think this was her plan from the beginning?"

Dom broke into a sprint. "Check her calls. I bet she called Phalanx. In Honduras. For Jose Onofre to kill Micah. Confirm there was a call."

"Poison of a viper is under their lips. Psalm 140. Holy mother of God, you think it was Yvette?"

"Yes!" Dom yelled from the door. "And Onofre didn't kidnap Hettie."

Forensics was on the second floor. It was staffed twenty-four hours a day. Fluorescent tubes glared unnaturally bright across rows of white laminate tables overflowing with machines and clinic boxes. Dom raced to Becky Turnball at the far end and skidded to a stop. "Where's that box of evidence from Hettie Van Buren's apartment?"

Becky Turnball darted to a shelving unit, yanked down a cardboard box, and set it at the end of the lab counter. "What do you need?"

"The stuff from inside the dishwasher."

Becky Turnball flicked a large sheet of white paper across the counter, and both women snapped on white plastic gloves. They set down five glasses wrapped in Ziploc bags—three mismatched highball glasses and two matching short crystal glasses. Dom pointed to the matched set. "Those. Those two. I need to know if there's residual."

Yanking a cotton swab, Becky Turnball squeezed liquid from a plastic bottle on the tip, ran it inside the glass, and immediately followed with a dry swab. Hurrying to the gas chromatography–mass spectrometry machine, she inserted the swabs and hit start. The machine kicked up a whir.

She said, "It will take a bit."

With a racing heart, Dom marched across the room. If her suspicions were proven, the whole investigation had just turned on a dime.

Stewart Walker whispered, *Wait for it, Dom, wait for it. Let the evidence show you the way.*

When she reached the wall, she spun and marched back under the glare of the bright lights. As she reached the machine, it fell silent.

Becky Turnball glanced to the screen. "Yup. Evidence of benzodiazepine or GHB."

Benzodiazepine or gamms-hydroxybutyric acid were psychotropic drugs that caused loss of inhibitions or consciousness. Yvette had roofied her own daughter.

Stewart Walker murmured, *That's my girl.*

From the hallway, Lea skidded into the door frame. "Dom! You're right! Yvette called Phalanx. Last week!"

A thousand jigsaw pieces flew through the air and landed snugly in the image of pale, perfect Yvette. After returning from Honduras, Hettie threatened to testify at the trial against Claude. The testimony would ruin the family reputation. Yvette called Phalanx and arranged for their thug, Jose Onofre, to kill Micah Zapata. On the designated night, Yvette parked in the loading zone of the Washington Square building, took the elevator to her daughter's apartment, placed a pill in Hettie's drink, and waited. Sometime after, Hettie headed into the bedroom, stumbled, and fell against the wall, smashing the glass on the picture frame and overturning the jewelry bowl. Once the pill had taken effect, Yvette walked Hettie down the back stairs to the loading dock and into the car. The plan was to hide

Hettie outside Philadelphia at the family estate long enough for the trial to come and go.

Becky Turnball broke the silence. "Dom, do you know where Hettie is?"

Dom nodded. *I'm coming, Hettie.* In her mind, she dropped the FBI jacket on the lake's frigid bank, planted her feet at the edge of the lapping ice water, raised her hands over her head, and dove.

THE LANCIA WAS MADE for speed. At ninety miles an hour on the New Jersey Turnpike, the wide tires ate up the glistening wet asphalt and the engine hummed. Keeping a hand on the gear shift, Dom wove through gaps in the light traffic, her foot never touching the brake. Windshield wipers danced across a blurry screen.

She instructed her phone to call Fontaine.

He picked up on the first ring. "Walker, what have you got?"

"One of them broke. The wait is over."

"Talk to me."

"Sir, it's Yvette Van Buren. Yvette has Hettie. At her family home. Outside Philly."

Through the silence, Dom remembered sitting across from Yvette only hours earlier, in the darkened living room with the sliver of sunlight breaking through heavy curtains. The pale, graceful woman in a cashmere sweater had gulped the Manhattan. Dom, assuming she had been drunk, had pressed her. "Mrs. Van Buren, do you think your husband may be involved in Hettie's disappearance?"

Yvette Van Buren's gaze had turned distant. "I'm sure I can't answer that." Yvette had closed her eyes.

Dom had assumed the pale woman was shutting down mentally, distancing herself from a horror. "Mrs. Van Buren, I can protect you. If you are afraid, I can protect you."

Yvette had whispered, "You do not understand our world," before standing and weaving out of the living room.

The pristine matriarch of the wealthy Lowrance-Van Buren family hadn't been drunk—she had been acting. It had all been an act.

Fontaine demanded, "Repeat?"

"Yvette planned all this. She planned it. From start to finish."

"Fill me in."

The Lancia growled as Dom sped through an opening. "Yvette hears her daughter's threat may take down her husband and their empire. She calls in thugs from Honduras. She ordered the murder of Micah Zapata. She drugged Hettie with Benzo—there was trace in a glass from Hettie's apartment—and she has hidden her in Philly."

"What else?"

"I was with Yvette a few hours ago. As the case got closer to her family, she tried to implicate her own husband."

Dom remembered the full conversation in the dark apartment. She had asked, "Did Mr. Van Buren ever bully you, Mrs. Van Buren?"

"Define bully, please, Agent."

"Used his power or strength to coerce or intimidate you ... perhaps to do things you didn't want to do? It often takes the form of aggression."

With conviction, Yvette had answered, "Yes."

"How?"

"Many ways. Small and large."

"Regularly?"

"Yes."

"Habitually?"

"Yes."

"Have you told anyone?"

And even in her perverse theatrics, Yvette had tried to play Dom. The pale woman had said, "No. The lies we tell..."

Dom slammed her hands on the Lancia's steering wheel. God damn it, Yvette had played her.

Fontaine asked, "Where are you?"

The sports car threaded through the lights of slower cars.

"Yvette's phone is pinging outside Philly. Sir, Yvette's original plan was to hide her daughter till after the trial. But now she's trapped. I'm not sure what she'll do." *I'm coming, Hettie.* "I'm on my way to get Hettie."

Dom's anger surged, cutting through the exhaustion, the shock, the throbbing toes. She imagined standing in thick shadows on the edge of a dark property, reconnoitering a large mansion. She imagined pulling her Glock on Yvette and ordering that goddamned treacherous, malevolent, murderous woman to "Freeze!" Special Agent Domini Walker, with all her weaknesses, doubts, and Office of Professional Responsibility investigation, was going to get Hettie and end this thing. Tonight.

"Understood. But, Walker, we're going to do this carefully and methodically. This is how we're going to play this: I'm going to give you cover so you have time to ID Hettie at the location. I am not going to call Claude, the mayor, or the AG until sunrise. That will give you time to get eyes on her."

His words made sense and weren't too far off her initial plan. Sunrise was at 5:30 am—in six and a half hours. "Roger."

"Once you've ID'd her, we'll call in the troops from the

Philly field office. It will be lightning fast. No way for anyone from New York to interfere at that point."

It was a savvy plan from a politically savvy guy. It gave her six and a half hours to find Hettie and kept the NY field office out of play. "Roger." It was the second time in the past two hours that ASIC Fontaine had proven reliable, willing to work the political angles to keep the investigation moving. Maybe she would consider trusting him. Maybe. Later.

"But it means you need to go dark. If anyone ever digs into what went down tonight, they have to find you were on your own. Are we clear?"

He wanted plausible deniability. Going dark meant she was on her own. She wouldn't have Lea as back up for the next six and a half hours. "Yes, sir," she said. "This is our last call. I did not tell you where I was going."

The wet highway glared against headlights.

His voice was soft. "Safe hunting, Special Agent."

"Sir."

Two minutes later, Dom's phone rang.

It was Lea, "Hi, Dom. Where are you?"

"On the turnpike to the Lowrance estate. I'm going to get Hettie."

"Let justice roll on like a river. Amos 5:24."

"I just spoke to Fontaine. I'm going off-grid tonight. But first I need a favor, and you've got to make this fast."

"Copy."

"I need information on Yvette's family home. I need to know what I'm facing when I get there. Can you send that to me before—"

Lea dropped into a muffled whisper. "Dom?"

"Yeah?"

"He's walking to my desk—"

"Fontaine?"

"Yes."

Dom hung up. Damn. Fontaine was savvier and faster than she expected. She pulled the sports car into the slow lane. Damn. She pulled over into the emergency shoulder, clicked on her flashers, looked up a number on her cell phone, and dialed it.

The voice that answered was tentative. "Hello?"

"Mila?"

"Yes?"

"It's Special Agent Walker. I need your help."

"Yes?"

"As a researcher, I need your help."

"With finding Hettie?"

Dom spoke quickly. "I need information on the Lowrance estate outside Philadelphia. I need some kind of map. I need to know what's there."

"You think Hettie is there." It was a statement.

"Mila, I just need the research."

"You think Hettie is there."

Dom waited her out.

"Okay," Mila said. "I'll find architectural and landscaping diagrams, I can tap into university libraries—"

"Send it to my email." She spelled out her personal email.

"I'll send you what I find."

Dom hung up, threw the phone on the passenger seat, revved the sports car, and blasted back to the highway.

Cicatrices
@LastCurlew

slashes of malice delivered deftly across a heart
like smiles of a jester in a castle—
harlequin—in silk and gold—laughing, taunting, sneering
entreaties cloaked in satin endearments
as rancor strikes through dreams, slices
apart emancipation—
my dowager failed to crush
the aspirations, sureness of a muted offspring
with scarred husk—now
reassembling, buttressing for retribution.

AT NIGHT, the wealthy Philadelphia suburb of Gladwyne, with its steep hills, gated driveways, and huge mansions, felt sleepy and well protected. Ten minutes earlier, the Lancia roared through the main arterial intersection and into the parking lot of an organic supermarket where three shoppers were making their last rounds. Next door, inside a well-lit gas station with a twenty-four-hour convenience store, a teenage girl with braids had rung up Dom's coffee, two power bars, and a bottle of water.

Striding back to the sports car, Dom downed the stale coffee in three gulps and pulled out her phone. Mila sent an email with three attachments. The first was a series of photos from *Architectural Magazine* of an enormous estate captioned *Titus Hill*, comprised of three large buildings of light brown stone and peaked roofs encircling a large courtyard. It was an American version of a French nobleman's chateau situated in the middle of rolling green lawns, gardens, and woods. Dom shook her head. "Evil rolled in a dollar bill."

The second attachment was a written description. *"Titus Hill, an historic estate in Gladwyne PA, is set back from Monk*

Road. It was built in 1928 by Herbert Lowrance. The 14,000-square-foot, twenty-room manor home was designed by Edmund Daniel and features a French Normandy manor main house, a guest house, three staff quarters, a detached five-car garage, a barn, a pool and pool house, tennis court and tennis clubhouse, an aviary, and a greenhouse. The manor is approached by a long driveway that leads to a circular motor court with fountain. The estate sits on fifty-two acres of land that as variously been culti-vated as a formal garden, a maze, wild English garden, orchards, and grazing land. Titus Hill is still privately held by the Lowrance family."

She imagined high perimeter walls and security cameras. "You've got to be shitting me," she mumbled.

The third attachment was a satellite image of the property. It showed the main cluster of buildings set back from the road surrounded by a vast heavily wooded area. Yvette would be hiding Hettie in one of eight buildings. An estate this size required staff, so Dom ruled out the main building because Yvette could not easily hide a drugged Hettie among staff. That left seven possible buildings. Hettie could be hidden in one of the seven buildings. *Shit.*

Slipping into the car, Dom tossed the empty coffee cup and the phone on the passenger seat, turned the key in the ignition, and revved the Lancia. *Hettie, I'm close. The monster doesn't get to keep you.*

The towering trees along Monk Road choked out the moonlight. Passing Titus Hill's gated entrance, the high beams lit up a ten-foot-high stone wall as Dom pulled into a neighboring driveway. She pulled off the gravel into the impenetrable shadows of trees, silenced the car, and slowed her mind.

The presumed first fact was that Yvette had imprisoned

Hettie in one of the seven buildings surrounding the main manor. Five hours was not enough time for Dom to clear these buildings. The second presumption was that Yvette had kept Hettie alive for three days, which meant there was a feeding schedule. The only viable plan was for Dom to observe Yvette visiting Hettie and move in after for the rescue. Over the next five hours, Dom needed a hideout from which to observe the back of the manor and the seven outer buildings. In her favor were three bona fide facts: it was dark, she had the element of surprise, and she was alone and nimble.

Dom pulled up the satellite image on the phone. Situated behind and to the west of the main house was a pool, a pool house, a tennis court, and clubhouse. To the east was a cultivated square—three acres long and three acres wide—that might be a formal garden, a rectangular orchard of lined trees, and a long building. In the photo, the long building had an odd shine. There, inside the orchard. From a position inside the orchard, Dom would have direct line of sight if Yvette went to the clubhouse or the pool house and she would be situated along the path Yvette would use to the shiny building.

Snapping the phone off, she pulled a flashlight from the glove box and stood out of the car. Sinking into wet ground, she walked to the rear, popped the trunk, slipped on a pancake holster and locked in the Glock. She unfolded a camouflage jacket and slipped it on. In the jacket pockets, she slid in two rounds of ammo, an extra battery for her phone, high-powered binoculars, the power bars, and the bottle of water. As she pulled a baseball hat snug, memories crashed over her like ocean surf, churning and roiling.

In a dark, damp basement in Cleveland, Darlin Montgomery stared listlessly at the ceiling from a stained, bare mattress. Dom placed a warm hand on the girl's brow, but the little girl didn't move. "My name is Domini, honey. I'm a police officer. I've come to take you home." Dom softly smoothed the brow. Blank eyes didn't flicker.

From the darkness, a man on the floor groaned.

"Just ignore him, sweetheart." She slid out her knife and sliced through the filthy rope tied around a tiny ankle. Her ponytail brushed the girl's face.

Darlin blinked.

"That's it, sweetheart. I'm here to take you home. You're safe now." Dom clasped the girl to her chest.

Skinny arms reached around Dom's neck and tiny hands gripped long hair.

"I've got you. I've got you. You are a strong girl. I've got you now." Dom squeezed the girl tight as tremors rattled the tiny body. "You just close your eyes, sweetheart. I'm gonna walk us out of here. I've got you. Just close your eyes."

At the back of the Lancia, Dom slammed the trunk.

"You hold on, Hettie," she spoke into the dark. "I'm coming. It's what I do."

48

DIRECTING the flashlight beam a foot in front, Dom took off at a jog across the neighbor's damp lawn to the Lowrance estate. Within minutes, she came to the towering stone wall and banked left, jogging deeper into the funereal woods and the back of the estate. The undergrowth was thick with spiked ferns and groping branches. Overhead, the straining limbs of trees interlaced like bony arms stretched tight. Blackish primeval moss blanketed the forest floor. Occasionally a thin shaft of bluish moonlight cut through the trees and into deep, shadowy gloom. Ignoring the pain in her toes, Dom kept a pace that was brisk and controlled.

Fifteen minutes out, she reached the northeast corner of the estate and flashed the light against the wall. Stacked stones glistened. She doused the light and slid the flashlight into a jacket pocket. Reaching high above her head, fingers felt for a slippery hold in the cold damp stone. Slowly, using only a sense of touch, she scaled the fifteen-foot-high wall and hoisted herself onto the foot-wide berm. After pulling out the flashlight, she cast a beam into the estate's woods like a lighthouse beacon against a sea of inky foliage.

She dropped the flashlight on the ground below and lowered herself. Resuming a jog, she weaved through trees in a diagonal route to the center of the estate.

After ten minutes, the woods thinned and a tree line emerged. Beyond, an overgrown meadow stretched from the border of the woods to the edge of a manicured lawn. Within the eastern portion of the lawn, the windows of the tennis club-house glinted in silvery moonlight. In the center of the lawn, lights from a swimming pool shimmered eerie blue against the pool house. To the west, rows of shadowy scraggy trees resembling goblins marched toward the darkened three-story manor that dominated the center like a dark medieval fortress against a moonlight sky.

"Yvette, I'm here."

She jogged along the edge of the woods north of the pool to the top of the orchard. The cracked and shattered windows of a greenhouse glistened in the moonlight. Neat rows of gnarled trees led down a soft slope, their buckled branches spread overhead in a thin canopy. Across soft damp earth, she moved slowly down a row. Near the manor she found a stunted tree with a droopy overhang of branches and a solid line of sight to the tennis court, the lit pool, and the pool house. The gravel path that led to the greenhouse passed within ten feet of the stunted tree. She pushed the branches aside, knelt into the space, hunkered to sit cross-legged, and trained the binoculars on the back of the mansion.

Fontaine would call in the cavalry at sunrise. She had four hours for Yvette to make a move and lead her to Hettie. "Yvette, I'm right here."

An hour later, a cicada clicked from a nearby tree, and an owl hooted from the woods. The moon, high in the sky, cast a bright glow across the damp meadow and lawn. The swim-ming pool swirled with phosphorescent aquamarine phantoms.

Dom had imagined Yvette inside the dark house lying in a huge canopied bed, her pale hair and perfect face resting on a satin pillow. Was Yvette so delusional that she believed she could get away with hiring an assassin to murder Micah Zapata and kidnapping her own daughter? What level of moral corruption, what variation of pure depravity, had driven this woman to such demented acts?

Dom unwound herself from under the gnarly tree, stood, and stretched against stiff, aching muscles. Toes throbbed. She began a slow walk up the row of trees to the greenhouse, making sure to frequently look back at the darkened manor. The damp soil smelled of charcoal and fertilizer as the trees gave way to an overgrown vegetable garden, wild with haphazard weeds. The glass panels of the greenhouse glinted in the weak moonlight. Was Hettie inside, tied up and terrified? Dom glanced over her shoulder at the manor. How long would it take to clear the building?

If Yvette chose that moment to visit Hettie, perhaps to another building, Dom would miss her only opportunity.

"Damn you, Yvette." She turned and headed back to the small gnarly tree lookout.

Forty-five minutes later, the moon disappeared behind a cloud bank and cast the manor and the grounds in a deep black cover. Something small scurried past the stunted tree. Dom felt her brain slowing and stifled a yawn. She cracked her neck and gulped some water, but still her lids flagged and her eyes burned. She unbent herself from the gnarly tree, shook her arms, and bit hard on the inside of her cheek. A flash of pain followed by the iron taste of blood brought back memories of the Cleveland basement.

She had clasped the trembling Darlin to her chest, tiny hands entangled in her ponytail. "Close your eyes, sweetheart."

She turned to the door just as the man on the floor groaned. Tiny arms squeezed.

"Don't you worry about him, sweetheart. I've got you. I'm going to walk us out of here."

In the darkness of a long dank hallway she carefully found her footing and walked slowly to the stairs and the anemic light from the landing above.

Heavy footfalls smacked across the floorboards overhead.

She took the wooden stairs slowly, crushing the tiny girl against her chest.

Above them, an agent appeared in the doorway.

"I've got her. I've got her."

It was only later, after Darlin had been handed over to a victim specialist, after the Cleveland team had called it a success, and after all the navy windbreakers had gone home, that Domini Walker rested her forehead against her arm and cried deep neck-straining sobs for the children they saved and the ones they let slip away.

In the orchard, she blinked.

"I'm here, Hettie. Hold on," she whispered.

The Hettie Van Buren case was supposed to have been easy. A rich girl partying in Las Vegas. It was not meant to have been the case given to a Special Agent under investigation by the Office of Professional Responsibility for unprofessional conduct during one of the FBI's grisliest cases.

Her phone vibrated. Hiding the screen within the folds of her jacket she read the message from Lea. *Fontaine was here. The AG called him. Quote: Tell Walker to move faster.*

Shit, shit, shit. She glanced at the dark manor. How was she to move any faster if she was forced to wait for Yvette to show her maniacal self?

From somewhere beyond the orchard, deep in the woods, swiftly moving footfalls rustled leaves. Adrenaline shot through her veins. Holding her breath, she followed the trajectory of the runner. Branches broke, bushes swished. Whoever it was, they were moving deep into the woods.

49

RAPID BLINKING WOKE MILA. Even after she opened her eyes to the dark, the twitching of the muscles continued for seconds. In the dream, she had been standing on the corner near the elementary school, waving to Jimmy as he raced away. Lightning had burst across the sky, and a swirling ash cloud had appeared over the horizon, moving quickly toward them. She yelled to Jimmy to hurry inside the school, to get to safety. His little legs scissored faster, bright yellow tennis shoes whirling over the gray sidewalk. He glanced over his shoulder, the white of his rabbit teeth radiant against the gray of the storm. She had screamed as dust enveloped him.

She must have been blinking in her sleep. Night noises emanated from the window—a passing car, the tinkle of a dog collar, the soft traffic from Houston Street. The clock read four am. What was Special Agent Domini Walker doing at the Lowrance estate? Had she found Hettie? Had she found her alive?

Her thoughts were interrupted by the loud creak of an old step on the stairwell two floors below. Her neighbors were quiet folks. Who could that be at this time of night?

She held her breath. A second stair squealed as someone placed their heavy weight on it. A big person was climbing the stairs two floors below. The steps were methodical, one after another.

The heavy boots rounded the landing one floor below. Clomp, clomp. The boots strode the hallway below.

Under a single sheet, naked except for a T-shirt, her skin froze. The curtains ruffled in a slight breeze as moonlight lit the room. Her eyes cast across the darkened room to the white door. Surely this intruder wasn't going to come up the last set of stairs. No one ever came up to the fourth floor.

A heavy thud landed on the first step of the final set of stairs. She sat upright.

Clomp, clomp. The heavy boots climbed.

This couldn't be good. Whoever it was, whoever this terrifying intruder was, it couldn't be good.

The realization slammed through her in an instant. She had forgotten to use an encrypted service to send the email to the precinct chief. The dirty cops had tracked the email back to her ISP location. Terrifying Dirty Cop was here to silence her.

In a shot, she was out of the bed and slipping thin legs in shorts. She jammed her cell phone in the shorts' pocket and yanked a hoodie from a chair, zipped it quickly.

Clomp, clomp. Terrifying Dirty Cop was only a few stairs below.

Rookie mistake, Mila. So dumb. So freaking dumb.

Darting to the table, she grabbed the kitchen chair, raced it to the door, and jammed it under the doorknob on a reckless angle.

You freaking ridiculously dumb rookie sleuth.

Out in the hallway, the climbing stopped. Raw fear washed over her spine. Terrifying Dirty Cop was on her landing, on the other side of the flimsy door, listening.

Clomp, clomp down the hall.

She spun, grabbed the key to the park below, and raced to the window. The curtains undulated in the bluish moonlight. There was only one escape route—through Elizabeth Street Park.

The door shook with a huge bang as a thick fist crashed against thin wood.

She dove through the window onto the cold metal of the fire escape. Four stories below was a black canyon ready to swallow her should she stumble, should she career off the slippery metal. Grabbing the railing, scratchy with rust, she inched bare feet across to the platform to the first leg of ladders. Tremors gripped her hands. Facing the ladder, she gripped the rail and set one bare foot down followed by the other. She descended to the third floor platform. Clutching the rail, she shuffled past her neighbor's dark window. Descending the next leg of the ladder, she did not look into the yawning darkness below. On the second floor, she glanced down. The drop into the darkness was alarming. If she jumped, she would surely break a leg. Shuffling to the far end, she grasped the hook on the final piece of the ladder—a straight length to the ground—and yanked for its release. Nothing moved. She put both hands on the hook and jerked. The ladder held tight. She yelped into the night. The intruder would surely follow her here. This last straight ladder must release to the ground.

A cloud gliding in front of the moon doused the park in blackness. Shaking fingers clamped on the hook. With a mighty yank, the hook squealed open. The ladder slid to the ground.

Blindly she set one bare foot on the first rung and leaned her weight on it, the metal digging into her arch. The ladder wobbled. The ladder stilled and held. She set her other foot on the rung. Foot over foot, hand over hand, she slowly descended into the dark emptiness. The moon broke through the clouds.

The ground was ten feet below. She took shallow breaths, leaned back off the ladder, and let go.

The grass met her as she tumbled onto her backside, hands digging into damp ground. She scrambled to the shadow of bushes.

Above, her apartment windows were black. Was Terrifying Dirty Cop looking out? Could he see her? *You freaking ridiculously dumb rookie sleuth.*

Jumping up, she sprinted across the grass, past shadowed bushes, demonic statues, and stone carvings. She would escape through the park gate. Moonlight streamed white on glistening grass. Ten yards out, her feet hit the gravel path and sharp rocks cut through her flesh. She yelped. Her fingers clutched around the gate key in her pocket as she raced to the gate.

Ahead, a silhouette appeared. On the other side of the gate.

Mila skidded into a dive off the path into shadowed bushes.

Terrifying Dirty Cop had a partner. And they were here to silence her.

50

DOM SQUINTED through binoculars into the deep shadows of the woods. Thirty yards out, a dark figure dressed in black moved quickly to the back of the estate. *Shit all over my surveillance, who is that?*

She took off in a slow smooth jog through the orchard and into the woods, leaving a wide berth between herself and the black figure. Low bushes grabbed at her jeans, and leaves brushed her cheek, but her controlled jog didn't falter. The black figure slowed to a walk and approached the tree line north of the pool. He had a distant but clear line of sight across the entire estate.

She circled behind him deep into the woods and stopped.

The black-clad figure stood inside the tree line, confidently staring down over the manor, unaware of her presence. His hands rested calmly at his sides below broad square shoulders with a professional poised stance. A holster on his right leg held a sidearm.

She slowly clicked open the latch of her holster, slid out the Glock, and silently clicked off the safety. Silently, she moved up behind him. With each step, she nestled her foot into leaves on the wet forest floor before pressing her weight into the stance. Silence.

Fifteen feet behind the intruder, she sighted the Glock on his leg and hissed, "Freeze. FBI."

The black intruder stiffened.

"FBI. I have a gun aimed at the back of your leg. I'm a good shot."

He didn't move.

"On the ground."

The black figure dropped to his knees, fell to a push-up, and lay on the ground. He spread his arms wide.

She approached with the Glock aimed at his calf. "Who are you?"

"Private security. Greystone."

Shit on my surveillance parade. Claude and Runner had called in a team.

She stepped back and holstered the Glock. "You can get up. How many of you on the property?"

"Three of us." He stood and brushed himself off. "They didn't tell me Feds were here."

He was tall, maybe six four with hair high and tight, regulation length. Former something—she guessed Ranger. "What're your instructions?"

"Secure the mother. Find the girl."

She didn't trust Claude or Runner. In fact, she didn't trust anyone related to the fucking Van Buren family or Rittenhouse Equity. "That's it?"

"That's it. Secure the mother. Rescue the daughter."

"And then do what with the daughter?"

He frowned. "What do you mean?"

"Did they tell you what to do once you have the daughter in hand?"

"Only to call it in. Await instructions."

Innocent enough. He was here to help Hettie.

He said, "But my sense is the client is on their way. We are to secure both mother and daughter till the client arrives."

Claude was on his way. Since he was coming from New York, it meant he would arrive between one and two hours. "What's your name?"

"Moose."

"All right, Moose." In the dark she couldn't make out an earpiece. "You got coms to your team?"

"Affirmative."

"What are their positions?"

He instinctively motioned right and left with two fingers. His guys were on either side of the house, outside the perimeter of the lawn and in the woods.

"I'm the point on this, understood? We hold until the mother leads us to the daughter. We hold until the mother comes out and leads us to the daughter. I do not want the mother to panic, maybe kill the daughter. Understood?"

"Copy that."

With the three additional assets, she could clear the buildings. "In the meantime, you're going to be my eyes. I'm going to check out the greenhouse first. If you see the mother heading to the greenhouse, secure her."

"Roger that."

"After the greenhouse, I'll recon the pool house and the tennis house. In that order. The rules of engagement are the same. If you see the mother heading to either while I'm inside, you secure her. Understood?"

"Roger that."

"Otherwise, you stand down till I make noise. Don't worry, I'll make noise. Operational priority is retrieving the daughter. Once I do that, you are cleared to enter the manor and secure the mother."

"Roger."

"Okay, relay that to your team."

He repeated the instructions softly into his neck mic. When he was finished, he nodded at Dom.

"You a former Ranger?" she asked.

He gave her a small smile. "How'd you know?"

"Gut feeling. Thanks for your service."

He nodded.

They didn't have much time till Fontaine called in the FBI cavalry. "Stay frosty. It's go time."

The greenhouse glass glinted in the fading moonlight. The glass panes rattled against steel frames as she threw open the wobbly door. Inside, the air was sweet and earthen. Underfoot, shards of glass crackled on tiles. A long row of wooden potting tables ran the center of the space, creating two outer aisles. She took the right aisle first, weaving through vines and brushing away stretched cobwebs. A bat dive-bombed her head, and she crouched as it buzzed past.

She moved further down the right aisle and hissed, "Hettie? Hettie? It's FBI. Hettie?"

Nothing.

Between a row of wooden tables, broken ceramic pots lay shattered, their inhabitants long ago withered, their brown roots webbed around dry dirt.

"Hettie? Hettie. It's FBI!"

Only silence.

At the back of the building, she crossed to the left aisle. In the tepid ray of moonlight through dusty glass, the area was empty. Her phone vibrated with a message from Lea. *Fontaine was just here. Tell Walker I'm calling in our local squad.*

The Philadelphia FBI Hostage Rescue Team would be here

in thirty minutes, forty minutes max. Dom had to clear the pool and the tennis house immediately before the onslaught of sirens panicked Yvette into doing something dangerous to Hettie.

Shit on my surveillance stick. Time to move.

She sprinted down the aisle.

51

DOM SPRINTED through the wobbly door into the fresh night air and froze. As if conjured from a dream, Yvette stood at the edge of the pool like a translucent phantom in the swirling lights. Dropping to a low crouch, Dom drew the binoculars to her eyes. Yvette's magnified face was tight with lips in a clamped straight line. Her features were perfect even in the eerie light.

"It's about time, Yvette," she whispered.

Dom knew firsthand the traits of a psychopath with antisocial personality disorder—charm, extreme arrogance, compulsion for dominance, exceptional manipulators, and lacking remorse. None that she had met ever came close to the complexity of Yvette.

At their very first meeting, Yvette misdirected the investigation toward Micah Zapata. She said, "My side, the Lowrances, have been a family of privilege ever since my great- grandfather discovered oil. We must protect our family. I'm not happy she's wrapped up with a man who may not have her best interests at heart."

Dom asked, "Why do you think he may not have her best interests at heart?"

Yvette said simply, "His family does not have money."

In that one beautifully crafted line, Yvette acted the part of the proud mother while casting suspicions on the gold-digging boyfriend.

In the shimmering aquamarine light, Yvette cast her eyes to the pool house and walked around the pool's edge. A heavy canvas bag smacked against her leg.

Dom held the binoculars steady. Hettie was in the pool house.

During their second meeting, Yvette reverently stroked a leather photo album and shared intimate details. "People used to remark that we act more like friends than mother and daughter." She had utilized physicality to display fear—touching her neck, wrinkling her face, and closing her eyes. The facade was immaculate.

Swinging the binoculars, Dom skimmed the back line of trees for any movement from Moose. There was nothing. She searched the tree line around the estate, but there was only stillness. The Rangers were following orders—hold for her signal. Arms bent, she returned the binocular focus to the pool house.

At the door of the pool house, Yvette stopped and listened to the night noises before slipping into the dark building.

During their final meeting, Dom asked her, "Does your husband bully Hettie?"

"Oh, yes," Yvette replied.

"Regularly, small and large?"

"Oh yes. And my Hettie is very quiet—she is not able to stand up to him." She finished her cocktail with a final gulp, a desperate woman pushed to drink.

"Mrs. Van Buren, do you think your husband may be involved in Hettie's disappearance?"

Yvette's gray eyes glazed over as she set down the glass and whispered, "I'm sure I can't answer that."

"Mrs. Van Buren, if it would help find your daughter... I believe you must answer it."

In the final stage-crafted act, Yvette whispered trancelike, "Our world is different. You do not understand our world." It was a stroke of genius stroke to distract by playing equally on Dom's concerns about abuse and her own working class insecurities. Genius.

An owl hooted from the woods. Dom swung the binoculars around the tree line, but still the Rangers held fast. The front windows remained dark. Inside, Yvette was either working in the dark, or she turned on a light in a back room where the windows were curtained. Was she talking to Hettie? Was she feeding her? Had Yvette heard that the FBI were on their way? Was she hurting Hettie?

In the pool house, a ghost floated past the front windows, and Dom straightened. Yvette emerged into shimmering blue light. Dom gripped the binoculars.

Yvette had almost gotten away with her crimes. *That's right, my Dom, almost.* Stewart Walker whispered. *But she hadn't counted on you.* Yvette was not prepared to go head-to-head with a special agent whose tenacious grit grew out of a father's suicide and a mother's exodus.

Yvette slid the door closed, strode around the pool's edge, cornered the hedgerow, and disappeared into the manor.

Go time. Dom slung the binoculars to the ground, surged to her feet, and shot down the path. As her feet spun gravel into the air, her soles hit the damp pool deck with loud slaps. Yanking open the pool house door, she raced inside and snapped on the flashlight. The beam traced across the front room—two couches, a coffee table, a pool table, a pinball machine, and a huge television on a wall.

"Hettie?" she hissed. "Hettie, it's FBI. Are you in here?"

Sprinting into the back room, the smell of pungent flowers hit her nostrils like the overly sweet scent of burned sugar.

52

AT THE ENTRANCE of Elizabeth Street Park, Terrifying Dirty Cop's silhouette rattled the iron gate. The chain jangled, but the lock held. A shaft of light from a heavy-duty flashlight sliced through the dark. Mila pressed into the shadows of the bushes as the beam swept inches away. The light sliced out across the lawn and statues, casting ominous shadows like awakened souls in a ghoulish cemetery. The flashlight clicked, and the park went black. The hinges of the gate creaked under a heavy load. Fiendish Partner was climbing the gate. To come get her.

She crawled through the underbrush to a tall statue, stood, and peered into the gloom. If she made it quietly over the damp grass to the back of the park, she could climb to the top of the gardening shed and swing herself over the back wall.

At the gate, Fiendish Partner grunted as he dropped to the gravel.

She sprinted across the cold damp grass, arms slicing, feet racing.

Behind her, the high-powered beam blazed into the night sky.

Weaving through statues, she veered around an unruly flower patch and hit the gravel path at full speed. Small stones slashed the skin on her soles.

The beam methodically sliced left and right, dipping under bushes like a hunting dog rattling out a rabbit.

Racing across the path, the stones slicing her skin, she reached the far side of the park. Lungs pulled in air. Against the back wall, the gardening shed with its rickety roughhewn plank walls was bathed in a pale moonlight. The roof of the shed was low—only seven feet high—and precariously flimsy. Would it hold her weight? Cracked earthen planting pots sat on a bench set against the foot of the shed. When she set her right foot on the bench, pain flashed. The bench wobbled but held. In a swift move, she heaved her weight up on the bench, her lacerated soles burned like a lit flame against skin. She stretched for the roof edge and grasped the damp wooden planks. She hung, the relief instant in her feet, for only a second before she threw her right leg up—a movement she had used with her bike a thousand times—and hooked the ankle. The heel dragged across wood, driving splinters deep into her skin. Breath caught in her lungs. Thrusting the leg straight, she shoved her knee over the lip and onto the roof. With a mighty last pull and a grunt, she pitched her full body onto the planks.

The beam flashed on a nearby tree.

She dropped her forehead to the damp wood and panted against mildew.

Close by, heavy feet crunched gravel.

She rolled across the damp wooden slats away from the roof's edge and flattened herself against the wet bricks of the wall. Her hands and feet burned, and slats dug into her shoulder blades.

The flashlight sliced over the shed.

She held her breath.

The shed door blasted open with an enormous crack, and the thin walls shook. She froze, eyes wide against the pitch black as adrenaline surged. Heavy breathing from inside the shed as the flashlight sliced left and right, a wolf hunting prey. Light flashed through the cracks of the thin planks, the glimmer casting across her skin.

From the other side of the wall on Mott Street, a sound approached. *Clink, clink, clink.*

Below, in the shed, the light was doused.

On Mott Street the noise moved quickly. *Clink, clink, clink.*

She recognized the sound. It was the scraping of a shoe clip on the pedal of a bike. A lone biker was riding in the night, his clip scraping against cement on every rotation. *Clink, clink, clink.*

The sound passed down Mott Street. *Clink, clink, clink.*

From inside the shed, the Fiendish Partner waited for the sound to recede before crunching across gravel into the park.

She released her lungs.

Soon, there was only silence.

The moon peeked from behind clouds as her heart rate returned to normal. Maybe it was the adrenaline in her bloodstream or the near brush with capture, but the air that filled her lungs felt silky and new. Against the burning pain in her feet and hands, tears of frustration crept from the corners of her eyes and slipped off her cheeks to the rotting wood. Who sends an email outing corrupt NYPD officers from a trackable wifi? *A rookie sleuth, that's who. One who was now being stalked by Terrifying Dirty Cop and his Fiendish Partner.*

The inky darkness of the sky looked miles away. The

universe was not ready for Mila Pascale to disappear. Stars blinked like millions of beacons just for her. It was not time for Mila Pascale to disappear. No way. The universe wanted Mila Pascale to hone her skills, become an FBI agent, and find Jimmy. That's what the universe wanted.

She wiped away the tears.

53

IN THE BACK room of the pool house, the flashlight beam slashed over a large white bed and blonde hair splayed across a white pillow. On a nightstand, medicine bottles and syringes lay next to a timer set for three hours. She had found Hettie.

Dom leaned into Hettie Van Buren's still face and whispered, "I'm here, Hettie. I'm here."

Behind closed lids, eyes rolled. Hettie was barely conscious. Yvette had been immobilizing her daughter with pharmaceuticals.

Dom positioned the flashlight on the table and placed both hands on either side of the young woman's face. "It's the FBI, Hettie. I've come to save you. You're going to be okay. Try to open your eyes, Hettie. Just try for me."

The lids fluttered.

"That's it. You almost got it."

They fluttered and opened to unfocused blue corneas with dilated pupils.

"That's it, sweetheart. I'm here."

Hettie's cracked lips shuddered, trying to speak through the haze of drugs.

Her will was still strong, she was fighting. "I'm going to make sure you're okay now, Hettie. It's going to be okay now."

Dom slid her hands to Hettie's throat and felt a steady pulse. Her temperature felt normal. Brushing the sheet off Hettie's shoulders, she smoothed her hands down both arms checking for injuries. There were none. Below the sheet, Hettie was dressed in a clean white nightgown that ended at pale bare ankles. Below the nightgown, Hettie's torso was distended, and Dom pressed softly to discover that Yvette had wrapped her in adult diapers.

Dom shifted to Hettie's face where tears streamed and looked into her blue eyes. "I know. I know, sweetheart. It's going to be okay. Your body looks okay. You hear me?"

Hettie moaned one syllable: an unmistakable, "no." The tears streamed faster.

Hettie was getting her strength back by the minute. "I know, sweetheart, it's going to be okay."

Hettie's head twitched, and she moaned against the paralyzing drugs.

"You keep fighting, Hettie. That's good. Can you nod for me?"

Hettie groaned, but this time her head wobbled.

"That's it, my girl. Good job."

Hettie's head rocked back and forth as the groans grew louder. Suddenly, Hettie went still. Tears streamed onto the pillow as blue eyes stared at the ceiling.

Dom moved in front of Hettie's eyes. "You know what, Hettie? I know a secret. Something you don't know. Do you want to know what it is?"

The eyes focused on Dom's face.

"I know that you are strong. I know all about you. I know everything you have done over the last few months. I know you saw the protest at the museum gala. I know you went to CAN and learned about what happened in Rapoosa. I know you suspected your father's company. I know you and Micah went down to Rapoosa to confirm your suspicions about Rittenhouse's investment. I know you are planning to testify at the trial in Canada. Because you are strong, you are courageous, and you'll even take on your father for justice. See, Hettie, I know you are strong. Because you *are* strong."

Hettie blinked, and the tears slowed.

"That's it, my girl. Now I'm going to get under you and lift you up. Then you and I are going to get the hell out of here."

Hettie's head wobbled. Yes.

"Okay. Now I'm going to get underneath you, and you're going to concentrate. You're going to help me, because we both know you're strong."

Hettie mumbled. It sounded like a yes. The tears had stopped.

"That's my girl."

Dom flicked off the flashlight and shoved it in her jacket pocket, grabbed Hettie's ankles, and shifted the pale feet to the floor. Leaning in, she wrapped Hettie's arms around her neck. With a quick breath, Dom grabbed Hettie's waist, hoisted her to a stand, and jammed a shoulder under Hettie's armpit. Hettie's full weight bore down on her, heavy but manageable. "That's my girl. Okay, Hettie, you lean against me. Use that strength to lean against me. We're going to walk right out of here."

Hettie grunted, and her head canted forward.

Dom took a step, and Hettie's feet dragged behind, but Hettie shifted weight to Dom. "That's it. Just like that. You lean on me, stay stiff. That's it, Hettie."

As Dom shuffled toward the bedroom door, Hettie grunted.

Dom shuffled them into the game room. "That's it! Just outside now."

One step at a time, they made their way across the room. Sweat dripped from Dom's hairline.

They passed through the open door and into the fresh night air. "Hettie, we're doing it! We're doing it!"

Hettie moaned.

Swirling blue lights washed over them. Did Moose see them? Did Yvette? At the corner of the pool house, Dom banked and shuffled them down the side of the building.

Reaching the back, she leaned Hettie up against the wall. "I'm just going to set you down here Hettie—"

Hettie wailed a thick-lipped "No."

"It's okay, Hettie. I'm not leaving you. I just need to call in our backup."

The moan was small. "No."

"I'm just going to get reinforcements. You have to hide here for just a few minutes. I'm right here. Okay? Nobody will find you."

Hettie gave a limp nod.

Sliding Hettie's body into a seated position, Dom turned and sprinted from the shadows of the pool house out onto the damp lawn, clicked on the flashlight, and slashed the light across the sky. She opened her lungs and bellowed, "Move out! Move! Out!"

From the impenetrable woods at the back of the estate, there was movement as the inky silhouette of Moose emerged. He signaled with two quick flashes from a flashlight. A second black shadow stepped onto the tennis court. A third dark shape jogged swiftly from the gloom of the orchard.

Far in the distance, the faint wail of sirens pricked the night's silence. The Philadelphia FBI Hostage Rescue convoy would be here in minutes.

Dom yanked out her phone and dialed Fontaine.

Like trained ninjas, the three dark shadows covered ground quickly to a rendezvous point at the edge of the pool.

Fontaine picked up. "Hostage Rescue is on—"

Dom barked, "There are private security on premises. Armed. Three. Moving on the house."

The black ninjas converged at the hedgerow by the pool's entrance and formed a single line. The pool's oscillating blue lights flickered over their dark forms.

The sirens wailed closer.

"I repeat," Dom said. "Private armed security heading on the main house."

"Roger that." Fontaine hung up.

Across the pool, the three ninjas drew guns. Moose flicked two fingers by his ear and led the unit to the manor, guns drawn. The three disappeared into the silent house.

Sirens keened.

Dom jogged back to the pool house and sat by Hettie. "I'm back. It's going to be okay."

Hettie's breathing was louder, stronger. One of her hands squeezed Dom's arm.

Sirens blared as vehicles turned onto Monk Road.

Dom slipped an arm around the young woman's shoulders and pulled Hettie close. "It will all be over soon. You stay strong, Hettie."

Through the night air, the shriek of sirens blasted and flashing red and blue lights slashed across the brick walls of the manor, across the glistening meadow, and up against the thick ancient tree trunks. From inside the manor, a single gunshot cracked.

54

IN THE CIRCULAR COURTYARD, white and red lights blinked frenetically against the spray of a fountain and flared across the manor's brick walls. Light streamed from the open back doors of an ambulance where an EMT was soothing Hettie on a gurney. Two rescue agents in green camo and tactical vests, packing guns and ammo, questioned three Titus Hill staff on the portico. Three rescue agents took statements from Moose and his two ninja warriors by a black SUV. One of the ninjas had a bandaged shoulder where, during the initial breach, a panicked Yvette shot him. They subdued her quickly.

Dom pushed off from the hood of a car, fatigue weighing like ankle anchors, and shuffled to the back of the ambulance. Her toes throbbed. Inside, the EMT was holding an oxygen mask across Hettie's mouth.

Dom leaned in. "Can I get a moment with Hettie?"

He nodded and climbed out.

Dom took his seat and gave the young woman a sad smile. "How you feeling?"

Hettie nodded, her eyes clear and focused as she lifted the

oxygen mask off. Her voice was scratchy from disuse. "Thank you." A single tear dropped.

"You're welcome. I was very worried about you. I was always going to get you."

Hettie just nodded.

"I'm very sorry about everything that has happened."

Hettie stared at the ceiling of the ambulance with blank eyes.

"It will not make sense for a while. It's going to take some time to sink in. You take all the time you need."

Hettie's brow wrinkled.

"Hettie, do you remember what happened in your apartment?"

Hettie shook her head and whispered, "No," before looking into Dom's eyes.

The Rohypnol had done its job—it had wiped her memory. It meant Hettie didn't know what her mother had done to her. Or that Micah was gone. Dom took a deep breath. "I have something to tell you that is not going to be easy to hear. Are you ready?"

With wide eyes, Hettie nodded.

"Hettie, your mother drugged and kidnapped you."

Hettie's face wrinkled.

"Then she bundled you up and brought you here to Titus Hill. To keep you from the trial in Toronto."

Hettie stared at Dom's lips.

"Trust me when I say that all this will be your past. You will have your future. It will be yours. You will be in charge of your future. Not your mother. Not your father." Dom swallowed. "Hettie, there's one more thing."

Hettie waited.

"Your mother also hired someone ... to kill Micah. Hettie, Micah is dead."

Hettie's eyes dilated.

"I'm sorry."

Hettie blinked.

"I'm so sorry."

Wait for it. Wait for it.

The blue eyes froze, locked on Dom's.

It was shock. And shock took time. Hours. Maybe days.

Dom squeezed Hettie's hand. "You are strong, Hettie Van Buren. I know all about you. Remember, you are strong."

From the end of the drive, a large black Mercedes roared up the drive and squealed to a break.

With a final look at the dazed young woman, Dom crouched out from the ambulance.

In the center of the brick drive, Claude threw himself out of his car. "Where is my daughter? Where is Hettie?!"

A rescue agent pointed at the ambulance and Claude broke into a run.

Dom stepped out of the way and approached the front of a black SUV in the convoy line. Inside, Yvette stared contemptuously past the windscreen at the manor, ignoring her surroundings. Dom leaned close to the glass and tapped it. Yvette turned with hard eyes and a small confident smile.

"I have evidence, Yvette. Plenty of it. I'm going to send you away for a very long time. Oslo Bockel won't be able to help you. Oh yeah, I've got the evidence. I've got you."

The smile faded, and Yvette glared.

"Oh yeah, I've got the evidence."

In Dom's mind, Stewart Walker whispered, "*See, my Dom, you are enough.*"

In the dark of the neighbor's drive, cocooned in the silence of her car, Dom cracked her neck. Time to check in. She dialed Fontaine's number.

He answered quickly. "You out of there?"

"Yeah, the Philly field office has it under control. I left Hettie with the EMTs. Claude just showed up."

"And the private guys?"

"They're fine. Pretty professional actually. They were invited on the property by Claude. So, in the end, there was no illegality on their part. Yvette shot one of them when they breached."

"He okay?"

"Yeah, it was a graze."

"And Yvette?"

There weren't many words to describe Yvette Van Buren or the feelings Dom had about her. "She's in custody."

His voice turned soft. "And Hettie?"

Dom stared into the darkness. Hettie was strong, but what she needed to recover from this diabolical situation was resilience. "I dunno. You never can tell."

"You found her, Dom, alive. That's all that matters. It's a win."

It didn't feel like a win. How often in her FBI career had the *win* turned out to be pretty horrible? Too many. Too many to think about right now. There were too many monsters destroying lives. "Yeah, I guess."

"It's the best possible outcome."

"Sure." The sadness felt infinite.

"Take the weekend off. We'll wrap up the paperwork on a school day."

The gentleness in his voice made her close her eyes.

"And Walker?"

Whatever he was about to say, she wasn't ready for it.

Coming so close to Yvette's evil and having witnessed Hettie's devastation, Dom Walker wasn't ready for kindness.

"You did really good. You're a solid special agent, Walker. Come on home." Then he was gone.

Her throat thickened, and the back of her lids stung. Pride nudged the sadness. Fidelity, bravery, and integrity. She would always fight the monsters. It's what she did.

The phone vibrated with an incoming call. She clicked it on.

"Special Agent Walker? It's Mila Pascale." The faint voice sounded exhausted. "Can you pick me up from the hospital?"

THE NEXT WEEK

The male called wildly for her to follow. The terror of the ground had not yet left him. But the female didn't move. He circled and recircled above and his plaintive cries must have reached her, but she didn't call back. A long time later he overcame the fear and landed on the ground close to her.

    —Fred Bodsworth, "Last of the Curlews"

55

ON THE FOURTH-FLOOR landing of the Mott Street apartment building, Dom unlocked the door and felt it push against a wedged chair. Cracking the door open, she hooked her hand through, grabbed the chair, and wiggled it aside. Inside the raw floorboards creaked under her feet. A blue bedspread was lumped near the end of mattress on the floor. A small kitchenette table sat at the end of a long laminate counter and a battered leather armchair was hunkered by one of the tall windows. The bright sunlight, white walls and white-washed floorboards made the small room feel large. The place was incredibly clean—no dust balls, no dirt. A glass jar held hundreds of pennies, but otherwise, there was very little color and no knick knacks or photos. Most young women had stuff, but she and Beecher learned over the weekend that Mila was not most women.

A breeze billowed white gauzy curtains. The last time Dom had entered another woman's empty apartment, the pungent smell of lilies jarred a warning. So much had happened since last Tuesday. Micah's torn chest. The Zapatas wailing. The ghost-like cement of Port Morris. The Aerie view of the city from Rittenhouse Equity. The glistening highway on the way to Titus Hill. Hettie's hair brushed back over a white pillow. So much tragedy at the hands of a single demented woman. Life was fragile and transitory.

Had it really already been three days since she raced from Gladwyne back to New York's Bellevue Hospital?

Dom found Mila sitting upright on a hospital bed in the emergency section, pale and thin, an oddly serene creature in the midst of the medical chaos. Machines pinged, children screeched, a drunk rambled incoherently, and Mila's bandaged feet rested at the foot of the bed.

A young doctor, working with tweezers on her hands, glanced over his shoulder as Dom stepped into the antiseptic room. "Well, now I get to meet the family of my bravest patient."

Mila glanced up at Dom with a pleading look.

Dom asked, "What happened?"

The doctor said, "Looks like Mila got in a fight with some very sharp gravel and a whole farm of splinters. I'm working on her hands. Glad to see someone's come to get her home."

"She okay?"

"You're going to be just fine, aren't you, Mila?"

Mila nodded, her eyes on Dom.

He returned attention to the splinters in Mila's hands. "We're getting all the offending culprits out. She's had a tetanus shot, we have her on antibiotics, and we'll bandage her up in a few minutes. She'll be good to go home soon. A few days and she'll be back to fighting fit."

Over his head, Dom nodded to Mila. "Okay, good. Thanks, Doc."

Mila gave her a timid smile.

· · ·

An hour later, Dom had settled Mila into the Lancia. "What happened?"

Bandaged hands rested in her lap, and bandaged feet wore hospital slippers. "I appreciate you coming to get me."

"What happened?"

Mila's eyes were sunken. "It was a bad night."

"I left you at the coffee shop near CAN a few hours ago. What happened?"

Mila gazed across the hospital parking lot. "A lot."

"Start talking."

Mila bit her lip before slowly relaying the story of her research on the Filthy Five and the lists she discovered in the New York University Law School's Police Records Project.

The Filthy Five. Dom's stomach dropped. It had been a long time since she heard that reference. She relived the march down the steps of the courthouse, the press yelling questions, her hand squeezing Beecher's, and Esther following behind. It had been the beginning of the rest of her life. Her chest clenched.

Mila's voice was small. "I wanted to help find Hettie."

"So why research me?"

"I wanted to know if you were a good agent or a mediocre one." The bandaged hands bobbled in her lap. "I did research. That's what I do. I chase rabbits wherever they lead me. The Filthy Five seemed relevant—"

"They're not," Dom said tightly.

"Not to this case—"

"Not to anything."

"Well, I deduced you chose the FBI to prove yourself. To prove that you are a good person. That was useful data."

This young woman's black-and-white view of the world was unnerving. Dom was used to secrets and maneuvering. "So then what happened?"

Mila whispered, "The Filthy Five are regrouping."

Breath caught in Dom's chest.

"I figured I should tell someone. So I sent a note to their Chief. Told him about the leader, Robert Gessen and his crew. I thought I had sent an anonymous email. But they tracked me down through my ISP. It would have been in the metadata of the email. It was a really, really dumb mistake. A rookie move." Mila dropped her chin. "So dumb."

"Why on earth would you send your findings to the Chief of the Precinct?"

Mila turned to her, eyes clear and open. "Because it was the right thing to do."

Dom hadn't met someone like Mila in a very long time. Just a good, good person. Odd. But good. "You could definitely have gotten hurt. NYPD do not mess around." She pointed at Mila. "When this is all over, you and I are gonna have a long talk about your research."

Mila whispered, "You can't stop me."

Dom gaped. "What did you just say?"

Mila stuck out her chin. "You can't stop me from researching. It's what I do. I want to be an FBI analyst. That's why I'm a researcher."

Dom blinked.

Mila stared.

Dom was the one to break the stare. "Where's your family?"

Mila glanced away.

Was she alone in New York? "Do you not have family in New York?"

Mila's voice was small. "No."

Her tone implied she had no family at all. A pang of guilt pricked Dom's stomach. "Do you have family?"

"No."

Dom exhaled. "Well you can't go home while two crooked cops are chasing you. You'll come stay with us till I get this sorted. Did they give you pain meds?"

"I said no."

"Why?"

Mila shrugged. "Drugs are bad."

Tinks met them with a tap dance, a dangling tongue, and a chiming collar just before sunrise. Mila crouched and stroked Tinks gingerly with bandaged hands. It was the first smile Dom ever saw on her.

Beecher stepped into the kitchen, blonde hair askew, eyes blinking over a big grin. Easy-going, ever adaptable, never-surprised Beecher. "Hey. You both are either up really early for church or coming in really late from a boozy bender. From the look of those bandages, I'd guess the bender."

Mila stood.

"Mila, this is my brother, Beecher. Beecher, this is Mila Pascale."

"Did you win or lose that fight?" he chuckled.

Mila's face was blank, but her eyes were curious.

Dom said, "Mila had a run in with some bad guys. Unfortunately, she also had a run in with gravel and splinters, but she's fine."

"Huh. You want coffee or to go to sleep?" He glanced up at Dom. "The case?"

"Hettie Van Buren is safe."

Mila whispered, "We found her."

Beecher chuckled at Mila's interference.

Dom said, "It's a long story, and we need sleep. Beecher, do you mind showing Mila to the guest room?"

His hair flopped as he nodded. "This way, my friend."

Mila stared at Tinks. "Is she allowed in beds?"

Beecher laughed at Dom. "Oh my, Tinks is about to have a new best friend for life! Come on, Tinks, let's show our guest how you've perfected the art of sleeping."

A full smile broke across Mila's face as she shuffled across the kitchen floor after Tinks and Beecher.

In the apartment on Mott Street, Dom stepped to an open window overlooking a wild, unruly park. At this time of day, the gate was open but the park was empty. On Thursday night, it would have been very dark. Mila would have scuttled across the rusty fire escape, barefoot, made her way down the flimsy ladder, would have jumped down to the ground, would have landed on the gravel, and would have raced across the lawn. It would have been a terrifying flight.

Bastards. That had tracked her here. One of them, probably that bastard Robert Gessen, had lumbered up the stairwell and banged on the door while the other waited in the shadows by the gate. It had been a well-planned approach—calm and rational—and diabolically frightening. What had Mila called them? Terrifying Dirty Cop and Fiendish Partner?

It had been a spine-chilling stalking, but it was not criminal. Further, if they had wanted to actually kidnap Mila, they would have merely waited for her to come or go from the apartment. But calm, rational cops didn't just nab young women. That led to a lot of unnecessary hassles. Where to hide them? Who to watch over them? What to do with them when they were done? No, that bastard Robert Gessen and his partner had simply wanted to scare Mila.

Well, gentlemen, two can play that game. Once I've gotten Mila off your radar, I'm gonna dig into the Filthy Five reunion. Because you motherfuckers broke up my family.

Her phone pinged. It was a message from Fontaine. "OPR is ready for you. Interview is scheduled today for one pm. Javits floor three."

She headed across the creaky floorboards. The hits just kept coming.

56

TORONTO, Ontario

She didn't like Toronto. It was clean and the people had treated her nicely, but she didn't like the sun. Maria much preferred the yellow heat in Honduras that warmed her face and arms than the diluted glow this far north. They had put her in a hotel with a huge soft bed. But she had difficulty sleeping, sinking into the grasping mattress. She did not like being confined.

This morning they discussed the trial. They explained they would take her to a grand courtroom where a translator would help and a lawyer would ask questions. She thought of the office in Tegucigalpa with the large man with the thick neck and wondered if the courtroom lawyer would treat her dismissively. It didn't matter. She was here to tell the story. An arrogant lawyer could not stop her.

She sat on a large wooden chair staring over the courtroom and a sea of a thousand eyes. A young translator stood by her left ear. To her right, an imposing woman judge watched over her, a soothing guardian in a black robe and red sash. She never imagined a woman could be a judge.

The lawyer stood and walked to her. His eyes were kind and gentle. He knows, she thought. He knows what's coming. It is time to tell our story.

The lawyer said softly, "Hello, Maria."

She nodded as the young translator whispered in her ear.

"Maria, we would like for you to tell us about what happened on March 25, five years ago in Rapoosa. Are you able to do that?"

For my Ines, I am able to do this. "Si."

The translator said "Yes."

"Thank you," the lawyer said with sad eyes. "Why don't you tell us in your words what happened that night?"

She cleared her throat. "Early that night, at sunset, there had been a red sky and a sound over the lake. The sound wind makes when it is angry." She looked at the translator and said in Spanish, "Aullido."

He nodded. "Howling. The wind was howling."

She and the translator continued. "In the village, before that night, we taunted the children, told them bad things happen when there is a blood red sky that howls. I can't remember if we joked that night. But I remember the red sky and the wind." She swallowed. "We don't joke anymore." She wrung her hands and swallowed. "They came in the middle of the night when we were sleeping. They came quietly, like a pack of coyotes. They must have known that many of our village had gone to Teguci-galpa. Most of the men had gone. They must have known that they had gone to protest." She didn't know if she should explain the protests, the mining company Phalanx, or the new mine.

The lawyer said, "We know about your protests, Maria. No need to explain all that."

"I remember there were only three men left. Us women and

girls stayed behind. We woke to the fires. The smoke from the roofs. The reeds popped as they burned. I ran out of my home and saw all the homes on fire. They must have set all the homes on fire at the same time.

"There were ten coyotes. They were large men, dressed in black. They stood in a circle around our homes. We were in the center, trapped.

"We stood in a group, in the middle of the burning. Fifteen women, the three men, and the children. We were crying, our men were yelling—Miguel and Rodrigo were yelling the most, trying to be brave. We were terrified.

"Then the coyotes moved in, coming closer. Miguel and Rodrigo moved to meet them."

The memory slashed at her guts. She felt a tear drop. She should be embarrassed, with all these thousands of eyes staring at her, but it was a real tear for a real horror. It deserved to be. Funny what you learn when you face the unknown.

"Miguel and Rodrigo wanted to fight. But the coyotes were quiet. Rodrigo moved to one of the coyotes. That's when it started. Two of the coyotes grabbed him. Rodrigo was on the ground. We were screaming. A third coyote had a machete in his hand."

Memories blurred her vision. A thousand eyes stared at her.

The kind lawyer stepped into her line of sight. "Maria, are you okay?"

She nodded. "The coyote with the machete hacked at Rodrigo."

The young translator never wavered. He must have known the English word for hack because the thousand eyes blinked, and some of the women covered their mouths.

"We were screaming. In a huddle. Rodrigo was screaming the death screams of an animal. I did not watch. I could not watch. I closed my eyes. Then Rodrigo was silent."

The gentle lawyer nodded.

"Then they took Miguel. I heard him screaming too. Then he was quiet."

"What happened next, Maria?"

"The coyotes scared the children away into the prairie. They told us women to lie down in the dust. The burning all around us. The sky lit up. They raped us."

The thousand spectators gasped.

The lawyer raised his hand gently. "I'm sorry, Maria, but can you explain that to us?"

"There were ten coyotes. Some held us down while others raped us. They took turns. I fought, but their hands were strong. They held us down."

"Okay. Thank you for that. And then what happened?"

"They left."

"Did anyone come? Any medical people or police?"

"No."

"Did anyone come the next morning?"

"Yes, the next morning, some of the coyotes came back. They brought two foreigners."

As if in unison, the thousand eyes blinked and the spectators leaned forward.

The gentle lawyer took a step toward her. "Did you get a good look at these foreigners?"

"No."

The gentle lawyer nodded with a finality before giving her a sympathetic look. "One more thing, Maria. Can you explain why you have come all this way to tell this story?"

The thousand eyes stared.

She wiped her cheeks. The chair was stiff. "Because I know the difference between right and wrong. I may be poor. My people may be poor. But we know right from wrong. There was no justice for my village, for Miguel or Rodrigo, or for us women. The police did nothing to Phalanx. They coyotes have not been arrested. Not one of them. The foreigners—nothing has happened to them. They came and witnessed what had happened in Rapoosa, and still, they walk free, making money. There was no justice. Even if I am a small person in the eyes of the world, even us small people can stand up for what is right. Who would I be if I didn't teach my Ines right from wrong?"

The gentle lawyer nodded. "How old are you, Maria?"

"I am nineteen."

"And how old is your daughter Ines?"

"My daughter is four years old."

Across the room, chests held breaths. Ines was a daughter of the night of the howling blood red sky.

For the first time on this journey, Maria felt strong, right-eous, and protective. She held the stares of the thousand eyes. Funny what you become when you face the unknown.

57

THE BRIGHTLY LIT interview room in the NYC FBI building
was tight and stuffy. The walls appeared to be tightening. Two
attorneys from the Office of Professional Responsibility, a black
man by the name of Aaron Mele and an older white guy named
Landon Soble settled into seats across the scarred table.

Soble opened his notebook, reached to the recorder, and
turned it on. "This is the final interview on Office of Professional Responsibility investigation 4577. Attorneys Aaron Mele
and Landon Soble to question Special Agent Domini Walker."
He turned to Dom and place his hands flat on the table. "Special Agent Walker, Operation Saint Christopher was a big
success, right?"

Dom's pulse raced. "I'd say it was successful." The obvious
crack in her voice made her stomach lurch.

"As you know, we've been reviewing the St. Chris files and
talking to your fellow agents from that operation."

They think I'm guilty. She nodded.

"In summary, it was a year-long operation in which your
team identified a ring of child traffickers in ten cities across the
US. You were able to identify thirty-four perpetrators who,

combined, held over fifty children in various situations. These children were traded among the ring. They were sex slaves."

"Yes."

"Your team felt confident they had the locations of those thirty-four perps and you built an operational plan to secure the sites simultaneously at 02:00 on August 1 last year."

"Correct."

"It was a huge undertaking, this operational plan."

"It was."

"It required coordination across twenty-five field offices."

"Yes."

"By all accounts, you led a tightly run, buttoned-up operation."

As a statement, it did not require her consent. She watched him.

"Your teams were in place, fully briefed, on time. The order was given. All thirty-four teams broke down doors. We understand within thirty minutes of each other."

"We needed the element of surprise. We didn't want any one safe house to put out a warning."

"You were concerned that if word of the raids made it out, some of the perps in other locations would kill the children they held?"

"That's correct."

Mele smiled sadly. "For the record, we commend you on your investigation and the subsequent rescue operation. You did, by all accounts, a really impressive job."

That was unexpected. "Thank you."

"But you know why we're here today?"

"Yes."

"Because of your own actions during the raid on the Cleveland safe house."

"Yes."

"Can you explain to us in your own words what happened in Cleveland?"

Her heart clamored. For months, Fontaine had been telling her to lie. She took a sip of water and slowly set the glass on the table. "We were in the van outside the Cleveland location. There were only two of us, me and Agent Arturro. We were short an agent. We had to assign one of my guys to the situation room at the last minute, so there were only two of us outside the Cleveland location. At 02:00 we went in."

"Can you explain that for us?"

"We had a battering ram. We knocked down the door. Agent Arturro and I moved in, guns drawn. We announced ourselves. Two men were inside the house. One took off out the back. Arturro pursued. One took off down the stairs into the basement. I followed the perp into the basement."

"Is this the perp named Winston Jackson, aka Jacker?"

She nodded.

"Explain what happened next."

She closed her eyes, remembering the basement. "Dark, strong smells. Plywood walls. In weird places. As if they had built a maze. No noise. Oddly silent. Like a bunker. I pursued Jacker. He was moving quickly around corners. I was running. I yelled freeze four times. Exactly four times. Jacker kept running around corners through the maze. He was at the end of a long hallway. There was one lightbulb. No other light. He hooked into the room just under the lightbulb. He disappeared into that door. I slowed, then I cornered into that room, Glock drawn."

"What did you see in the room?"

"Another bare bulb. From the center ceiling. Under. A girl. A young black girl. Staring. Unmoving. On a bed. A filthy bed." She breathed in through her nose.

"Was the victim Darlin Montgomery?"

"Yes. It was Darlin. She was naked. Skinny. Ankles tied to

the bed. Rope. Dirty rope. As if it had been there around her a long time."

"Did Darlin see you?"

"No. She was staring. She was disassociated. My assumption in that moment was that she was disassociated. From what I could see." She closed her eyes against the image.

"Was Jacker there?"

She kept her eyes closed. "Yes. He was to my left. Against the wall. I heard him breathing."

They waited.

"I turned to him. His gun was drawn on me. Spotting at my head. I looked down the barrel."

"He was pointing the gun at you?"

"Yes." She cracked her neck. "I looked down the barrel."

"What did you do?"

"I stared at him."

"You what?"

"I stared him down."

"Did you say anything?"

"No. I wanted to use his fear against himself. He got squirrelly, started shaking. He was afraid of me. He was afraid to shoot me. He took a step back into the wall. He was afraid. That step back, it was defensive. He must have had some sense, inside all that meth, inside all that rot."

"And then?"

"His arm moved. He trained the gun on Darlin."

"What did you do then?"

"I trained my Glock at his head." She opened her eyes. In the interview room, her voice took on a sterile, robotic tone. "I said, 'This is how this is going to go down. You are going to drop your weapon. You are going to get down on the floor. This is going to go nice and easy. Because I know something you don't know.' Jacker jerked his eyes to me. Shaky. His gun was shaking.

Probably meth. I said, 'I am a very good shot. I will nail a single bullet through the middle of your right eye, through your brain stem mass, out the back of your skull, and into that wall behind you. Unless you drop that gun now, I will take that shot. Just like that.' I snapped my fingers—"

"You snapped your fingers?" Mele asked.

"Yes. With my left hand."

"You took your left hand off your weapon?"

"I'm a solid shot with either hand. I don't need both."

"What did he do?"

"He blinked. I knew I had him. I said, 'Lie on the floor.'" She shrugged. "He did."

Mele asked, "So what happened next, Special Agent Walker?"

"I kicked his gun under the bed. I leaned down to make sure Darlin Montgomery was okay."

"Jacker was on the floor behind you?"

"Yes."

"And?" Soble asked.

She imagined Fontaine watching from behind the two-way glass of the interrogation room. He had advised her to lie about the next part of the story, to say everything went according to the rule book. It was her word against Jacker's. They would believe an agent over a convicted pedophile.

She thought about the last week. About how Hettie and Micah had gone to Honduras to find the truth, how Micah had been killed to protect that truth. Dom thought about Mila, how she had persisted in her research, how she had told the truth to the NYPD precinct about the Filthy Five because it was the 'right thing to do.' All of them telling the truth, letting the chips land as they may.

She didn't want to lie. "I felt his hand on my ankle. I looked down. He had a razor in his hand. He was going for my ankle."

"There was no razor found at the site," Mele said.

"I believed, I saw, that Jacker had a razor."

Soble asked, "So what did you do then?"

It was as if the silence in the interrogation room emanated through the walls, through the neighboring witness room, and down the long fluorescent hallways of the Javits building like a seismic shift daring these bureaucrats to understand the reality of the streets. Into this silence, Stewart Walker whispered, *"You don't have to lie, my Dom. You and your truth are enough."*

Dom straightened her shoulders and pulled down on the navy FBI jacket. "I kicked him in the face. A solid connect. His nose crunched flat, his cheeks took a hit. I heard the bones snap."

Soble blinked.

Mele leaned over the table. "You had him down. The perp was down. The gun was under the bed, out of reach. There was no razor at the scene. And you're telling us, the Office of Professional Responsibility, that you kicked a civilian in the face? You crushed his face?"

Dom leaned back and crossed her arms. *Fidelity, bravery, and integrity. And truth.* "Yes."

Soble closed his notebook and clicked off the recorder. "Okay, Special Agent Walker. That's all we'll need for today."

58

TORONTO, *Ontario*

The courtroom was smaller than Hettie had expected and oddly outdated. Three of the four walls were wood paneled, the fourth was a checkered brick montage from the 1970s. The female judge, an imposing woman in her fifties with tight hair, a handsome countenance, and a black robe with a red sash, listened to the morning's introductory remarks from Mr. Davidson, the lawyer for the plaintiffs. Five suited businessmen and lawyers crowded the defendant's table. The crowded room was quiet.

Mr. Davidson, a medium build man in a blue suit and a pink tie, spoke directly to the jury with gentle calming voice. "This morning we heard of the severe human rights abuses rained down by security personnel of Phalanx Limited on the villagers of Rapoosa, the plaintiffs in this case, my clients. As we prepare to hear our second round of testimony, let me briefly revisit the facts as we know them. Five years ago, Rapoosa had the misfortune of being the planned site of a Phalanx nickel mine. The villagers spent months protesting the planned mine. They built roadblocks and went to Tegucigalpa to carry signs outside Phalanx offices. On March 25, the day before the ground was to be broken on the mine, Phalanx security arrived in the middle of the night and committed heinous crimes against the villagers. We have come to know that during this time period, Rittenhouse was in the processing of selling their equity in Phalanx to Orion Extractives. No police report was ever filed. Not a single person was punished. These are the facts." Davidson's posture was ramrod straight. "We contend that Orion Extractives must assume all liabilities of its subsidiaries. In particular, our suit alleges that Phalanx, Rittenhouse and Orion, one, failed to establish a code of conduct, two, failed to put in place rules of engagement, and three, had no policy to protect human rights." Davidson hung his head, letting a pause hover in the courtroom. "It is our contention that above and beyond the failure to enact these basic codes of conduct, in fact, Rittenhouse and Orion were very much aware of the abuses that took place March 25th—despite their vociferous claims of innocence. We will prove that today." Davidson looked to the judge. "Your Honor, I call our next witness, Miss Henrietta Honor Van Buren."

Hettie's heart clanged in her chest. She rose slowly and made her way to the witness chair.

Davidson used a gentle voice. "Please tell the court your name, Miss."

Her throat was tight and dry. "Henrietta Honor Van Buren." The mic crackled.

He nodded. "But you go by Hettie?"

"Yes."

"May I call you Hettie?"

"Yes."

"What do you do, Hettie?"

"I am an ornithologist at the American Museum of Natural History."

"You study birds."

"I do. My specialty is the Eskimo curlew."

"It sounds like a commendable career at a prestigious institution."

"It is."

"Thank you for your work on behalf of our planet, Hettie."

She nodded.

"Recently, you've had a very traumatic experience."

She clasped her hands tightly as cold sweat crept up her neck. "Yes."

"According to the police report, you were held captive by your mother using a cocktail of immobilizing drugs. Is that right?"

All eyes in the room were glued on her face.

"Yes," she said softly.

"And you were rescued in a nighttime FBI raid four days ago, is that right?"

"Yes."

"Are you doing okay?"

"I'm okay."

"Do you know why your mother kidnapped you, Hettie?"

"Yes."

"Can you tell the court?"

She breathed deeply. "To prevent me from coming here. Today."

"And why is that?"

"She believed my testimony would destroy my father's firm."

Davidson let the moment lengthen. "What is the name of your father's firm?"

"Rittenhouse Equity."

"The same Rittenhouse Equity that held majority investments in Phalanx Limited that were sold to Orion Extractives?"

"Yes."

"Hettie, can you tell us why you are here?"

"To explain what we found."

"And who is we?"

Talons pierced organs. "My boyfriend, Micah Zapata, and I."

"Where is Micah?"

When she closed her eyes, Micah smiled at her. She threw her lids open. "He's dead."

"I'm sorry."

She swallowed.

"So Hettie, can you tell us what you found?"

"Four months ago, I learned about what had happened in Rapoosa. An environmental nonprofit in New York City, CAN, told me what happened. CAN told me that they believed my father's firm was an investor during that period of time. They suspected my father knew about the crimes. They told me this trial was going to take place."

"And what did you think when you heard this from CAN?"

"I found it hard to believe. I didn't want to believe my father would be involved in something like that."

"Did you confront him?"

"Yes. I told him what CAN had told me."

"What did he say?"

"He denied it. Said it was all a big sham, that they were trying to muckrake ahead of this trial. We got in a fight."

"Is it normal for you and your father to fight?"

She shook her head. "No."

"Why is that?"

"My father is a belligerent man. I do not fight him."

"Okay. I understand. After this fight, did you believe him?"

"I wasn't sure what to believe."

"You didn't believe him?"

"Not completely, no."

"Were you upset?"

She stretched her fingers releasing a clench. "Yes. The accusation against my father was ... terrible."

"What did you do?"

The tears stung the insides of her lids. "Micah and I planned a trip. To go to Rapoosa ourselves. To learn the truth. I made up a ruse for work. I pretended that the trip would be about research on the Eskimo curlew."

"Did you go there?"

"Yes. Three weeks ago."

"What did you do when you got there?"

"We talked to the people, the villagers. We asked about the incident five years ago. They told us what happened."

"You heard that this violence had occurred?"

"Yes."

"What else did you learn?"

"A young woman named Maria Cardona—"

"Yes, we heard Maria's testimony this morning here in this courtroom."

"Maria Cardona told us something. She told us the next day two white foreigners had come to Rapoosa, had seen the aftermath."

"What did you think about this information?"

"I wondered if one of those men had been my father."

"You suspected your father had been there, in the village of Rapoosa, after the violence?"

"I did not know. I did not want to believe that. But yes, I suspected it."

"That must have been unnerving."

"Yes."

"What did you do?"

"I showed her a photograph on my phone."

"Of whom?"

The hum of a ceiling fan purred. "Of my father."

"Did Maria recognize him?"

She released a breath. "No."

"What did you do?"

"Micah and I went to the nearest hotel. It's a nice hotel."

"What's the name of the hotel, Hettie?"

"Paradise Villa."

"What did you do at the hotel?"

"I showed the staff the photo of my father."

"And?"

"They recognized him. From five years ago. I asked them to look up their records. They confirmed that he was there during the time the crimes were committed in Rapoosa."

Gasps escaped lungs in a collective exhale. She closed her eyes against the shame and the pain.

"Is that all, Hettie?"

Her heart raced against her neck. She released her lungs and opened her eyes. "No. Maria Cardona said two white foreigners were in Rapoosa after the atrocities. Micah and I googled for photos of people we thought may have been with my father."

Collectively, the crowd leaned in.

"And?"

"The staff of Paradise Villa recognized the other white foreigner."

"Who was it, Hettie?"

"John Abbott. The chief risk officer for Orion Extractives."

With a single movement of finality, the spectators pushed back against benches, eyes wide, mouths slightly ajar. Hettie Van Buren just implicated her father and Orion Extractives.

Davidson hung his head to mark the moment. Lifting his chin, he nodded. "Thank you, Hettie. That's all." He turned to the judge. "No more questions, sir."

The judge turned a sharp disapproving eye to the defense table. "Your witness."

The prosecutor shook his head. "No questions, your Honor."

Hettie rose, gingerly stepped down from the podium, walked past the throng of spectators, and left the courtroom behind.

59

IT WAS ALMOST midnight as Dom cruised the quiet street in Staten Island. There were no other cars on the road and only a few lit windows in the neat townhouses. Families in this neighborhood were all tucked asleep in their beds. The GPS on her phone confirmed the location. She pulled the Lancia to the curb and turned off the engine. In the dark, the silence was ominous.

Across the street, a two-story white trim and brick home of Robert Gessen and his family sat daintily at the top of a steep driveway.

That early Friday morning after Mila had gone to bed with Tinks, Beecher heard the full story. "So you're kinda responsible for her," he said, leaning the kitchen chair back on two rear legs.

Dom had scratched nails against scalp. "Yeah. That's where I am too."

"I mean, what are we gonna do? Those assholes are still out there."

"First of all, this isn't a we. This is a me. And I'm gonna take care of it."

"I mean, holy shit. These are the Filthy Five we're talking about."

"I'll handle it. But Mila stays here till it's sorted." As she stood, every fiber in her body ached. "But now I need some sleep and some kind of splint for my toes."

Beecher gazed at an envelope in the middle of the kitchen table.

She shot him a look.

He nodded. "It's her letter."

"I told you to throw it out."

"I didn't." He crossed his arms. "I think we should meet with her."

"No."

"But—"

A headache crawled across her scalp. "No."

"She says we don't have the right story—"

"She's full of shit. We know what happened. He was dirty, he went to jail, he killed himself. Esther left us. That's the story. End of story."

"Isn't it kind of crazy timing that Mila dug into the Filthy Five—"

"No."

"I mean, what if Esther is right, and there's more to the story. And now the Filthy Five are getting back together—"

"No."

"Just think about it."

"No."

"Dom, what if we have the story wrong?"

In the back of her mind, Stewart Walker released a ragged sigh as if the truth was finally released from confinement. With her last ember of anger, Dom turned and headed to bed.

In the rearview of the Lancia, a pair of headlights flashed as a car turned onto the street. It approached slowly, routinely. A Ford sedan pulled past and swung up the sloped driveway. A moment later the Ford's headlights switched off.

Let's get this game started. She flicked on the Lancia's high beams and a spectral shaft illuminated fifty yards into the pitch-dark night. She rose out of her car, softly shut the door, and leaned against the cold metal.

At the top of the drive, the Ford's driver side door opened and the dome light winked for a moment like a shadowbox. A lighter's flame flashed and a cigarette tip glowed as Robert Gessen assessed the Lancia's beam.

Stewart Walker whispered, *Hello, Bob.*

The Lancia was hard and solid against her back.

Gessen walked slowly down the driveway, into the street, and stopped ten feet out. He took a long drag and the embers flared. In the shadowed edge of the Lancia's beam, his face appeared angular and sinister. His gray hair was close cropped and aggressive. "What do you want?"

"Here's the thing about Feds," she began silkily. "We have amazing access."

Gessen squinted and pulled hard on the cigarette. He was nervous.

"You see," she said, "Feds have access to an incredible array of surveillance and data that isn't available to your below average, run-of-the-mill cops. NSA signal intelligence, surveillance, wire-tapping, internet tracking. All this amazing technology is at our fingertips. Most of it doesn't even need a warrant or a judge. You can just dig in to your hearts content."

He glared.

"It just doesn't take much to flay someone's life open, like slicing a chef's knife right down the chest cavity, exposing the heart and the guts. Wide open."

He took a final deep drag and flicked the cigarette to the asphalt and crushed it underfoot.

She opened the Lancia's door, leaned in, picked up a manila file from the passenger seat, turned, took a few steps to him and handed it over. "Everything about a person's life can be put into one neat file. All in one place." She pulled out a flashlight, clicked it, and shined it on the folder. "Here, take a look."

Under the light, he flipped the documents. The first few items were photos of his wife outside a supermarket, his son on a high school sports field, and his daughter walking a plump yellow Labrador. His jaw tensed as he flipped through bank statements, cell phone usage, a copy of his mortgage. He refused to look at her.

As his fingers turned the second to last paper, she said, "I especially like that last one."

Eyes narrowed as he read the list of his misconduct charges for the last ten years, courtesy of Mila's research. He closed the folder and glared at her.

"That's where I'd start," she said softly, "if I wanted to flay you open."

"Who are you?"

"I'm pretty sure you don't want me to start turning over the rocks where you hide, do you, Officer Gessen?"

"Who are you?"

"Just know that I'm federal."

"Do I know you?" he asked.

Stewart Walker whispered, *"Not yet, Bob, but you will. My Dom is more than enough."*

She clicked off the flashlight, blinding him momentarily in darkness.

He asked, "What do you want?"

She stepped close, and he leaned away. Her voice was low. "No more sinister stalking of a young woman who lives on Mott Street. That means no more of your second-rate, clumsy creeping-around-in-the-middle-of-the-night Keystone Cop antics. You stay clear of her. She's protected."

He blinked.

She clicked the flashlight beam on the folder.

He nodded.

She clicked it off. "Good."

"Wait. That's it?"

"For tonight. But trust me, I've got eyes on you now." She opened the Lancia's door. "Have a good night, Officer Gessen."

TUESDAY

May those last of the curlews prevail. —Fred Bodsworth, "Last of the Curlews"

60

THE TANG of coffee permeated the bright kitchen. Outside the day was brilliant. Tinks followed Dom into the room, tiny toenails tapping on the tile.

Beecher, hair tousled and reading from his laptop while sipping a coffee, said, "Yo."

"Morning," she mumbled through sleepiness.

Moments later, Mila shuffled in and Tinks tap-danced around her ankles.

Dom handed her a coffee, "You want pancakes?"

"You have pancakes?" Mila's eyes were wide.

Dom grinned. "Beecher makes killer pancakes."

Eyes glued to the screen, he smiled. "Easy done if that's what you guys want."

Mila said, "Yes, please!"

Beecher waved them over to the table. "But come check this New Yorker article."

They read over his shoulder.

The Fall of a Private Equity Firm: Human Rights Abuses in Honduras

The New Yorker

A trial in Toronto this week has thrown the private equity world into chaos. At the heart of the case are allegations that human rights abuses conducted by a mining company in Honduras were witnessed by investors—one of New York's premier private equity firms, Rittenhouse Equity—in the midst of a sale to a Canadian conglomerate. Rittenhouse Equity is owned by banker Claude Van Buren, whose wife, Yvette Van Buren is the sole heir to the Lowrance fortune. In a shocking twist, the daughter of the Van Burens, Hettie Van Buren, testified yesterday that she discovered her father witnessed the aftermath of the atrocities. To make the remarkable story even more sinister, Yvette Van Buren, in an attempt to prevent Hettie Van Buren from testifying, abducted her.

Regardless of the ruling by the Superior Court of Justice of Ontario, many investors, much of New York's high society, are appalled by the crescendo of scandals and are demanding redemptions of their investment from Rittenhouse Equity.

From the counter, Dom's cell phone vibrated. The screen read *Fontaine*, and her stomach clenched.

Clicking it on, she walked out of the kitchen. In the silence of the hallway, his voice was loud. "OPR finished the investigation."

Her heart clanged. "Yeah?"

"They cleared you."

Her lungs released.

"I've got the report right here. They put in your testimony word for word. They noted that your honesty was exceptional, a real testament to the Agency. They said it had been a complex situation with months of preparation that led to a harrowing— they used the word harrowing—scenario. Their conclusion was that they believe you acted within the letter of the law, that you saw your life in danger, and that you acted accordingly."

The truth worked.

"It worked for you, Walker. The truth was the right way to go."

"I guess it was."

"Congrats."

"Thank you, sir."

"Take the week off. I'll see you next Monday."

"Thank you, sir."

Back in the kitchen, Beecher was cracking eggs into a bowl, and Tinks had made her way onto Mila's lap, his chin on the young woman's arm, eyes closed. It felt like Mila had been part of the small family for years.

61

The Sound of a Furious Sky
@LastCurlew

A childhood fraught with complications
within a rhythm of constant tension
while the world lusted all the opportunities.
Only inside a maternal orbit. Her world. My world.

Moving past the constraints, perception emerged
from isolation to find a gentle soul
beside me. Evenings. Laughter and touches
bathed in the scents of novelty and love.

Discovery a lightning and thunder
that broke apart the structures of solidity
in a single blow of righteousness.
Breadcrumbs to follow. Our journey. My journey.

The sound of a furious sky
sliced through innocence, revealing flesh.

Inhumanity, torture, neglect,
approached from a distance without shame
to goad us to action. We sprung

to uncover the secrets hidden
in the dry dust of tragic prairie.
Grace. Humanity. Hoped to redeem,
but underestimated the potency. They lost. I lost.

62

RAPOOSA, *Honduras*

The prairie grass rustled a warm greeting. Over brightly colored marbles strewn across deep red dirt, the ruffle of downy hair beckoned. Hearing footsteps, Ines glanced up before hurtling down the path across dusty earth. Maria clutched the small body against her chest, grateful for the density of flesh and bones, and felt the saturation of a mother's love.

###

Want more HN Wake? .....

1. Grab Dom Walker Book 2.

In ebook, click here or on the image.

2. Get a FREE Mac Ambrose book when you sign up for my newsletter at www.hnwake.com or click on the image.

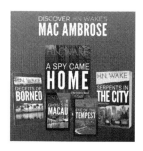

Made in the USA
Columbia, SC
21 March 2022

57950636R00219